DEAD CROWD

Also by Dan Barton

Heckler
Killer Material
Relife
Banshee

DEAD CROWD

DAN BARTON

THOMAS DUNNE BOOKS
ST. MARTIN'S MINOTAUR
NEW YORK

THOMAS DUNNE BOOKS.
An imprint of St. Martin's Press.

www.minotaurbooks.com

Library of Congress Cataloging-in-Publication Data

Barton, Dan.
    Dead crowd : a mystery starring Biff Kincaid / Dan Barton.—1st ed.
        p. cm.
    ISBN 0-312-29034-9
    1. Comedians—Fiction. 2. Hollywood (Los Angeles, Calif.)—
Fiction. I. Title.

PS3552.A76785 D43 2002
813'.6—dc21

                                                      2001058551

First Edition: May 2002

10 9 8 7 6 5 4 3 2 1

To Mom.
Ever onward.

Acknowledgments

Thanks to some people who helped me out along the way . . .

Mom, Dad, Ted, and Jean, a.k.a. my family.

In New York: Ruth Cavin, senior editor at St. Martin's Minotaur, Matt Bialer of Trident Media Group, and Robert Youdelman.

At E! Entertainment Television: John Rieber, Gary Snegaroff, Scott Woodward, and Edward Zarcoff. I have the best job in show business.

And he can't read, but I wouldn't have gotten all this work done if my cat, Russell, didn't wake me up so damn early to hit those keys.

DEAD CROWD

PROLOGUE

I woke up with a fractured skull.

That's what it felt like. I could feel the bandages on my head without touching them. It hurt bad. It hurt without my moving or doing anything. That's what happens when someone hits you so hard they knock you out cold.

The whiteness of the hospital sheets and the robin's-egg blue paint on the walls let me know where I was. The clock on the nightstand showed the time and date. Twelve hours ago I'd walked in through the back door of Flugelhorn's Comedy Cabaret. I'd thought it was empty, except for Bernie Coleman, the owner.

I'd found Bernie with a knife sticking out of his chest, and after that it all went black.

I found the call button and pressed it, waiting for the nurse with my eyes closed.

By the time the nurse showed up, I had passed out again, trying to remember what had happened the night before.

ONE

It was a funeral.

No, not a real funeral, with a dead body and a minister and flowers and a hearse waiting outside. Funeral is comedy talk, like when one comic asks another, "How was the gig?" and the other one would say, "Man, it was a funeral," meaning that the show didn't go very well. Few laughs, sparse crowd, low bar sales. No rebooking.

The eleven o'clock show that Saturday night at Flugelhorn's Comedy Cabaret was a funeral.

I was wrapping up my third show of the night, one every two hours. The seven o'clock had been light, the nine o'clock had almost sold out, but the eleven o'clock made the seven o'clock look like standing room only. Fewer than twenty chairs were occupied, the back rows so empty when I walked among them I could smell the hot wax from the table candles.

Flugelhorn's was built in a semicircle, the stage set along one long side of it. The design was meant to give everyone a good view. ("Not a bad seat in the house!" a brochure read. "When you think of your next corporate function or company party, think Flugelhorn's!") After I did my set and got offstage to the mild applause—hands making a light slapping sound like a dozen fish flopping on a flatbed truck—I went straight to the bar at the back and traded in my drink ticket for a pint of Guinness thoughtfully stocked by Rick Parker, the bartender.

"Nice job," Rick said.

"More like nice try," I said, and tipped him a dollar.

I turned around. The owner himself, Bernie Coleman, was on-stage, exhorting the crowd to drink and tip and also plugging the upcoming calendar of events at Flugelhorn's, including a twelfth-anniversary show. Bernie liked to emcee. It made him feel like he was a comedian, too. He had never learned that being onstage wasn't necessarily enough for a performer; you had to look like you belonged there.

Bernie was a short man well over the dividing line of middle age. He had large round eyes, a thin sharp nose dotted with large black pores and small teeth spaced too far apart. His hair poked up from the back of his head as though he combed it forward with a garden rake. He wore a white short-sleeve dress shirt over a tank top, and the tank top showed through. His pectorals were sagging, and he was carrying half a soccer ball above his belt. Only five-five, small-boned and pale, he looked like a hungry bird, nervous and scratching.

He was, in fact, none of those things. After working for him half a dozen times over the course of five years, I would use the adjectives hard-nosed, driven and cold-blooded. What humanity he had left after what seemed like a life of nothing but hard knocks had been systematically driven out by the practices and procedures of owning a comedy club.

Bernie ended his between-comic patter and brought up the headliner, Tim Scofield. Bernie stepped off and headed for his office in the back.

I looked back at Rick. He was shaking his head. "This place is going down the tubes," he said. "I give it six months at most."

"You ever here in the old days?" I asked. We were both keeping our voices at a whisper while Scosh started his opening bit.

"No, but I heard," Rick said. He was taller than my six feet, but skinnier. He had pale, blotchy skin over taut ropy muscles, with hair the color of iron filings cut above the ears. He was older than I was by maybe five years. He had a pack of cigarettes loose in his stained white shirt, the sleeves pulled halfway down his forearms to hide the bluish dye of crude tattoos. I had the feeling he wasn't spending his days studying for his Pepperdine MBA.

"Five years ago this place was packed," I said. "Every night. The comics used to have to wait in the parking lot because there wasn't anyplace for them to sit or stand inside. There was a speaker rigged up so we could listen to the show for our intro."

I looked at the empty seats with electrical tape stripped over the cracks in the upholstery, the lights set low to hide the stains on the carpet, the collection of framed flyers with yet-to-be-famous names of the last decade lining the walls like trophies from battles gone by.

"Leno played here. So did Seinfeld. Robin Williams used to drop by. The crowd would go nuts. One time Letterman was in town during a writer's strike and read a top ten list of—what was it? Top ten drink specials at Flugelhorn's Comedy Cabaret."

"What happened?"

"Original owner left," I said. "Bernie took over."

"When was that?" Rick asked.

"Five years ago," I said.

"What happened to the original owner?"

"Mel? He retired. Mel Sikorsky. Like the helicopter. You never heard of him?"

Rick shrugged. "I've only been working here six months," he said. "My first job in show business."

"Hey! Kincaid!" This was coming from the stage. Tim Scofield, the headliner, was yelling at me. "Shut the hell up during my act! I'm the one that got you this gig!"

I raised my right hand like a basketball player assessed a foul. Scosh needed all the help he could get tonight. His act was a series of spot-on celebrity impressions, sometimes accompanied by music. We had met on the road and when he was looking for a middle this weekend he had had Bernie Coleman give me a call.

Without another word I nodded at Rick and headed for the back of the showroom. There I sat and drank my stout while Scosh fought the good and glorious battle against the silence of the empty seats. He sang, he danced, he twisted his face into a dozen different shapes, pulling a handkerchief from his pocket to wipe the sweat off his brow. It was the mark of a true professional. Not one remark about the light turnout or the late hour. He didn't care about either. Dammit, he was going to put on a show.

I watched him work. Forty minutes later he left the stage, bowing to as much hand noise as the twenty people there could muster. He went to the back, got himself a drink and flopped in the chair beside me.

"Jesus Christ, what a goddamn night," he said, combing his lanky brown hair over one eyebrow with his free hand. He was long-limbed and willowy and wore a white suit onstage.

"Sorry about talking during your act, Scosh."

He shook his head and swallowed alcohol before he answered. "It was so quiet in here you could hear the mice fucking the cats." Tim's act was clean as a Disney musical onstage, but once off he swore like a sailor having phone sex.

"Good show."

"I felt every minute of it," he said. "Look at this." He indicated the last of the audience as it filed out to an Eric Clapton tape. "I can remember being at the Laugh Factory wondering how to get into this place, now I'm in this place wondering how to get booked at the Laugh Factory. What the hell happened to this club?"

"Nobody knows," I said.

"No, everybody knows," he said. "Bernie Coleman's what happened to this club." He slapped me lightly on the leg. "Let's go see the man and get our money before Bernie launders the green out of it."

I followed him past the bar, where Scosh nodded at Rick as Rick was busy cleaning what dirty glasses there were left in the bar sink, supplied to him by the lone cocktail waitress.

"What's her name again?" Tim asked.

"Cynthia," I said.

"God, what an ass. And that bartender. He wasn't here when I played here last year. You see those tattoos?"

I shrugged. "I just met him tonight." We passed the bar and were headed toward a hallway that ran all the way across the back of the club. I stopped at the men's room. "I'll meet you in Bernie's office," I said. "I got to make a pit stop."

"Mention my name," Tim said. "You'll get a good seat."

The bathroom was out of paper towels. I got some napkins from the bar and when my hands were sufficiently dry I headed for Bernie Coleman's office. The door was a quarter of the way open and over the music I could hear an argument heating up, on steam and beginning to boil.

I waited in the hall and heard Bernie say in a consciously calm voice: "I'll have the rest of it Monday. I promise. Here's another drink ticket. Take a bottle from the bar. Go have—"

"Hey, Bernie, fuck you and your goddamn drink tickets," Scosh said. "Fuck your club and fuck your goddamned mother."

The door flew open and Scosh stormed out, angrily stuffing a wad of bills down his inside suit pocket. "He's short," Tim growled through his teeth. "Last time I play this fucking shitbox."

"Did you have to say that about his mother?"

Tim stormed off, heading straight past the bar, stopping only to tip a table on its side as he banged the back door open so hard it slammed against the concrete exterior of the club.

This didn't look good.

I walked in.

TWO

Bernie's office was the size of a few phone booths shoved together. It had enough space for a desk, a filing cabinet, and a TV/VCR combo set on top of the filing cabinet. That was it. A booking calendar hung on the wall to his left, and a smoked yellow window reinforced with chicken wire was on his right. It was open to the parking lot. I could hear Scosh grind the starter as he revved the engine in his car, put it into gear and screeched out of the parking lot.

"Nice show tonight, Biff," Bernie said. His voice was high and froggy. It didn't sound any better over a microphone.

"Thanks," I said. "I'm here to get paid."

"Uh, yeah. About that." Bernie pulled open a drawer on his desk and reached in to unlock a metal box.

"What about it?"

Bernie looked up with an obsequious smile. "Nothing."

He handed me a paper-clipped bundle of twenties. I stood and counted it in front of him.

"I'm short," I said.

"I'm sorry?" He pretended he didn't hear me right, but I knew he did.

"I'm short, Bernie. We said one-twenty-five a show. I did two shows last night and three tonight. That's six-twenty-five. There's only five hundred here if I counted right and I did."

Bernie shut the metal box and quickly relocked it, closing the desk drawer. "We said one-twenty-five a show?"

I automatically took the twenties. "One-twenty-five a show."

"I thought we said a hundred a show."

"One-twenty-five."

"I never pay more than a hundred a show for a middle."

"I don't know what you pay your other middle acts," I said. "And I don't care. I know what we said over the phone. I've headlined this club, Bernie, just a little over a year ago. You were looking for a middle for Scofield. Desperate, if I recall your phrasing."

Bernie continued to look puzzled. "I'm not saying you're *lying*, Kincaid . . ."

"No. I'm saying you owe me another hundred and twenty-five bucks."

"There's no need to get *confrontational* . . ."

"There's no need to short me, Bernie."

"Do you know what the bar did tonight? Third show? With twenty people?"

"That's not my problem."

"And never mind the *door* . . ."

"We set a price. It's pay or play in comedy. We've both been in this business too long to pretend otherwise."

He reached into another drawer and pulled out a checkbook. "Okay. I don't *remember* saying one-twenty-five. I mean I can't remember the *last* time I paid a middle act one-twenty-five." He opened the top of the checkbook. "But if it's worth *that much* to you . . ."

"No checks, Bernie," I said. "Cash and carry. You give me the cash and I carry it out."

"Cash?" He made a face like I'd said something obscene about the Tooth Fairy.

"A Ben and an Abe and a Jefferson. I know you got it. I saw more dead presidents in that cash box than in Arlington Cemetery. Fork it over."

He put the checkbook away as though it was sleeping and he didn't want to wake it. "Kincaid, are . . . are you threatening me?"

I sighed. "Bernie, I know Flugelhorn's is on the ropes."

He started shaking his head. "If only you knew . . ."

"The glory days are gone."

"You said it."

"And it's at times like these that we as fellow entertainment professionals need to band together. Later this month, we celebrate Thanksgiving."

"It means so much to me to hear you say . . ."

"So cut the shit and pay me. I'm not leaving until you do. I don't want any free booze, I don't want any promises and I don't want any delays. I want the hundred and twenty-five bucks you owe me."

He steepled his fingers together. "Let me tell you what I worked out with Tim Scofield."

"Tim Scofield who just barged out of here?"

"We reached an agreement . . ."

"He told me you shorted him, too."

". . . and I'd like to think we could do the same."

"You didn't reach any kind of an agreement with Scofield, and I don't care if you did. I'm talking about you paying me in the very near future."

"I got big money coming in."

"Great. You've got a hundred and twenty-five going out. Now. Tonight."

"Let me show you something." He reached into a drawer.

"It better be green and crispy."

"It's golden."

"I can't pay my rent in gold, and all the pawnshops are closed."

He pulled an unlabeled videocassette out of the desk drawer and a secretive smile out of his back teeth. "You'll think differently."

"And that's not gold or silver or even a bucket of loose change," I said. "It's a blank tape."

He stuck it in the VCR and grabbed the remote to turn on the TV. "Not blank," he said. "Golden."

"You keep saying that and I don't know why—"

The TV screen was filled with a slate and I read it as I kept talking. This was the tenth episode of the second season of *Eyewitness Crime*. The producer was S. Temple and the Exec Prod

11

(shorthand for executive producer) was K. Matthews. The slate was replaced by a countdown. Five, four, three, two—

"—you think I keep wanting to hear—"

Bernie shushed me. "Watch."

"I'm giving it two secon—"

The tape started. Accompanied by a rush of music and sound, the show graphics flashed by accompanied by an authoritative voice-over that barked: "Tonight on *Eyewitness Crime!*"

"You seen this show?" Bernie asked.

"Just the promos," I said. "I never—"

The voice-over cut me off: "How stand-up comedy goes from bad—"

Then I saw an image that made me instantly shut up. A comedian stood onstage in front of a mike in a grainy home video. He was cut off in mid bit—the sequence was edited so tightly I couldn't even tell what he was saying—when another man stepped forward and stabbed him in the stomach.

The voice-over: "—to worse—"

The stabbed comedian immediately doubled over, clutching his stomach as the attacker drew his hand back for another strike.

Both men were wearing orange jumpsuits.

There was a white flash and the next shot was of a large room filled with men in orange jumpsuits fighting, running and hurling furniture as guards tried to contain them.

Voice over: "—and starts a prison riot."

"What the hell?" I said. "Let's see that again."

"Didn't you see anything about this on the news when it happened?" Bernie asked.

"When I was on the road I saw a story on a prison break during a talent contest," I said.

"This is it."

"But I didn't hear anything about it being a comedy show and I sure as hell didn't know someone videotaped the whole thing."

"You watching now?" Bernie said sarcastically. He freeze-framed the image. "You interested now?"

"Yeah."

"Then hold on to your hat," Bernie said. "It's a wild ride from here on."

He hit PLAY.

12

THREE

Bernie fast-forwarded through the rest of the *Eyewitness Crime* cold open. I had never seen the show itself before, just promos for it. *Eyewitness Crime* was a TV news magazine dedicated to stories featuring shocking or bizarre videos. There was another video of looters running wild through a trailer park in the aftermath of a tornado and images of someone drawing a bead on a bear as he attacked a campground tent.

The video sped through the entire opening show graphics, which introduced a host and three reporters. Bernie slowed the tape when the host was seated in what looked like an information center, with shadowed figures sitting at computer monitors and television sets tuned to trouble spots in the world.

The host was identified with his name bannered across the bottom of the screen: "Darren Mitchell." He was in his rugged mid-forties, and handsome in the style of catalog models who are wearing a new type of elastic socks. As the song says, I coulda been an actor, but I wound up here.

"Good evening. Welcome to the *Eyewitness Crime* News Center. I'm Darren Mitchell."

Cut to a different angle, closer on Darren, so graphic art could be flown in over his left shoulder: two hands reaching through prison bars, clutching a microphone. It was titled "Comedy Behind Bars."

"Stand-up comedy is usually found inside the comfort of night-clubs or on TV, harmless jokes meant to entertain an audience out for an evening of fun and relaxation."

He should have seen tonight's crowd, I thought.

"But when the tried-and-true combination of setup and punch line is brought behind the walls of a prison, the results can be dangerous. Jeff Elliott has our first story."

Whooosh. More music, swirling graphics and wind tunnel sound effects.

When the pixels had settled, the first shot was of the razor wire topping a chain-link fence at least twelve feet high. As the camera pulled back, I could see more. A guard tower. Inmates walking by.

"This is Ojai Correctional Facility, a private prison just a few hours north of Los Angeles. Here, first-time criminals are sent to pay their debts to society. Although security at Ojai was meant to be minimal and the prison was built to house nonviolent offenders, it was the scene of a full-scale riot . . . a riot triggered by a comedy show."

"I'm up in about fifteen seconds," Bernie said.

What followed on-screen were a series of images from inside the prison: prisoners' feet as they walked by in single file, inmates working out in the yard and a lone soul reading in his cell. Care was taken not to show any faces. It was all feet and hands, elbows and necks, and lots of orange jumpsuits.

"Life here on the inside is hard, with long hours of monotony and few distractions outside of work, reading and exercise. Only a few years old, Ojai had yet to establish a full slate of rehabil-itative activities for its occupants. It was here—"

"There I am," Bernie whispered.

"—that comedy club owner Bernie Coleman decided to bring a little light and laughter."

Sure enough, on mention of Bernie's name the screen dis-solved to show Bernie walking up to and opening the front door of Flugelhorn's during the day. Another quick shot showed him working at his desk, talking on the phone and writing on the booking calendar with comedians' headshots scattered across his desk. The dedicated club owner at work.

"Do they ever show you not paying anybody?" I asked.

Bernie stopped the tape and rewound it a few seconds back. "Will you *watch?*"

I had talked over Jeff Elliott's last line: "—a little light and laughter. Even he had no idea what the outcome would be."

Cut to Bernie sitting in a chair, his face made up to look five years younger. He was sitting in the showroom, just twenty feet away from where I was standing, with the stage and the Flugelhorn's sign hanging in the background, but carefully lit and photographed to make the club look warm and inviting, not old and run-down. Like most of what you see on television, it looked better than the real thing.

I looked at the real Bernie, watching himself on screen, his face aglow in the light from the television monitor. He could not have cared less about his troubles of just a few minutes ago, his dilapidated club, his sagging finances, or the comedians who needed to be paid. He was mesmerized by the sound of his voice and sight of his face now embraced by that holy of holies in our culture, the force that bound us all together more tightly than any political or spiritual faith: television.

"My original idea," the TV Bernie said, his face suffused with soulful yearning, "was to bring laughter where there might not have been any for a long time."

His name and title—comedy club owner—was superimposed just beneath his chin for five seconds.

Back to the reporter, now standing outside Flugelhorn's front door. "So Bernie Coleman—"

"They cut the shit out of this," Bernie muttered.

"—started to book the same comedians from his highly successful comedy club in Los Angeles to perform behind the walls of Ojai prison."

Back to Bernie for a quick sound bite: "Not every comedian wanted to do it. Some of them were intimidated."

"Why didn't you call me?" I said. "I would have done it."

"Hush," Bernie said.

"I've done prison shows before," I whispered.

The tape cut to another man working at his desk. He was

introduced by a shot of an inmate walking around the exercise yard and pulling back to reveal that the inmate was being seen through the glass window in this man's office.

"But when Bernie Coleman approached Ojai warden O. V. Douglas—the man responsible for the security, safety and welfare of the fifteen hundred prisoners—Douglas had a different idea."

Cut to Douglas in a chair with his picture window view of the yard behind him. He was a heavyset man with a thick neck and beefy hands. He cut his hair to military length and apparently bought his eyeglasses by the pound. In his interview, he made no pretense at spiritual compassion; he looked and spoke like a man who was used to rolling his own cigars.

"My policy toward live entertainment is to try to involve the prisoners in some way. We had a music night here where a blues musician headlined but inmates got to perform as well, and some of them were very talented. When I was approached about putting on some stand-up comedians here, I thought it might be worth investigating to see if there were some inmates who wanted to get up onstage and do a few minutes. I'm not in show business, I'm in law enforcement, so I just had no idea how to go about it."

Warden Douglas's face froze.

"Jesus, why did they have to give this guy more screen time than me?" Bernie complained, his finger still on the pause button. "He makes it sound like it was all his idea." He turned to me. "You know what he told me? He had never been to a comedy show. I mean like, in his life. He asked me to bring him one on tape."

"Bernie, how long ago did this happen?"

"Three months ago," he said wearily. "In August." He hit PLAY.

The interview close-up of Warden Douglas dissolved to a shot of Bernie and Douglas walking into the cafeteria at Ojai, Bernie talking animatedly and Douglas listening, his hands clasped behind his back in a quasi-military pose.

Jeff Elliott resumed his voice-over: "So in August of this year the prison warden and the comedy club owner decided to start a series of comedy nights for the inmates of Ojai Correctional Facility in the form of a contest. Once a week for six weeks, inmates would get a chance on Sunday nights after dinner to perform five minutes each. Winners would be determined by an applause vote taken at the end of the show. After six weeks, the six winners would be gathered again for an hour-long finale. The prison comedians would perform ten minutes in front of a crowd of fellow inmates."

During Elliott's narration, clips flashed by of various inmates performing onstage. Someone had taped the shows. Some of the faces were blurred out. The audio was turned down so low I couldn't hear what the individual acts were saying, but . . .

Comedy behind bars. I would like to have seen it, listened to the inmates' material, watched them work the stage. Even there, even then, the impulse exerted itself. Watching even five-second clips, I could see what some of them were tasting, perhaps for the first time in years.

Freedom.

Back to Darren Mitchell in the *Eyewitness Crime* News Center.

"But the show would end far from the good time both the comedy club owner and the prison warden had in mind," Mitchell said.

"God, could they say my name any less?" Bernie whined.

Mitchell: "When we come back . . ."

I saw the video repeated of the inmate getting stabbed behind the mike as another prisoner leaped onstage from the crowd.

Mitchell's voice intoned: "Comedy turns deadly."

The screen faded to black.

FOUR

Bernie hit the FAST FORWARD button to speed through the next few minutes of black tape. "Dammit, I asked them to give this to me without the commercial breaks," he said. "They're doing like three segments on this. It's their lead story. I'm only in this next segment for a little bit."

The stabbing incident was replayed after the break, dissolving back to the *Eyewitness Crime* News Center and Darren Mitchell, looking somber in his anchor chair. The graphic titled "Comedy Behind Bars" reappeared. Darren decided to recap the story so far for people who had a tendency to forget everything they had just seen. "For those of you just joining us, as a caution to our viewers, this story contains scenes of graphic violence and parental discretion is advised. Jeff Elliott has the story."

"You know what the executive producer told me?" Bernie said. "Anytime they include that warning, the ratings go up a tenth of a point."

"If they said it was educational and helpful to watch, would people tune out?"

Bernie snorted. "I would."

Back to reporter Elliott standing in front of the chain-link fence surrounding the prison. "It was here at Ojai Correctional Facility—a privately run prison—that comedy club owner Bernie

Coleman and Warden O. V. Douglas decided to put on a weekly comedy contest. The winners would get to perform onstage for the entire prison population. It was meant to be an evening of laughter and fun—a break from life behind bars. But it turned into a nightmare no one would ever forget."

Cut to home video of the prison dining area being transformed into a performing stage. A camera was set up high, on a second-floor railing, shooting down. Guards supervised burly inmates at work.

"There it is, Kincaid," Bernie said. He paused the tape. "That's my footage. Right there. On TV."

"You videotaped the shows?"

Bernie nodded. "And guess how much they're paying me?"

"I hope it's enough to cover what you owe me and Scofield," I said.

"And then some."

"Good."

"But for the interview and the footage and everything. Guess how much?"

I shrugged. "I don't work in TV a lot."

"Fifteen thousand," Bernie said in a near whisper. He clutched the remote like it was a set of prayer beads. "I get it all on Monday. Enough to pay all my bills and put me in the black for the next two months."

"Cashier's check?"

Bernie shook his head. "Better than that. Wired directly into my account. They can do that these days, you know." He flipped the remote in his hand like a lucky quarter. "Like I said. Gold."

"The stabbing your footage, too?"

"Yeah."

"Let's see it."

"Okay. This is where it gets good." Bernie fussed with the remote control until I reached out and pressed the PLAY button on the VCR myself.

The story did not cut away from Bernie's footage. "For the night of the performance, the lunchroom was turned into an ersatz comedy club." There was a dissolve to a point later in time, when the tables had been cleared away and replaced with chairs. A portable stage had been erected. A lone figure stood onstage, checking the microphone and stand that had been placed at the center and making sure the sound system was operational. Bernie.

"At five P.M.," Elliott intoned, "Bernie Coleman checks the sound system."

Dissolve. Prisoners filed in and took their seats for the show. "At seven P.M., the audience arrives and the show begins."

There was a quick montage of a few different inmates as they performed, some with their faces blurred out, but all in various stages of their acts: some held the microphone out of the stand, close to their chest, others used it like a prop, and one nervous soul clutched it with both hands like he was going to fall over without it. "Six inmates—for one night transformed into would-be stand-up comedians—make their stage debuts."

The montage stopped as a final performer got onstage. I recognized him. He was the inmate I'd seen in the cold open and in the teases. He was the prisoner who had gotten stabbed. Right now he was walking toward the microphone in its stand.

Jeff Elliott's voice: "But when the last of the inmate comedians got up onstage . . ."

On the tape, Bernie shook his hand and left the inmate in front of the microphone. He surveyed the crowd, said hello, and took the microphone out of the stand.

Jeff Elliott's voice-over continued: ". . . everything goes horribly wrong."

The inmate started his routine. I couldn't tell how tall he was exactly because the camera was looking down on him. He looked to be in his thirties, trim and muscular, but with hair that had gone prematurely gray. He had a face lined with scars, as though his features had been stitched together from different pieces of skin. His eyes were so dark they looked black in his skull, and when he smiled I knew that I was not looking at a man who was innocent of the crimes he had been convicted of or would ever pretend to be.

"Who's that?" I asked.

"One of the bad guys," Bernie said.

The voice-over: "It was while this man was in the middle of a routine about the food at Ojai—a common topic among the prison comedians—that another inmate climbed up on the stage . . ."

The video slowed, the entire frame darkening except for a small circle that focused on a burly figure clambering up over the lip of the stage. He was wider than the other man, broad in the shoulders and thick throughout his whole body, not fat. His head was shaved completely bald.

He had something in his hand.

Voice-over: ". . . and put a stop to the entertainment. His way."

The video resumed normal speed. The performer turned to face his attacker. His face registered a modicum of surprise. He dropped the mike to the stage with a thud. His hands went out in front of him, bent at the elbows. Bad move. His attacker swung his right hand from underneath, toward his victim's stomach.

The gray-haired man bent over, clutching his abdomen, as the bald-headed attacker moved past him. The gray-haired man fell to the ground, his legs bicycling in front of him, trying to walk on his side, red spreading through his fingers.

Back to Darren Mitchell in the *Eyewitness Crime* News Center.

"When we come back," he said, "the shocking aftermath."

The screen went black again.

FIVE

Bernie shut the tape off. This time he got the remote control to work.

"That airs next month," Bernie said. "Wednesday night, nine o'clock." He held a finger up in the air. "That's during prime time, my friend."

"Congratulations," I said. I was still looking at the blank TV screen.

"The executive producer wants to see what other video I have—you know, shows I booked on the road, shows here at the club—especially of comics in their early days who became famous later. He's producing another show for a cable channel called *Before and After* and it's about celebrities who—"

I interrupted him. "What about the 'shocking aftermath' at Ojai the host was talking about?"

Bernie flipped the remote control in his hand again. "They haven't done that part yet," he said. "They're still in the edit bay on that one." He smiled. "Listen to me, talking edit bays and ratings and segments. I sound like I work in TV. I tell you, all the ideas I got, this could be the start of a whole new career for me as a television producer. Sounds like I should be driving a Jag with a blonde in the front seat, huh? Yelling at my assistant on my cellular. That's what this guy does."

"Who?"

"The executive producer of this show. You should see the chickie he's got cutting his segments for him. Hoo-boy. And his office on the lot? You could almost fit the showroom in it, it's so big. And he likes me, he likes what I've given him. So if—"

"Bernie."

"Yeah?"

"What happened?"

"What?" He was confused. I'd interrupted his ever-expanding fantasies of wealth and success. "When?"

"At Ojai," I said. "After that white-haired guy got stabbed."

He put the remote down and sat back in his creaky wooden chair behind his sagging wooden desk in his cramped office that needed a new paint job and had no heater or air conditioner. Reality was not nearly as much fun as the imagined future.

"It got a little out of hand."

"Out of hand like here?" I looked over my shoulder at the showroom of the comedy club we were in. "People heckling the comics?"

"A little more out of hand than that."

"In the cold open on the tape the anchor said something about it starting a full-scale prison riot. They showed video of prisoners assaulting guards."

"I wouldn't call it a riot exactly . . ."

"What would you call it?"

He shrugged. "A few prisoners started fighting. Tossing some chairs around. Yelling at the guards. Stuff like that. I got a few minutes of it on tape."

"I'd like to see it."

"It's on the original tape."

"Where's that?"

"It's in a safe place."

"What happened to the comedian that was stabbed?"

"Hey, Kincaid." I was beginning to pain him. "If you want to find out the whole story, tune in and watch when this airs. For fifteen grand, I don't ask those kinds of questions."

"I'm not trying to get fifteen grand," I said. "I'm trying to get one-twenty-five a show."

He immediately dropped his defensive posture. Like a lot of

people I'd met in show business, Bernie could change attitudes and personalities with the same ease as trying on different kinds of hats.

"Why don't you come by the club Monday night around ten o'clock?" He spoke with soothing confidence, as though I was the one who needed to be trusted. "The showroom's dark, but I'll be here. Knock on the back door. I'll have gone to the bank by then and I'll have your hundred bucks."

"Bernie, it's a hundred and twenty-five you owe me," I said.

"Oh, yeah, right. I appreciate your professionalism here, Biff, I really do." He smiled gently.

"No problem, Bernie. Just one other thing."

"Sure."

He was seated and I was standing. I reached out and pressed the EJECT button on the VCR. The dub he'd gotten of the finished *Eyewitness Crime* segments slid out and into my hand. "This your only copy?"

"Yeah."

"Good." I tucked it in my jacket.

"Hey, what—?"

"You'll get it back Monday," I said. "When I get my money."

"Kincaid." Bernie was up and on his feet. His gentle smile fell on the floor. "That's mine."

"Wouldn't do me any good if it wasn't," I said. He didn't come out from behind his desk and I did nothing to encourage him. "See you Monday night."

I turned and left his office, walking back out into the showroom. Rick Parker was leaning against the drinking side of the bar, smoking a cigarette, and it wasn't the first he'd lit waiting for me to get out of Bernie's office. "What took you so long?" he asked.

"He shorted me," I said.

Rick smiled, showing his missing tooth. "You and Scofield both, huh?" He leaned over the bar and lifted the bag that was the night's bank from the cash register. It hit the countertop with a metallic chink of coins, muffled by bills. "Then this ought to be fun. We barely covered the power bill tonight."

I didn't mention the tape I'd just taken. "Good luck in there."

Rick exhaled the last of his smoke, stubbed it out in the ash-

25

tray, and said, "Ain't it the fuckin' truth. I'll need it." He picked up the bank and walked toward Bernie's office.

I went out the back exit, hitting the metal door hard enough so everyone would know I was leaving. I froze just outside, in the parking lot, until the door swung back into place with a bang.

I wasn't going home yet. I just wanted everyone left in the club to think I was.

A comedy club owner could short his comics—even stall them twenty-four hours—but if he shorted his bartender then he was in all kinds of trouble. Comics were overhead. The bar was profit, and the bar had not done well tonight.

On top of that, Bernie was coming into fifteen thousand dollars Monday. I wondered if Rick knew that yet.

If there were going to be a fireworks show between Bernie and Rick I didn't want to miss it.

I was not to be disappointed.

SIX

I bent down low and silently walked over toward Bernie's half-open office window. I heard Rick's voice and then Bernie's. I crouched underneath the windowsill so I could hear what they were saying. Surprise! They were arguing about money.

Bernie: "How bad's the news tonight, kid?"

Rick: "We barely covered overhead."

Bernie unzipped the bag. I heard Bernie make a disapproving sound. "Six hundred forty . . ."

"Six-forty-two-fifty-seven."

"Still . . . is this from all three shows?"

"Yeah."

"You clock out?"

"No."

"Go clock out. We got other business to take care of."

"We take care of business, and then I clock out."

"I'm the fucking boss and I make the fucking rules," Bernie said, as casually as if he was updating a score on a baseball game.

Rick sighed and walked out of Bernie's office. I heard the metallic *chunk* of a time clock on the other side of the club, near the kitchen. While he was gone I heard the soft whisper of bills as Bernie counted money and then the papery crackle of an envelope.

Rick: "The comics say you shorted 'em."

"I did not. I paid 'em some tonight and I'm paying 'em some Monday."

"Monday you get paid for the tape, right?"

So Rick knew about the tape.

"Supposed to," Bernie replied.

"How about me?"

"You're getting your money tonight. Here."

I heard Rick open an envelope. Now it was his turn to count.

"Don't worry," Bernie said. "It's all there."

"Bernie, there's only five hundred bucks in here."

"Yeah?"

"You said we'd go fifty-fifty."

"Yeah. When the deal was a thousand. It went up from there."

"They're paying you fifteen grand Monday—"

"It was a thousand when we said fifty-fifty. I'm paying you half of a thousand. That's five hundred bucks."

Rick's voice was rising in heat and volume by degrees. "I set up that deal," Rick said. "I'm the one who called the executive producer to see if they were in the market to buy something like this."

"And I'm the one who owns the copyright on the tape. The lawyer for the network said so."

"So it was fifty-fifty until I handed over the tape, is what you're saying . . ."

"I already paid you for your time when you were there: ten dollars an hour, just like bartending."

"You said we were partners . . ."

"The extra five hundred was a bonus. Found money. Like when you skim off the till."

"There was just that once, and I was going to pay you back, every dime . . ."

"Then what the hell are you bitching about? You were looking for a chance to make it up to me, and you did. Now we're even. Five hundred bucks. It's more than you deserve."

I heard the wooden rattle of chair legs scooting back.

"I took twenty dollars from you so I could eat the next day and you cost me thousands."

"Get the hell out of here," Bernie said. "Don't come back."

"There wouldn't be a tape if it wasn't for me!" Rick was yelling now. "There wouldn't be a prison show or a TV deal if I hadn't set them up! I'm the one who put this money in your pocket!"

"You said you wanted to know how the big boys play in Hollywood?" Bernie roared back. "Now you know. My ass is sore how many times I been bent over a barrel. How many guys you think come through here go on to their own sitcoms? Their own hit movies? And where do you think the industry sees 'em. Here! I've comped more tickets and drinks for those high-rolling assholes with their cell phones and fancy cars it's no wonder I'm going broke!"

"Bernie—"

"Shut up!" Bernie roared.

Even crouching outside the window I cringed at the pent-up rage in Bernie's voice. There was no mask in place now. This was the real man we were hearing.

Now I heard his chair go back. Bernie was standing, pacing in his cramped office, his voice moving to and from the window. "Who put Jack Taylor onstage when no other club would touch him? Me! Night after night, telling those same stupid wife jokes he did when he hosted the Emmys. No manager, no agent, no nothing. Spending the night in his car in the lot out back. Eating leftover pizza from the kitchen. I was here the night Howard Schultz saw him and signed him as his latest client. Did you hear what his latest syndication deal got him? Two hundred million. And it's seven years later and I'm looking for change in the carpet here. Not a phone call, not a fucking thank-you, and he sure as hell didn't come back here to shoot any of his HBO specials."

"Bernie . . ." Rick said.

"That's just one story I got." Bernie's voice had dropped to a growl. He wasn't talking to Rick. He was playing the tape loop that ran continuously in his mind. "One story out of dozens." He snorted. "Comics. They squawk when you short 'em a dollar, but don't go looking to them for a dime. They don't remember, they don't appreciate. They dump you as soon as they don't need you anymore—like Hillary Thomas." He changed his voice to nastily mimic a woman's, nasal and high. " 'You're gonna be my manager, Bernie. When I get my show. You're going to be executive producer. You and me, Bernie, all the way to the top.' Yeah, big talk as long as I kept her in weekend spots. As soon as NBC waved a development deal at her, she lost my number. I left so many messages for her I must have broken her answering machine. Next thing I see, she's making a hundred thousand a month on her syndicated talk show."

He sat back down. "And you're busting my balls over a few lousy grand."

A respectful silence went by. Then Rick Parker did exactly what he wasn't supposed to do.

"Bernie—"

"What?"

"About my money—"

"You got your money."

"About the rest of my money—"

"Go home, Rick."

"Bernie, if you don't make good with me—"

"You got paid more than you deserve."

"—I swear to God I'll—"

"You'll what?" Now Bernie's voice was light, breathy. Taunting. "Turn me in to your parole officer? As far as he's concerned, you're still washing dishes in the kitchen. You're not supposed to be inside the showroom, where they serve alcohol. You make one move on me I'll turn you in for lifting that twenty bucks out of the till. You'll be in handcuffs and in front of a judge so quick you won't have time to take a piss." Bernie chortled darkly. "But, then again, maybe you miss getting your jailhouse jollies every night. Hey, how does that work, anyway? Which one were you, the husband or the wife? You lie there in bed, waiting for Bubba to grease you up like a Thanksgiving turkey?"

Bernie laughed.

When he stopped, I heard Rick's voice, and it, too, had changed.

"Maybe it's time," Rick said slowly and carefully, "I showed you everything I learned in prison."

Bernie was silent. Rick walked out of his office.

I realized he was coming out into the parking lot, and when he cleared the back door there was a good chance that he'd see me crouching under Bernie's office window. I scooted over to the shadows offered by some bushes growing against the fence that separated Flugelhorn's from the bagel shop next door. I knelt in the garbage and dead leaves. The back door banged open and Rick Parker walked out, his shoulders bunched, the muscles in his arms tense. He stopped under a streetlamp to light a cigarette and he stood there smoking, illuminated in a halogen glow. My car was a block away, and there was no other way to it, so I squatted in the dirty shadows and watched him inhale and exhale swirling boas of smoke in the still night air. Then Rick heard or saw something that made him stub out his butt and start toward Ocean Park Boulevard at a trot. Within seconds I heard it, too: the diesel rumble of a bus engine.

I listened for the gassy sound of the doors opening, Rick's voice as he said something to the driver. The night was so still and quiet I could hear the tinkle of coins as he dropped his money in just before the doors closed. I could see why he wanted fifty-fifty on the money; he didn't even own a car. In L.A., it's like not having citizenship papers.

I listened to the bus doors close and then I jumped as the back door of Flugelhorn's opened one last time and Bernie Coleman stepped out, less than ten feet away from me. I couldn't see his face as he shut the door firmly and tested it to make sure it was locked.

He walked to his car on the far end of the lot as the bus carrying Rick Parker pulled away. Bernie got in his ten-year-old Toyota and started the engine and drove away. His face was a blank. Monday was going to be better. Monday he was going to get fifteen thousand dollars.

I straightened up and brushed debris off the legs of my pants and started walking toward my car. Time for me to go home, too.

SEVEN

The next day was Sunday. I watched the tape I'd taken from Bernie again. There was something I hadn't noticed before. Most of the convicts who performed comedy had their faces blurred out deliberately, except for the man who was stabbed.

Who was he? Why was he stabbed? Did he live? Did he die? Was he interviewed later on? And why wasn't his name mentioned?

Maybe all of those questions were answered in the next segment.

Monday afternoon I called Bernie.

"You got my money?" I asked.

"Sure. You got my tape?"

"I watched it again."

"Don't wear it out. Are we still on for ten o'clock or do you have a spot somewhere?"

"I got an eight-forty-five spot at the Comedy Store, but they may run late."

"See you some time between ten and eleven."

"Don't ditch me and don't short me, Bernie."

"Kincaid, I got your money. I'll be in my office or out in the showroom. Ring the bell by the back door and I'll let you in."

"Bernie, one question."

33

"What?"

"Who's the guy that got stabbed?"

"I did know his name," Bernie said, "but I forgot it."

I hung up. He was still mad at me. I'd ask him again when he wasn't.

At fifteen minutes after ten I pulled into the lot behind Flugelhorn's. The parking lot was empty except for Bernie's car. There was a light on in his office window. I parked and rang the bell on the back door, the tape tucked under my arm. No answer.

I was going to bang on the back door with my fist but I noticed it was ajar. I pushed it with my fingertips. It opened.

Uh-oh.

I walked in slowly, looking around for some sign of trouble or safety. "Hello?" I called out.

I heard something dripping. I turned and looked in the direction of the bar.

Someone had smashed the bottles behind the bar with a heavy object. Dozens of bottles of liquor and mixers lay in shards, their contents running onto the floor.

"Bernie?" I said as I walked toward his office.

The door to his office was closed so tight it didn't open. It wasn't locked. It had been jammed shut by force. I put a shoulder to it, the wood gave and the door swung back on its hinges and that's when I saw what had happened to Bernie.

"Bernie," I said. "Oh my God."

Bernie was sitting upright in his chair, his eyes almost completely closed, his hands dangling at his sides. A long knife with a dark wooden handle was protruding from the center of his chest, blood running out from the wound to gather in his lap.

He was trying to breathe, but the act was so painful to him that his chest hitched and spasmed as he drew only the minimal amount of air into his lungs. His eyes fluttered in his head as he did it. I wasn't sure he knew I was there.

I looked around the office for a phone. There was one on his desk. I picked it up and dialed 911. I set the tape down on Bernie's desk while I was connected to an operator.

I said who and where I was. I had to read the address for Flugelhorn's off a piece of stationery taped to the wall. I told the operator about Bernie and the knife in his chest. While I was describing the knife wound, Bernie took in another breath, his hand twitching with pain. I told them to please hurry.

The operator had one last question before I hung up: "Is the assailant still in the building?"

"I don't know," I said.

"An ambulance is on its way. So are the police."

I hung up and looked around. It hadn't occurred to me that whoever did this might still be there. The back door had been opened when I came in. It locked on the way out. Maybe . . .

I stepped out of Bernie's office to look around. I didn't have any weapon with me. I wondered if Rick kept something behind the bar.

I stepped over to the bar to look behind it. There was a small baseball bat taped underneath, big enough to be held and swung in one hand. I wrenched it loose and hefted it, feeling safer immediately.

Then I heard something swish in the air behind me and before I had a chance to duck, block or turn, it connected with the back of my head and I fell to the floor amidst the broken bottles and spilled spirits and everything went black.

That's how I woke up in a hospital bed feeling like my skull was fractured. I pressed the call button for the nurse, but by the time anyone showed up I'd passed out again.

When I woke up the second time, it was not a nurse who was standing at my bedside, it was a lab-coated doctor. Tall and with a scraggly beard, he looked younger than I was. A resident.

"Hi, Brian," he said, tucking my chart under his arm to shake my hand. "I'm Dr. Marsten. It is Brian, isn't it?"

The handshake movement cost me a little pain, but it was less intense than before. "Actually, most people call me Biff."

"Biff?" He made a note in the chart. "Don't think I've ever really met a Biff before."

"It's a family nickname," I croaked. "The initials from my first and middle names."

"Brian Francis Kincaid . . . B . . . F . . . Biff . . ." He tossed his head from side to side like a surfer shaking water out of his ears. "I get it."

"I don't," I said. "Where am I?"

"Cedars-Sinai. You have a rather nasty cut on your head. Do you remember how you got it?"

"Someone hit me on the head from behind," I said. Talking hurt.

Dr. Marsten blinked. "Well, now . . . that's not good."

"What happened to Bernie?" I asked. "Is he dead?"

"Bernie?"

"I was in a comedy club," I said. "The owner was stabbed in the chest. I was knocked out."

"I don't know about anyone else, Biff," Dr. Marsten said. "I'm just here to treat your injury. The police want to talk to you about what happened, though, as soon as I feel you're ready."

"Bring 'em in."

"I want to run some tests first," the doctor said. "I'm afraid you might have a mild concussion."

"If this is mild, I'll bet a serious one hurts like hell."

"It can do more than hurt. We x-rayed you while you were unconscious. You're lucky you don't have a fractured skull."

"I was making a joke," I said. "I'm funnier without bandages on my head."

He smiled patiently and set his clipboard aside and started his examination. It involved some following his finger, closing and opening my eyes, and reacting to needle pokes in the ends of my feet. He used one of those small rubber mallets to test my knee reflexes; he called it Marsten's Silver Hammer. Comedy. Then he sent me downstairs for some more X rays. That involved a ride in a wheelchair and posing for a camera the size of an engine block.

"I'm going to keep you in the hospital for another day," Marsten said when it was all over, "just for safety's sake."

"Okay."

"But for the next week I need you to rest, change your bandages daily, avoid alcoholic or caffeinated beverages and call me immediately if you feel dizzy, faint or experience serious pain. And I want you back here in two or three days."

"How soon until the bandages come off?"

"A week."

"And until the stitches come out?"

"Another week."

I looked at my left hand and right knee. There were bandages there, too: places I'd sliced open when I fell amongst the broken glass. I inventoried a few more light cuts and bruises. He was right. A week.

No coffee and no beer sounded like no fun. I couldn't go onstage looking like I'd just had a brain tumor removed. The next seven days were going to be a drag. I was going to have to get a hat.

"When can I talk to the police?"

The doctor looked at a business card in his pocket. "I'm supposed to call a Detective . . . Gilmore. Knowing the police, they have a habit of showing up without an appointment."

"I'm ready."

"What did you do," he asked on his way out, "that caused you to get such a nasty bump?"

"I'm a stand-up comedian."

"Didn't know you could get your head split open being a comedian."

"You'd be surprised," I said.

He didn't know what to say to that. He nodded once and lifted his clipboard in farewell and walked out. I leaned back against my pillow, closed my eyes and waited for the police to come.

EIGHT

"Mr. Kincaid?"

I opened my eyes. A man wearing a department store sport coat, dark slacks and a serious face was standing at the foot of my hospital bed.

"Who are you?" I said.

He produced a badge. He looked to be about ten years older than me. He had graying hair cut close to his head in a Caesar cut. He had a jaw I could use to corner a house and eyes the color of menthol drops. His white dress shirt was tucked neatly inside his pants and that still left some slack. Even under the sport coat I could see he had the muscular build of a beat cop. He stood over six feet tall. A nurse walked by and slowed to look.

"I'm Detective Sergeant Stephen Gilmore of the Ocean Park Police Department," he said. "How are you feeling?"

"Well enough," I said. "How about Bernie?"

"Bernie Coleman?"

"Yes. Is he dead?"

Gilmore nodded. "He died of his injuries en route to the hospital."

I took in a breath and let it out. I looked at a spot on the wall and listened to the beating of my heart as it rose out of my chest and filled my ears and made my head wound throb. I closed my eyes and leaned into the pain, holding it tight against me.

"Are you all right, Brian?"

"Sure." I opened my eyes. Bernie was still dead. He always would be from this point forward. There wasn't anything I could do about it. "Most people call me Biff."

"Okay. Biff. Feel up to answering a few questions?"

"Please."

"What do you remember about last night?"

I used my arms to sit up straight in my angled hospital bed. I told him what I remembered.

"You were showing up to get some money?"

"Money he owed me from that weekend's shows."

"So you're a professional comedian?"

"Yes."

His head moved slightly to one side and then back to its original position. "Don't think I've ever met a professional comedian before."

"Amateurs are flooding the market," I said.

"How much money did he owe you?"

"A hundred and twenty-five dollars."

"And he was going to pay you cash?"

"Yes. He'd only paid me five hundred after the last show."

"When was the last show?"

"Saturday night," I said. "Eleven o'clock."

"Why didn't he write you a check for the rest?"

"You don't take too many checks in my business."

"And how did you work out this arrangement?"

"For collateral, I took—" I looked at the detective anew. I just remembered something. "The tape."

"Tape? What tape?"

"I took a tape from Bernie," I said. "It had two segments of a television show on it." The whole story came spilling out of me in bits and pieces, me having to back up and explain about the prison show and the footage Bernie had shot.

"I left it on his desk when I called 911," I said. "Was it there?"

Gilmore shook his head. "I'll go back and look for it."

"Maybe it's what they were after," I said. "And he didn't have it. I had it." I looked up at Gilmore. "If I hadn't taken it from him, maybe he'd still be alive."

"There's no way of knowing that for sure at this point." He gave me his business card. "If you think of anything else, any other details you might have left out, please give me a call."

I held his business card in both hands. "Okay." It was all I could think of to say.

"I'm going to need phone numbers as to how to get in touch with you," he said. "Dr. Marsten tells me that you're going to be in the hospital just one more day."

I gave him my home number and my pager number. "And most nights I'm at the Comedy Store. If I'm not there you can try the Improv or the Laugh Factory."

"Aren't you supposed to take it easy for a while?"

"I probably won't be onstage," I said. I touched the bandage on my head. "Just hanging out."

He nodded. "Think about what happened," he said. "If you have any new information—anything at all—call me."

"I will."

"I'm sorry about your loss. Was Mr. Coleman a friend of yours?"

I couldn't think of a way to explain what Bernie was to me so I nodded.

"Nice meeting you, Biff. I wish it was under better circumstances."

We shook hands.

"Me, too."

He turned to go.

"Detective Gilmore?"

He stopped and looked back.

"Why didn't whoever kill Bernie kill me, too?"

"I don't know, Biff," he said. "They should have. It was sloppy of them."

Then he left.

I pulled my legs up to my chest and folded my arms across my knees, leaned my head forward and wished there weren't so many bad people in the world.

NINE

The story made the Tuesday evening news.

I sat in my hospital bed and watched a reporter from Channel Seven standing in front of Flugelhorn's—now surrounded by yellow police tape with a patrol car parked in front—tell the general populace how owner and manager Bernie Coleman had been murdered inside the comedy club last night.

The screen was filled with a driver's license photo of Bernie. Why did news reports always feature the deceased's driver's license photo? It was routinely the worst picture anyone had of themselves. I was going to file away one of my headshots taken by a professional photographer along with my will. In case of my death, use this photo.

The reporter said Coleman's body was discovered by a stand-up comedian who performed at the club, and police were interviewing him to see if he can supply them with any leads. Right now police had very little to go on.

The story ended on an ironic note, the reporter in his live shot commenting how Flugelhorn's had been the site of many nights of laughter and a favorite drop-in spot of such comedians as Jay Leno, Jerry Seinfeld, and Robin Williams. Now, there was only silence—and sorrow—at Flugelhorn's. Back to you in the studio.

Dr. Marsten let me go the next morning. He saw me a little

after nine in the morning, after I had more X rays of my skull taken. When he walked into my room, he had the X rays of my head in a sleeve marked RADIOLOGY. He slid them out one by one and held the ghostly reversed images up to the light of the window. "Uh-huh . . ." I could see my jaws, teeth and the outline of my skull. Not my best angle. Even worse than my driver's license photo.

"I see . . ." Views were recorded from the front, back and sides. I felt a little outside of myself, watching them, perhaps because from the pictures you couldn't tell who it was and whether that person was living or dead or just needed to floss more.

Marsten slid the films back into their sleeve. "Biff, you're looking good."

"It's the blue eyes," I said. "The strawberry blond hair."

"Well, the X rays don't show any injury to the skull or the sack of fluid that surrounds the brain. You got hit, but not hard enough to do any real damage. Besides the stitches, of course."

"So I can go?"

He smiled. "You can go. I want to see you again before the end of the week."

"Great."

"I can tell you can't wait to get out of here," he said. He stopped smiling. "The police detective . . ."

"Gilmore."

"Gilmore. He called. He told me what happened. I'm sorry about your friend who was killed."

I nodded with no expression.

"There were some press here trying to get an interview with you but I shooed them away."

"Thanks," I said. "I only like to be on TV when I'm being funny."

"You have someone who can come and get you?"

"My car's at the club," I said. "I'll take a cab."

"Detective Gilmore said he'd like you to call him before you left," Marsten said. "I think he had some more questions."

We shook hands and he left and I called Gilmore. I caught him at his desk.

44

"I was just about to check out," I said. "Take a cab over to Flugelhorn's and pick up my car."

"I'll meet you there," he said. "I'd like for you to take a look at the crime scene. See if we can find this videotape you were talking about."

After I was discharged, I rode in a wheelchair down from my room to the lobby. I hailed a cab out front and rode through morning traffic to Flugelhorn's. My car was still there, next to Gilmore's unmarked car. He got out and greeted me.

"You feel well enough to come inside and take a look around?" he asked, eyeing the bandages on my head. I still needed to get a hat.

"Sure."

The unlocked back door of Flugelhorn's was marked with yellow crime scene tape. I stepped under the tape and walked into the club.

It was dark inside even though outside it was a sunny day. The houselights were dimmed to candle level, and I needed a few seconds for my vision to adjust. I looked to my right and saw that the bar bottles hadn't been replaced. The smell of their contents filled the air: sickly sweet mixers along with the pungent vapors of distilled spirits.

I looked around the club. I couldn't help but think that there was something else wrong, something else out of place . . .

"See anything?" Gilmore asked. He stood just a foot or two behind me.

"No. I mean, not yet." I turned and looked at the police detective. His face was still as a lake made from melted snow. "Maybe it'll come to me."

"Do you want to take a look at the office?"

"Sure."

I led the way. The door to Bernie's office was half-open, and I pushed it back with my fingertips. Light came in through his window, and a feeble fluorescent desk lamp had been turned on.

"The tape's gone," I said. I looked over my shoulder at Gilmore. He squeezed his massive shoulders in through the doorway. It was cramped, the two of us standing there. I could smell his shaving lotion. I pointed to a spot on the desk. "It was right there."

"Anything else missing?" Gilmore said. His breath was clean. I could feel it on my face, we were standing so close. He'd brushed his teeth since breakfast.

"Not that I can tell."

"Take your time. Look around. I'll be out in the club."

He stepped out of the office. I looked at Bernie's chair. There were dark stains on it. Blood. Some had gotten on the papers on his desk. I looked at the booking calendar. I wondered if anyone had bothered to call the comedians who were supposed to play the club this weekend and tell them that Bernie had been murdered. I just assumed Flugelhorn's was going to be dark. If it was going to be open, I wondered who would run it.

"Where's the knife?" I called to Gilmore.

"We didn't find the murder weapon," Gilmore answered from the club. "Someone took it."

The desk drawer had been pulled out and the contents were in disarray. The cash box Bernie had used to pay me was missing.

I walked out of the office and found Gilmore standing in the middle of the club, looking at comics' headshots hung on the walls.

"Bernie used a metal cash box to pay the comics," I said. "He kept it in his top desk drawer. He used keys to unlock both the cash box and the drawer. Did you guys find it?"

Gilmore shook his head. "How much money do you think was in there?"

"Bernie was supposed to pay me the rest of the money he owed me," I said.

"A hundred and twenty-five dollars, if I recall," Gilmore said.

"But he owed the headliner, Tim Scofield, even more," I said.

"Another two hundred?"

"Maybe. Maybe three," I said. "But Bernie and Rick Parker—the bartender—had had an argument about money. Thousands of dollars. I don't know if they had had another discussion since then, but either way Bernie was going to have at least a few hundred in cash on him. Maybe more. He said fifteen thousand was being wired into his account."

"It got there," Gilmore said. "I checked his deposits and withdrawals at the bank where he had his business and personal accounts. He did get fifteen thousand wired into his checking account, and took ten thousand out in cash."

"What day?"

"Monday, the day he was killed. The cash box was taken. So was his wallet—along with his ATM card. Someone hit the money machine a few hours after he was murdered, taking out three hundred before midnight and three hundred after. That's the maximum Bernie's bank allowed per day. The card hasn't been used since, which wouldn't do them any good because the account has now been frozen."

"So you're thinking the motive was robbery?"

"At a comedy club that was closed that night?" Gilmore said. "And—correct me if I'm wrong—Flugelhorn's was not exactly in its salad days."

"No," I said. "It wasn't."

"The back door was not forced," Gilmore said. "Someone was let in. I'm thinking it was an argument—maybe about money— that got out of hand."

I felt a tingling sensation along the edges of my fresh stitches in my head. "What does Rick Parker have to say about all this?"

"We haven't been able to find Rick Parker," Gilmore said. "We checked his apartment in Venice. He's not there. He has a car registered in his name somewhere, but it hasn't been impounded and we haven't been able to find it."

"Last time I saw him he was taking the bus," Biff said.

"The registration on the car was last marked nonoperational," Gilmore said. "I think it's not running."

"But he is," I said.

Gilmore nodded. He took in a breath and let it out. "Anything else different, that you can see?"

"Uhhh . . . I'm not sure," I said. "Give me just a minute."

"Okay."

I had an idea. "Is it all right if I go behind the bar?"

"Why?"

"That's where the light and sound controls are."

"What do you want to see?"

"If they still work."

"Why?"

"You said to see if anything was different."

He made a gesture with his arm. "Go ahead. We haven't cleaned up back there so look out for broken glass."

I stepped gingerly among the pools of drying liquid and shards of broken bottles where I'd fallen toward the panel that controlled the lights. I pushed the controls up and down, setting the gels and spots for a performance. Then I turned on the amp and found a cassette—the same tape Rick Parker had played the other night—and popped it in and hit PLAY. Nothing.

I twisted more knobs and touched more switches. Nothing came out.

I wasn't sure how the entire sound system worked, but I knew for sure how to set the mike level. I'd done it just a few nights ago when Scofield and I were alone in the club before it opened. (He had taped music in his act.) I found that dial now, turned it up to an acceptable level, came out from behind the bar, walked through the tables and chairs, and stepped onto the stage.

"Hello," I said into the mike. "Testing, testing. One-two-three."

Nothing.

"Sound system not working?" Gilmore asked.

"No," I said. "That's not it." I stepped off the stage and walked back toward him. "You hadn't been in here before Bernie's murder, right?"

"No."

"Then you wouldn't notice." I stood at his side, turning around to face the stage again, pointing first to one side of the stage, then the other. "See? It took me a while to catch it."

"What?"

"The speakers are missing," I said. "They've been stolen, too."

TEN

On the way home I stopped at a department store and got a hat. Having ancestors from the Emerald Isle, with the strawberry blond hair and freckles to prove it, I had quite a collection of hats as well as a working knowledge of every sunscreen on the market, but the bulk of the bandages covering my head wound called for something a little more pliant than the dozen or so baseball caps I had stashed in my closet back home.

I found a rather stylish tweed beret, bits of color woven into the fabric, and as I looked at myself in the mirror I thought it gave me a rather dashing romantic air. Ah, my love, I would stay wiz you, but zee war, she iz the cruel mistress, *non?*

I bought it and wore it home.

I live in Beachwood Canyon, which is a peaceful oasis in the middle of Hollywood. One minute you're driving along Franklin, edging through the lanes leading under the 101 freeway, and then a quick left at a light takes you up into the hills, heading right toward the Hollywood sign. Side streets branch off, twisting and turning among the trees and hillsides, and within minutes one can be looking at greenery and listening to the quiet while your fellow Angelenos play bumper cars for the rest of the afternoon.

I live in a circular apartment building with only a dozen units at the end of Beachwood Plaza, a tree-lined cul-de-sac walking distance from the noise and schmutz of Hollywood. I slid my RX-7 into my covered parking space, petted one of my neighbor's cats, and walked up the stairs to my apartment. I was looking forward to sitting out on my balcony with a view of the Hollywood sign and pondering the fates or taking a nap or alternating between the two when I found a wrinkled note jammed between my doorknob and the frame.

It was a flyer for a local Thai restaurant that had been left hanging on my doorknob. Someone had taken it and scrawled an unsigned message on one side with a dull pencil. I spread it out and read the words carefully.

KINCAID, it read. WATCH YOUR BACK.

Something red and rectangular fell out from the note. I picked it up. It was a drink ticket, with the date of the last show I performed at Flugelhorn's written on the back and initialed in Bernie's handwriting. Only one person besides the police would have these in their possession.

Rick Parker had been here.

So there I had it: Bernie Coleman had been murdered. The motive? Apparently to steal a videotape and some speakers out of the club. I was the closest thing to a witness and my life had been spared. The detective investigating the case told me I should be dead. Rick Parker had left me a warning.

I had a choice: I could sit and wait for the other people involved to fumble around and hope they caught whoever had killed Bernie Coleman or I could see what I could find out on my own. I wanted to find the killer before the killer found me. I had a lot more to lose here than just a hundred and twenty-five bucks. I'd probably piss off Gilmore by playing amateur detective, but I didn't want to die of politeness.

I walked down to the newsstand on Franklin called the Daily Planet. They sold books, comics, magazines and the industry trade papers. I picked up a copy of *Variety* left over from the day before. Today was Wednesday, but every Tuesday *Variety* runs a listing of shows currently in production and names the producers and companies involved. I looked up *Eyewitness Crime* and found it was produced in-house at Global United Network

Studios. The executive producer was Kyle Matthews. That was all the information listed, except for an address and a phone number where potential contributors could submit tapes.

Back home, feet up on the balcony, cordless phone in hand, I made my first call of the day.

"G-U-N." A female voice.

"Kyle Matthews's office please, or the offices of *Eyewitness Cri—*"

I didn't get to finish my sentence before I was put on hold. I held.

Hold-hold-hold . . .

"*Eyewitness Crime.*" A male voice.

"May I speak to Kyle Matthews please?"

Hold-hold-hold . . . A tape loop bleated out GUN's current lineup of shows, and welcomed their new affiliate in Kentucky. Check out our web site at www-dot-Global . . .

"Kyle Matthews's office." Another female voice.

"Yes, may I speak to Kyle Matthews, please." I wondered if politeness was my problem. Maybe if I barked and snapped at people in television they'd respect me more.

"May I ask who is calling?"

"This is Biff Kincaid. I'm a comedian."

"May I ask what this is regarding?"

All these may-I's. People in Hollywood were at their most courteous only when letting you know your place in the food chain was beneath theirs.

"It's regarding Bernie Coleman," I said. "He sold a tape to your show."

"Just a moment," she said. "I think Kyle's in a meeting . . ." She was setting me up to take a message. "Let me check."

Hold-hold-hold . . .

"Matthews." A male voice. I guess it was him.

"Kyle Matthews?"

"Yeah, yeah, yeah. I know who I am. Who are you?"

"Biff Kincaid. I'm the comedian who found Bernie Coleman after he'd been stabbed in the heart."

"Oh wow! Really? Man! I read about you in the papers. And saw the stuff on TV!" For the first time it occurred to me that Kyle Matthews was younger than I was. "Thanks for calling!"

"Bernie was very excited about the work you two were doing together," I said, "and I'd like to learn more about it. I was wondering if there might be a time in the near future when we could talk in person."

"Oh! Yeah! Sure!"

"How about today?"

"Today would be awesome."

Awesome? Definitely younger than me.

"Let's say two o'clock?" he said.

"I'll be there."

"You know where we are?"

I looked at the address on the trades. Santa Monica Boulevard and Gower. "You're right down the street from me," I said. "I live in Beachwood Canyon."

"Man, that's great! Can't wait to see you and hear all about what happened."

He said he would leave a pass at the gate. I said my good-byes and hung up.

At one-thirty, after lunch and a nap, I drove down to the GUN studios and onto the lot. I parked my car in a visitor space and tried to follow the map the guard had handed me at the gate through the trailers and bungalows. Once you're past the entrance, most studio lots look the same.

I found Kyle Matthews's parking space first. He had a red Ferrari parked in front of a sign that read RESERVED FOR KYLE MATTHEWS. In front of the building just beyond the Ferrari was a sign that read *Eyewitness Crime* in the same lettering as the show opens.

I walked in at a quarter of two. It look me that long to sign in and negotiate my way past security guards and receptionists and three assistants until I was actually guided to a building behind the one I had walked into and up a flight of stairs to a corner office that overlooked the lot. You would have thought these people were making biological weapons.

"Kyle is in an edit bay right now, looking at a segment," the third assistant told me. "He'll be right with you. Can I get you anything?"

"Yeah. An office like this would be nice."

Her mouth tried to lengthen. I was not a person who could

significantly advance her career and therefore not useful. "Everyone says that."

I shut up and sat down. It's so great to be different.

On the walls of Matthews's office were photos of law-enforcement officials handing plaques and awards to the same person, a short, thin slip of a guy who looked like he was barely out of college, always wore a vest and small glasses with very thin frames in a variety of styles. On the wall next to the pictures were the awards themselves. Dozens of them. Holy cow. I guess *Eyewitness Crime* had its fans.

I looked at the desk. There were a few pairs of glasses scattered across the top, in styles to match the many different moods of Kyle Matthews. I looked back at the photos of him. This was not a guy who got picked first for the football teams in high school.

I was looking at a bookcase that was built to house legal texts but now was holding cassettes of episodes of *Eyewitness Crime* as though they were of equal importance when Kyle Matthews came bursting through his own office door. He lunged at me as he said his name and shook my hand before I had a chance to get out of my chair. Then he dived behind his desk and landed in his own chair and spoke into a wireless phone that he held in his hand all the time. It let out bursts of static like a walkie-talkie.

"Brenda, I'm in a meeting. Only interrupt if I get a call from a senior VP or above."

He put the phone in a handle meant to recharge its battery before Brenda could reply. I was right, he was younger—and shorter—than I was, maybe by as much as ten years and five inches. That would put him in his early twenties.

"Sorry to keep you waiting," he said. Today he was wearing an argyle sweater vest and a pair of round specs with red frames. As he spoke he took the glasses off and laid them down and put on another pair with tortoiseshell rims. He was like Elton John with his glasses. "What happened with Bernie?"

"Well, he's dead," I said.

"Right, right, right," he said thoughtfully. "Sorry to hear about that."

"The night before he was murdered—"

"Murdered? Why do you say murdered?"

"Well, when I found him he had a knife sticking out of his chest. Then someone hit me over the head hard enough to give me stitches." I pointed to the beret on my head. "Now call me crazy, but—"

Kyle laughed, a short barking sound I was sure I never wanted to hear again. "You didn't by chance happen to get this on video, did you?"

"No."

"Okay. Sorry." He shrugged. "The question was in bad taste, I know. But I had to ask."

"Bad taste is what makes this business great."

I heard the laugh again. Dammit.

"Two nights before Bernie was murdered," I said, "he showed me two segments of an upcoming episode of *Eyewitness Crime* where he'd sold you some footage of a prison—"

Kyle Matthews rolled his eyes. "Yeah, I remember. I mean, no disrespect to the dead or anything, I mean, God rest his soul and all that but Bernie Coleman was a huge pain in the ass."

"How did you meet him?"

"Well, besides doing this show my deal with the studio includes four specials each year that I produce for sweeps. That's actually how I got the series. I did four specials last year and by the third one I was pitching *Eyewitness Crime*. Did you see any of them?"

"What specials?"

He ticked them off on his fingers. "Last year I did 'When Elevators Attack and Escalators Go Bad' which was all about accidents that happen at the office. Uhhh, 'World's Most Dangerous Birthdays,' we had that video of the kid whose hair is burned off by the candles on his cake, and 'Insect Invasion,' which was people getting stung to death by bees and that kind of thing."

"Of course."

"So this year I'm working on a series of *Eyewitness Crime* stories we're going to broadcast and reedit into a special called 'When Show Business Turns Deadly.' We have a magician who actually starts to saw his female assistant in half—don't worry, she lived. We interview him, her, an audience member who saw it, the ER physician who worked on her and she shows us her scar. In the video, we don't see any blood but you do hear her scream and the screams are real." He nodded vigorously as though he had said something of great encouragement to me.

"And you're going to put this on television?" I said.

"During sweeps."

"Too bad you couldn't film the operation."

"We're working deals with hospitals to put video cameras in the ERs and operating theaters for the series and a special I want to produce for the fall season called 'Death Caught on Tape.' I mean, in the moment when the soul leaves the body, can we see it on tape? With the use of special photography, of course. Infrared cameras, that kind of thing."

"Why don't you edit together a bunch of Holocaust footage," I suggested, "and call it 'When Nazis Attack'?"

"Ad sales shot me down on that one," he said. "Specials are getting harder to do. I tell you, everything's going into the show. That's why we run the stories on *Eyewitness Crime* first. Pretty soon were going to have to use re-creations, and those don't promo that well." He snapped his fingers. "But you were asking me about Bernie Coleman. For 'When Show Business Turns Deadly' we started calling around to the comedy clubs, trying to dig up footage. A lot of the show is going to be funny, with outtakes and people who became famous later on. We've got a few clips of hecklers getting onstage and duking it out with co-medians. Or the lights going out. One guy gets shocked from the mike stand real bad. Most of our deals are done quickly, like with someone who had the home video camera rolling when a tornado hit the trailer park. They tell us what they got, we tell them what we pay, send over the papers, cut a check, done deal, boom.

"But with Bernie Coleman . . . there was all this drama. Once we saw what he had, naturally we wanted to include it in the show. We made him an offer and then it was 'I have to be a producer,' and 'My name has to be in the opening credits of the show.' I told him we don't work that way. He finally settled for a special thanks in the end credits of the show and I also got him on camera. You'd be surprised what people will do for you if you get them on camera."

"In the footage I saw—" I said, but I was foolish to think I was going to finish my sentence.

Kyle interrupted: "And then when we finally did strike a deal, he had to come into the bay and personally supervise the dubbing of the video from VHS to Beta when we bumped it up. It was like he had the Zapruder film or something. There was stuff on that tape he obviously didn't want to air, even by accident."

"What else was on that tape?" I asked.

"We didn't get to see it!" Kyle waved his arms around, exasperated at Bernie's unprofessionalism. "All he sold us was the stuff about the inmates going on, doing their acts, the one guy getting stabbed, and then the riot afterward."

"Wait a minute," I said. "Riot?"

"Yeah, there was a full-scale riot. Didn't Bernie tell you that?"

"He downplayed it," I said. "Said there were just a few fights between prisoners."

Kyle shook his head, smiling. "Oh no, it got a lot more out of hand than that. You said Bernie showed you a tape of what we had done already?"

"Two segments," I said. "Leading up to a third."

"The third is where we cover the riot. It's something. Let me call Sharon Temple, she's the producer who's working on that show. I think the third segment's done except for the graphics and the music. I'll have her show you what she's got so far." He plucked his phone out of the cradle and started dialing a number. As it rang he looked at me and smiled. "Bernie didn't tell you what happened afterward at Ojai?"

"He said there were just a few scuffles, some chairs thrown . . ."

"Then you are not going to believe this, man. It is going to blow you away."

ELEVEN

The door to Kyle Matthews's office opened and Sharon Temple
walked in. "You rang?" She held up her pager to indicate she
had gotten her boss's message.

Sharon Temple was about five-seven and weighed a hundred
pounds and change. She wore her blond hair pulled back, with
thick, black-framed eyeglasses. She favored vintage clothing,
with an unbuttoned blue sweater and a long wool skirt and black
saddle shoes. No stockings. None of this hid the fact that she
was extremely good-looking. She had high cheekbones, icy blue
eyes, full lips and a peaches-and-cream complexion. She dressed
like a fifth-grade teacher, but if I'd had a teacher like her in fifth
grade I would have paid more attention in class.

"Sure," Kyle said. He introduced us. I wished I wasn't wearing
a beret. "Biff was the comedian who found Bernie Coleman when
he was murdered over the weekend."

"Oh, I'm so sorry for your loss," she said.

"Thank you."

"You didn't . . . get it on tape, did you?"

"No," I said. This business. All heart.

"Would you mind showing Biff the third segment of the Ojai
story, though?" Kyle said. "Bernie showed him the first two

and . . ." He turned to look at me. "What did you say your interest was?"

"I didn't get a chance to," I said. I was too busy listening to your life story. "I think that Bernie's murder might have had something to with the videotape."

Both Sharon and Kyle reacted to that. "What makes you say that?" Kyle said.

"The VHS dub you'd made of the first two segments was missing from Bernie's office after he was murdered." I didn't mention the missing speakers. "I'm wondering if whoever killed Bernie was after the original tape."

Sharon Temple and Kyle Matthews exchanged a look.

"Can you . . . ?" Kyle said to Sharon.

"I'm in the bay right now," Sharon said. "Be glad to."

"Be glad to what?" I asked.

"I'm going to have Sharon show you the third segment," Kyle said. He looked at his watch. "I've got to get to a focus group."

Since entering, Sharon had not closed the door behind her or stepped through the doorway or taken a seat. Now she held the door open even wider. "Follow me," she said.

That won't be hard to do, I thought to myself. Kyle waved good-bye as he started talking into his phone, instantly shifting his focus.

We wended our way through a hallway and down some stairs, outside the building and into a little courtyard and into another building.

"Did you ever meet Bernie Coleman?" I asked her.

She nodded. "I was the one who negotiated with him to buy the footage," she said. "I also did the field interview with him you saw in the first two segments."

"Kyle told me you were originally calling around to comedy clubs to find footage to put in a special," I said.

"That's right."

"Was that you specifically or someone else on your staff?"

"Me specifically," she said. "I was the first person to call Flugelhorn's."

"And was that how you met Bernie?"

"Actually, I got this guy Rick on the phone . . ."

"Rick Parker," I said. "The bartender."

"I guess that's who it was. I only talked to him once on the phone and I never met him. I described to him what I was looking for and before I was even through with my pitch he was telling me about this prison comedy show Bernie had shot."

"What did he tell you?"

"That he had been up at Ojai Men's Correctional Facility in central California shooting a comedy show. Bernie had footage of prisoners doing stand-up routines and during his act one prisoner had been stabbed by another inmate and that started a riot. Naturally, I got very interested. He took my name and number and I swear within five minutes Bernie Coleman was on the phone talking a mile a minute. He had seen the show, he loved the show, he definitely had something he felt we could use, when could we meet . . . I could hardly get a word in edgewise."

"That was Bernie," I said. "God rest his soul."

We were walking down a second-story hallway now, and stopped outside a door with a small glass panel in it. Through the glass panel I could see into a darkened room filled with editing equipment. A man was hunched over a control panel big enough to fly the space shuttle. At his eye level were a bank of monitors showing images of prisoners moving in slow-motion hand-to-hand combat. Bernie's footage of the riot.

"And what did Bernie say he had on tape?" I asked.

"He said he couldn't describe it to me," Sharon said. "He had to show me." We walked into the room and the man at the controls looked up. He had a beard and glasses. "Jim, did you want to go to lunch?"

Jim nodded and left without looking at me.

"You ever work in TV?" Sharon asked me as she slid into Jim's chair.

"I've been on a few stand-up shows," I said. "Most of them aren't on the air anymore except for cable reruns."

"No, I mean did you ever work as a producer?"

"No."

"Let me tell you the first thing I learned when I became a producer." She pressed some buttons and the tape began to rewind, images blurring backward so fast I couldn't tell what was happening. The sounds screeched until she turned a knob and it went to a low howl. "Editors make all the money."

I looked around for a place to sit. There was a small table with a phone and a laptop computer on it set back just six feet from the editing console. I took one of the three chairs. "So why don't you become an editor?" I asked.

She turned around and smiled at me like we shared a secret. "Because I want to be on-air."

"You mean like a reporter?"

She nodded. "I learned to work the editing console so I could view my tapes and cut together a reel after hours. Jim doesn't mind if I fool around while he's at lunch. Kyle lets me shoot stand-ups out in the field. Stand-ups being when a reporter's on camera, not your kind of stand-up."

"You shoot any for this?"

"I shoot some for every story," she said. "I'm sending out tapes all across the country to smaller markets, looking for a break." She laughed, far more pleasantly than Kyle Matthews. "This sounds so Hollywood. You know: 'But enough about me. What do you think of me?' "

"I think you're wasted not being on camera."

She smiled and turned a little red, and said, "Thank you. Sorry. I know this isn't what you came to talk about."

"And yet we fell into it so naturally, like old friends."

She pointed to one of the monitors, where an image of the riot was freeze-framed. "What we're working on now is laying in final voice-over tracks and music on the third segment." She turned back to the controls. "And this is what we have so far."

All three monitors went black. I picked the largest one to look at and watched as the black screen gave way to the *Eyewitness Crime* set and a somber Darren Mitchell. He looked into the camera with reserved concern. It's a dangerous world out there, his face said. I'm here to keep you informed as best I can.

"You ever work with him?" I asked.

"Darren?" she said. A touch of a button and the tape stopped. "Sure. I was on the floor when they shot this; otherwise, Darren misreads the scripts and won't watch the stories."

"Why does he do that?"

"See him? Right there? Sitting behind that desk?"

"Yeah?"

60

"Underneath that desk all he's wearing are cut-off shorts. From the waist up he's in a coat and tie."

"Uh-huh."

"And see that coffee cup? The one with the GUN network logo on it?"

"Yeah."

"You know what's in there?"

"Decaf?"

"Vodka."

"He drinks on the set?"

Sharon nodded. "And in his dressing room. That's why he has a limo service written into his contract. He's already been pulled over for a DUI. One more and he's fired. I think Kyle's going to fire him anyway. It's why he got fired from his last job." She turned and smiled at me again. "Welcome to TV."

I said nothing. She started the tape again.

"The comedy night at Ojai Correctional Facility had started out as a night to remember," a somberly drunk Darren Mitchell was saying, "one filled with laughter echoing off the stone prison walls as inmates enjoyed each other's routines about life behind bars. But after one performer was stabbed by a fellow prisoner onstage, it instantly turned into a night that no one would ever forget." He paused dramatically. "Jeff Elliott has the shocking conclusion."

Darren's face was no longer moving. Sharon had stopped tape again. "They hate each other," she said.

"Who?"

"Darren and Jeff."

"Why?"

"They both auditioned for the anchor chair. Darren got it. Jeff didn't. They have the same agent. Kyle's been talking to Jeff about taking over when Darren's contract is up."

"The backstage drama," I said. "I had no idea."

"Sorry," she said. "I love dirt. I love gossip."

"There any I should know about you?"

"Unfortunately, no," she said. "I could use a good rumor or two. Everyone thinks I'm a Goody Two-shoes."

"Not me."

That made her smile and look in my direction. She had a reply, but I wasn't going to hear it right then.

The tape started again. The screen was filled with the grainy home video footage of one inmate being stabbed by another in slow motion. Jeff Elliott's voice narrated. "This was the scene in February of this year during comedy night at Ojai Correctional Facility in California. What followed was a full-scale riot."

There was a white flash followed by a wide shot of the cafeteria-turned-showroom as prisoners fought with guards and with each other. The stage was cropped off at the top. This shot was followed by close-ups of different individual incidents, forming a tableau of violence and mayhem. One prisoner was on a table, being held facedown by four others as a fifth jumped up and down on his spine. A guard lost his hat as one prisoner in front pushed him into the waiting arms of two others. A second guard swung his baton in front of him, fending off inmates, connecting with the skull of one. He went down like a broken puppet, and the guard was overrun by other inmates and he disappeared under their faces and fists.

"Good God," I said.

Another wide shot, showing prisoners pouring out of the lunchroom and into the halls. The image froze. At first I thought Sharon had stopped the tape again, but she hadn't. This was a special effect. Low ominous music lent a scary atmosphere to the still.

"This was all of the Ojai riot that was caught on tape," Jeff Elliott said. "Bernie Coleman then grabbed the camera and fled for his life."

The image turned from grainy color to black and white.

"During the ensuing melee, as prisoners overwhelmed guards and briefly took control of a common area of the prison, thirteen inmates escaped, including—"

Dissolve to another still, this one of the stabbing itself. The picture darkened, except for a small circle that formed like a halo around the head of the man who had leaped on stage with a weapon.

"The attacker . . ."

That halo dimmed and another one formed around the head of the inmate who had been performing and was just a few frames away from being stabbed.

". . . and his victim."

I heard another voice. I recognized it as belonging to Warden Douglas. As he kept talking the image dramatically dissolved into Douglas's talking head.

"This videotape," Douglas said, "shows a man being stabbed. But it turns out that the alleged victim disappeared after we had gotten control of the situation. We found what looked like blood on the stage where he had been stabbed and then later—as the area was searched by local police—we found his clothes. There was no puncture or tear over the abdomen of his prison uniform. A knife never entered his body. And the uniform was stained red, although it didn't take our investigation long to determine that it wasn't blood. It was ketchup from the prison cafeteria."

Cut to Jeff Elliott walking around outside Ojai prison. "Of the thirteen prisoners who escaped, eight were recaptured that night. Another three were picked up within twenty-four hours. But the two men involved in the phony assault that started the riot—who apparently staged this bizarre stunt to gain their freedom—have yet to be apprehended."

The video dissolved to the time of the attack, freeze-framing the moving image and superimposing the prison mug shots of the two men.

"They are Johnny Whiteside of Los Angeles, convicted of grand theft, sexual assault, assault and battery and attempted murder."

Whiteside's headshot showed the same glacial features I had seen when he was performing, only in more detail: hair that had gone prematurely white, a heavily scarred face, lantern jaw and eyes the color and brightness of unfired bullets. He looked to be about forty years old and the ride had been rough for all parties concerned.

"And Sam Agar of Bakersfield, California, serving time for armed robbery and assault with a deadly weapon." Whiteside's headshot shrank to the size of a playing card and Agar's filled the screen. He was a heavyset man, fleshy around the eyes and jowls, his head shaved, his lips thick and full, with large ears, one gone cauliflower. He wasn't chubby and weak. He looked thick and strong, like an inbred cousin.

The two headshots then assumed equal size. "If you have seen either of these men, contact your local police at once. Tell them you saw it on *Eyewitness Crime*."

Back to Darren Mitchell in his anchor chair.

Sharon stopped the tape.

"See, this is the worst part about working in TV," she said. "I ran out of time on this one. I wanted to go into the rest of the story about how Ojai was a private prison and no longer considered an asset by the community. When American Rehabilitation Services—that's the parent company—contracted with the city to build it there, they said it would add jobs to the community and boost the local economy. That was a load of horseshit. ARS has done this in half a dozen cities around the country, getting a contract for millions and then farming out work to unqualified subcontractors. The plant is substandard, it has all kinds of operational problems that have yet to be resolved, and then Warden Douglas? He's never run a prison before. In his last job he was captain of the guards at a state pen—not in California. The day of the riot he didn't have his emergency beeper with him, the one that when he mashes on the button all guards are alerted. He'd left it in his office."

"Oops," I said.

"Also, ARS is importing prisoners from out of state to be kept at Ojai, and mingling high-security prisoners—such as those two jokers who escaped—along with low-security inmates." She punched more buttons and tapes eased themselves out of their playing decks. "You shouldn't have comedy night in a facility where there are maximum-security inmates. Douglas worked maximum security for six months in his entire career, then applied for a transfer. But does that stuff get ratings? Nooooo. Next up is video of a kid getting pulled into a gorilla cage." She looked at me. "Would you like to go to lunch?"

"Sure."

"Good." She smiled to herself and we got up and walked out of the editing suite. "Over lunch I'll tell you how I'm going to have to reedit that entire segment after I thought it was done." She touched me on the nose with an index finger. "And all because of you, blue eyes."

TWELVE

"Why do you think your story's going to change?"

We were sitting in the studio commissary. Sharon Temple was having a salad. I was having a turkey breast sandwich, and I'd watched the chef slice it off the bird. The food was good. Sharon had handed the cashier a pair of coupons as payment, and in line she'd told me to get whatever I wanted. Now this was show-biz.

"New elements," she said. "That's why I asked you if you had a tape of Bernie's murder or at least of the crime scene. Definitely would have wanted that. But now that Bernie's dead, that's a new wrinkle to the story and Kyle's going to want to either make that a fourth segment or cram it into what's already there, because now he has something he didn't have before."

"What's that?"

"You."

"What about me?"

"Kyle will want you."

"To do what?"

"To go on camera."

"On camera?"

"To be interviewed. About what it was like to find Bernie Coleman's body."

65

I'd finished one-half of my sandwich and was starting on the second half. "I don't think so."

"Why not?"

"I only like to be on camera when I'm being funny."

"Come on, it'll be good exposure."

"For who?"

"For you. Some casting director might see you and decide to put you in a movie or a sitcom—why are you laughing at me?"

"No, it's just—" I shook my head. "I hate to break the stereotype, but I'm not that desperate for fame that I'm looking for it on *Eyewitness Crime*."

Sharon Temple had yet to stop smiling.

"I mean, next time I go up at the Comedy Store, they're not going to put in my intro, 'as seen on *Eyewitness Crime*, so you know he's really funny, please welcome Biff Kincaid.' "

"But, see, if you agree to be interviewed—"

"Yeah?"

"Then I'll look good."

"You already look pretty good to me."

"Was that a compliment?"

"And there's more where that came from."

"I meant I would look good professionally. To my boss. On the job."

"I knew what you meant," I said. "And you know what I meant."

She finished her salad and sat back with her arms folded under her fabulous-looking breasts. She enjoyed this kind of repartee. It made her feel smart. "And then we'd get to see each other again."

"Who's to say we can't do that anyway?"

She shook her head. *Tsk, tsk, tsk.* "I heard you comedians were like this."

"Like what?"

"Always on the prowl, always looking to score . . ."

"You mean with women?"

"With everything. Always wondering 'what's in it for me?' "

"People say that about comedians?" I said. "All we want to do is bring joy and laughter to the world."

She was trying to not let her smile get any bigger. "And you're

66

something of a closed bunch. Live by your own rules. Kind of like a private fraternity."

"There's even a secret handshake. And a password. And a special knock. When we get together in private we wear those raccoon hats like you see on *The Honeymooners*."

"Come on, Biff." She clasped her hands and leaned forward, hunching her shoulders together. Her silk blouse and librarian's sweater were unbuttoned enough so that it created some Olympic-class cleavage. "Sit for me. We'll do hair, makeup, wardrobe . . ."

"Nope."

"Nice lighting . . ."

"No thanks."

"Take you out to dinner . . ."

"Are you asking me on a date?"

She sat back in her chair and laughed. "Do you know how many out-of-work actors call us? Saying they have this great footage they're willing to sell us—oh, and they need to be on camera."

I shrugged. "I'm not an actor. Not out of work, either."

"What can I do?" she said, bracing her hands against the table like she was about to stand up. "How can I close this deal?"

"You can let me see the footage you've got of Johnny Whiteside's performance before he got stabbed."

Her smile started to fade. We weren't flirting any longer. "Why?"

"I want to watch his act."

She looked at me. I heard other people at other tables in other conversations.

"His act?" she asked.

I nodded.

"What for?"

"I'd like to know if this was his first time onstage."

"How would you be able to tell that?"

"The way he holds the mike," I said. "His opening bit. What he does with the mike stand."

She shook her head. "I don't get it."

"Just humor me," I said. "We got time before your editor gets back?"

She looked at her watch. "Sure."

I stood, picking up both our trays. "Then let's go."

Back in the editing room, I watched as Sharon fast-forwarded through the tape of the prison show she had dubbed from Bernie's original.

"Why does it jump around like that?" I asked. Footage from Bernie's camera stopped and started at odd points. There were three inmates on before Johnny Whiteside. All of them started their acts in mid-sentence.

"Bernie would only let us dub certain sections from his original VHS tape," Sharon said. "Not only did he have to sit in the bay with me and the editor while we bumped it up to Beta, but he had to go into a separate room, down the hall, by himself, and cue the tape so no one could see what else was on that tape."

"Do you see what's missing?" I said. "See what he's edited out?"

"No, what?"

"The emcee," I said. "As soon as each comic is done, the tape is cut off. When another comic is alone onstage again, it starts back up."

Sharon rewound it and watched it again. "Huh," she said. "Why is that?"

"I couldn't tell you," I said. We came to Johnny Whiteside's part of the show. "Okay, let me see this."

The tape jump-cut to Whiteside alone onstage, taking the mike out of the stand and setting it aside with an ease and a practice the other inmates hadn't shown. He was grinning. His teeth glistened and looked gray in the fluorescent lighting from the cafeteria. He had a single black eyebrow that grew across his forehead in a straight line. With his gray hair, black eyes, gray teeth and scarred face, he looked like he was about to change into a wolf.

"We got any fresh fish in the audience tonight?" he asked.

The other comics hadn't known how to work the mike. Whiteside was talking right into it. The other comics had started out asking the crowd how they were doing or acting nervous or saying they had never done this before. Not Whiteside. He was going right into his first bit.

"Cause I loooooooves me some fresh fish," he said. He got a large whoop from the crowd on that one.

"You know, I logged this tape myself and I still don't get it," Sharon said. "What's he talking about?"

"New inmates," I said.

"Why does he call them fish?"

"Jail talk."

"I likes 'em so fresh, they's still floppin'." Then he dropped the mike with a thud and started gyrating around on stage like a man trying to keep something from being inserted into his rectum. It was fast and cartoony. When Sharon turned and looked at me, I realized I'd made a single "huh" sound.

"You think this guy's funny?" she asked.

"I think he's done this before."

"And what I likes to put on my fish—a' course—is some tartar sauce," Whiteside said. He grabbed his crotch and held it.

"He's disgusting," Sharon whispered.

"Or making a signal," I said. "How soon does he get stabbed?"

"Right . . . about . . . now."

Whiteside was in the middle of a setup. "Now this is the first time I been in the cafeteria when they ain't been serving food here."

Boos.

"So's I gots me a few recipes that Momma Whiteside sent to me," he said, reaching in his pocket and pulling out a piece of paper.

"That's it," I said. "That's the signal."

"Signal for what?"

"For Agar to come and stab him."

"—and I thought I'd read 'em to you," Whiteside said.

Just then Whiteside turned and looked off camera.

"Slow it down," I said.

Sharon pressed a button and the video slowed to a frame a second.

"Look at Whiteside," I said. "He's not running. He's not moving. Look at his eyes. He knows what's going to happen."

Agar's shaven head entered the frame, one arm drawn back,

ready to plunge a small black object into Whiteside's abdomen. Whiteside's smile dropped, his expression calm and set. He had rehearsed this part of his performance as well.

Agar knocked him down with a single blow and kept going, like a charging rhino. The ketchup exploded over Whiteside's stomach and he clutched his belly in mock agony.

The camera swung away, following Agar as he ran into a guard and knocked him down, too.

Cut.

The next shots were of prisoners fighting. Guards being over-powered. One wide shot of the cafeteria as it exploded into chaos.

"See," I said, "now why did he do that?"

"Why did who do what?"

"Why did Bernie only dub off certain sections of this tape?" I said. "Especially the riot footage. What does he not want you to see?"

Sharon stopped tape. "Biff, I was hoping you'd know."

I looked at her. "Bernie was here with the original tape?"

"Yes."

"He mentioned where he was keeping it?"

"No."

"He say anything to Kyle Matthews about it?"

"Not that Kyle told me."

"Hm."

"My turn for a question."

"Go ahead."

She popped the tape out and held it up in her hand. "You think Whiteside's done stand-up before this?"

"Absolutely."

"So what does that mean for my story?"

"I don't know yet," I said. "But I got a feeling from watching that show that he's going to try it again."

"You mean another bank robbery?"

I shook my head and smiled. "No. I mean another show."

Sharon did a slow take. "You mean he's going to try to get onstage somewhere?"

"He might," I said.

"That makes no sense," Sharon said. "He's a criminal at large."

"Yeah, but I know his type," I said. "This guy isn't doing it to be funny. He's doing it because he thinks he's a star. The ego that drives some people to the stage is out of proportion to anything you may have encountered before."

"Oh, I don't know about that . . ."

"I'm not talking about Kyle Matthews with his private parking space and collection of eyeglasses," I said. "I've met comedians who think that God speaks the truth to them. Guys who thought they were the smartest ones in the class when they were ten years old and thought the teacher should be taking notes from them instead of the other way around. Some comedians aren't trying to entertain, they have a message the world needs to hear."

"Who do you know like that?"

"You know Rory Callahan? The comedian that throws water balloons at the audience?"

"Yeah."

"Him."

"What? But . . . he's . . . he throws water balloons at people."

"He thinks it makes him a genius," I said.

"Why?"

"He was the first to do it. He thinks everyone else is following in his footsteps. They wish they were him."

"That makes no sense." She liked that phrase.

I nodded at the TV screen. "Neither does what Whiteside is doing. My guess is that he's going to hit the L.A. clubs. I'm going to keep an eye out for him. I'd like to get copies of those mug shots and pass those around."

"Biff . . ." She looked at me askance. "I mean, I just met you, but . . . don't you think that's a little dangerous?"

"Yeah," I said. "Especially for him."

THIRTEEN

That night I hit the clubs.

I started out at the Laugh Factory on Sunset, then drove down to the Improv on Melrose and hung out there for a few hours. I gave more answers than I got. Most comics had heard about Bernie's death and me getting hit over the head, so I spent my time telling my story and listening to Bernie Coleman anecdotes. I hadn't counted on that cutting into my gumshoe schedule. The mug shots stayed in my jacket pocket until I ran into Tim Scofield.

We were friends before, but Bernie's murder had bonded us like brothers. We hugged and went into a corner of Hell's Kitchen, the Improv's restaurant, to talk.

"Nice hat, Kincaid," Tim said.

I lifted the beret and showed him the bandages. "You heard what happened?"

"I saw the stories on TV," Tim said. "I guess they haven't caught whoever knifed Bernie yet."

"You talked to the police yet?"

Tim nodded. "Detective . . ." He fumbled for a card.

"Gilmore?"

He nodded. "That's him."

"What'd he tell you?"

Tim snorted. "Not much. It was mainly—" He hunched his shoulders and stiffened his neck in a reasonable imitation of the police detective. Scosh not only did famous people, he worked up impressions of other comics, bookers, anybody that struck him as a character. " 'And after you left the premises of the club, where did you go? Did anyone see you there? Approximately what time was this?' " Scosh was tall and skinny, so he didn't look much like Gilmore's compact physique, but he had his voice down so well—a soft low monotone—it made me laugh out loud. "Felt like I was talking to Joe Friday. And I've talked to him like three times since then."

"So have I," I said. "I have the dubious honor of being the guy who first found Bernie with a knife in his chest."

"And I'm the guy who last saw him without it," Tim said. "Except for the killer, I guess."

"What do you mean?"

"After Bernie shorted us, he told me to come by Monday."

"Yeah, me too," I said.

"What time?" Tim asked.

"Ten o'clock," I said. "That's when I found him stabbed."

"He had me come by at eight," Tim said.

"I didn't know that," I said.

"Gilmore didn't tell you?"

"No."

"He didn't tell me you came by at ten," he said. "He didn't even mention you. I found out it was you who found Bernie from the grapevine at the Store."

"Did Bernie say I was coming by at ten?"

"No," Tim said. "He said he had someone coming by at nine."

"Nine?"

"Yeah. Apparently he was paying people back and had them spaced out by an hour each."

"So what happened when you came by at eight?"

"He was on the phone, arguing with someone."

"Who?"

"Gary Ross," Tim said. "You heard of him?"

"Isn't he an agent?"

"A manager. Manages comedians."

"I can never keep those guys straight."

"Do you a lot of good if you could," Scosh said. "Ross represents some big people."

"Why was he on the phone with Bernie," I asked, "and what were they arguing about?"

"I don't know. Ross was yelling at him so loud I could hear him over the phone sitting on the other side of Bernie's desk."

"What was he saying?"

"I just heard his voice," Tim said. "I couldn't hear him well enough to tell what the words were. But he was plenty mad and Bernie was trying to calm him down."

"What was Bernie saying to him?"

"He was like . . ." Tim instantly slipped into a pitch-perfect impression of Bernie's high, whining tone. " 'Your client's face does not appear on camera," he said. 'He's never mentioned in the story, and you never hear his voice. It's been edited out.' "

"Who was he talking about?"

"I don't know, Kincaid."

"Who are Ross's clients?"

"That I know of? Barry Norton. Joe Concita. Susan Ying. She just got a development deal with ABC. Peter Marling. He's shot twelve episodes of a mid-season replacement that NBC is very hot on."

"Sitcom?"

"Sitcom. Yeah. And Elliott Able. I just saw him on Leno. Ross represents him."

"So it would be one of those people?"

"That I know of. I mean, I've been trying to get with Ross for two years now, but he doesn't return my phone calls. He's bigtime. You have to have something going on at the network level for that guy to pay attention." He looked at me. "Why, you know something I don't? I got the feeling I'm not the only one you've been asking questions."

"I'm trying to find a missing emcee," I said, thinking of the choppy editing job I'd seen Bernie do on his original tape. "So when Bernie said that his client—whoever it is—didn't appear on camera, did that calm Ross down?"

"I thought so at first. He stopped yelling. There was a moment of silence on the other end of the line. Bernie turned to me and gave me a look and held up the phone, like he was saying, 'See what I have to put up with?' I mean, I didn't know what was going on until after he hung up.

"But there was no sound coming out of the phone. I thought the guy had hung up. So did Bernie. 'Hello?' he said. 'Hello?' He even put him on speakerphone. 'Ross? Gary? Are you there?' And while he had him on speakerphone, Ross came back on. I think he had left the phone or put his hand over it or put Bernie on hold."

"So you heard him when he came back on," I said.

"Loud and clear."

"What'd he say?"

" 'If that tape airs, I'll kill you.' Then he hung up."

I looked at Scosh. He looked back at me and shrugged.

"You tell the police?" I asked.

"Sure."

"What happened after Ross hung up?"

"Not much. Bernie and I talked. I said what was that about. He told me about this prison videotape he had sold to some TV show, and then it made sense. He said guys like Gary Ross think they can tell everyone what to do. Then he told me some story about how Ross used to do coke in the bathroom of Flugelhorn's ten years ago and got thrown out. As he was telling me he counted out my cash and threw in an extra hundred for my patience. He said he'd offer me a drink from the bar but he had someone coming in at nine."

"And he didn't say who."

"No." A pretty waitress passed by and Scosh gave her a smile. "Sounds like the murder took place sometime after I left and before you showed up."

"And," I said, "after Gary Ross had promised to kill Bernie Coleman."

Scosh was silent for a bit. "Kincaid, you don't think Gary Ross murdered Bernie, do you?"

"If he didn't," I said, "I want to find out why he threatened to."

That night I was wakened by a pounding on my front door.

I sat up in bed. My alarm clock read two-thirty in the morning. I sure as hell wasn't expecting anybody.

I reached under the bed and got out my welcome wagon, a .410 pump shotgun. I put on sweatpants and shoes in case I needed to jump off my balcony for any reason anytime soon. I crept up next to my front door just as it exploded into another round of knocking. This was going to wake my neighbors up.

I racked a shell into the chamber of the .410, a sound loud enough that I knew it carried through the door. It was a universal greeting that roughly translated into all languages as "Hi! I have a gun!" I hit the porch light and peeked through the blinds. I left the peephole alone. I'd seen a movie once where someone got shot through the eye that way and had never used it since.

Rick Parker was standing in front of my door, blinking in the sudden light. He was so dirty and bedraggled it took me a moment to recognize him. Last time I'd seen him he was walking out the back doors of Flugelhorn's. He was wearing the same clothes as when he pulled his last shift behind the bar.

I didn't put the safety back on the shotgun but I kept it pointed at the ceiling as I opened the front door. Rick didn't wait for an invitation. He came stumbling right in.

"Kincaid, you get my note?" he asked, flopping his long lanky frame down on my couch. He smelled of sweat and dirt, and looked like he'd been working on a road crew for the last three days. Something had happened to his hands. Caked blood ran down from the fingertips across the palms and over his wrists.

"Yes. Rick, where have you been?" I asked. I slid the safety back on the shotgun and set it in the kitchen next to the fridge. "The police have been looking for you."

"Yeah, well, I figure if the police can't find me, no one else can either, right?" He looked around. "Hey, I hate to crash in on you at two in the morning like this, but I've spent the last few days walking here from my pad in Venice with about fifty cents in my pocket. Then I hung out in the Hills waiting for you to show up. Do you have anything to eat?"

I made him a sandwich while he washed up in the bathroom and put bandages on his fingers. I laid the sandwich out and when I brought him a glass of milk to wash it down with, the food was already gone. I made him a second one. The third lasted a little longer. He started to talk between the chews.

"Good ham," he said.

"Trader Joe's," I said. "The cheese, too."

"Yeah, I like that place." He gulped the last of the milk like it was a flagon of ale, favoring his unbandaged hand. "God, thanks, Kincaid. I was going through trash cans behind a Burger King looking for leftover french fries."

I looked at the bandages on his hands. "You want to tell me what's going on, Rick?"

"Yeah, I do," he said. The food was having restorative effects. "You don't smoke, do you?"

"No."

"Man, I haven't had a cigarette in two days."

"Good time to quit."

Rick laughed at that. His teeth hadn't seen a toothbrush in a while. I was concerned for his well-being, but I also wasn't crazy about smelly strangers getting too comfy on my couch.

"Last time we saw each other was Saturday night," Rick said. "You left before me, right?"

I nodded. I didn't tell him I'd hung around to eavesdrop on his argument with Bernie.

"While I was cleaning up, I overheard you and Bernie talking," he said.

So I wasn't the only one being nosy that night. "He shorted me."

"I figured. Then I overheard him show you the tape he'd gotten from *Eyewitness Crime*."

I nodded. "I met the producer."

"I think her name's Sheryl."

"Sharon," I said. "Sharon Temple."

He was using his finger as a toothpick, talking around it as he probed his gums. "So you know about those two guys escaped from prison?"

"Johnny Whiteside and Sam Agar."

Rick nodded. He took his finger out of his mouth and hunched forward on the couch. "They're here in L.A."

I was sitting at my dining table. Out of the corner of my right eye I checked on the position of the shotgun. Still there.

"How do you know?" I asked. "Have you seen them?"

"They were waiting for me when I got back to my apartment that night." He held up his bandaged fingers. "Who the hell do you think did this to me? Santa Claus?" He lowered his hand and looked at it. "The big one, Agar, tied me to a chair while Whiteside did the talking."

"What did he say?"

"He wanted to know where the original tape of the show was," Rick said. "I said I didn't know. That's when Agar split open my fingernail and peeled it back." He looked at me. "Slowly. They put a sock in my mouth to muffle the screams."

I felt a small cold stone in the pit of my stomach. "Uh-huh."

"Then he asked me again and I told them Bernie had it. Agar did another one of my fingernails just to make sure I was telling the truth." He held up his hand again. "Whiteside called it getting a manicure." He chuckled darkly. "And I thought those guys were nuts when I was on the inside."

I remembered the crack Bernie had made about jailhouse jollies. "What do you mean by on the inside, Rick?"

"Behind bars. Doing time. Walking the yard. I was a guest of the Ojai Correctional Facility for eighteen months."

"When did you get out?"

"Last year," he said.

"How'd you end up working at Flugelhorn's?"

"My probation officer sent me out on a job interview for a dishwasher. Once Bernie learned I tended bar and he only had to pay me minimum wage . . ." He shrugged. "He got an illegal alien to wash the dishes and I never told my probation officer the truth. Only talked to him on the phone once a month."

"So whose idea was it to do the show at Ojai?" I asked.

Rick pointed at his chest. "Mine from the start. They'd had music nights there before, talent nights. I knew plenty of funny guys there. Hell, I thought—why not a comedy night? Funny how I thought of the gig, but somehow my name and face never made it into the story on *Eyewitness Crime*. Bernie makes it sound like he did it for the good of his fellow man, but you want to know the truth he wasn't even interested—always turned me down until he learned there was money in it."

"How was there money in it?"

"Well, this wasn't entirely my idea," he said. "One of the comics at the club and I got to talking and I told him I'd been in prison and he says where and I tell him and he says right then and there he wants to do a show there—how about Bernie producing it? I said Bernie's only interested in money and then he says, Okay, I'll pay him a thousand bucks plus expenses for the night."

"Wait a minute," I said. "You're telling me someone paid to have an amateur night of comedians put on at a prison?"

"Yeah," Rick said.

"Who was this?"

"Peter Marling."

Suddenly the phone call Bernie had gotten from Gary Ross made sense. Marling was one of Ross's clients. A former prop comic who had hit the club and college circuit with trunks full of gizmos and gadgets, he hadn't earned the respect of his fellow comics as much as he had the favor of audiences and booking agents. Prop comics were considered too gimmicky by other comedians, who relied on material as opposed to visual gags.

In five years he had gone from his first comedy gig to his own sitcom. The sudden success had fed Marling's ego and it had grown so huge he was given hour and a half sets at the Comedy Store, the audience shifting uncomfortably in their seats and the comedians grumbling in the back as he often walked onstage during another comedian's act—with no previous call or spot in the show and no introduction—and told the other comedian to get lost.

A weedy six-three, Marling had pale skin, deep-set eyes, curly copper brown hair, with prominent front teeth and a bulbous nose. Marling's popularity on the college circuit was partly due to his naturally clownish appearance. His show had been originally scheduled for the fall, but now it was being held for mid-season.

Called *Class Dismissed*, Marling played a junior high school science teacher who was all thumbs. His character, Peter Martin, was perpetually having his students help him build strange Rube Goldberg contraptions that never quite worked. The machines would be plugged in and—instead of working—there would be visual and sound effects with words like KA-ZAAAPPP!!! and BOING!!!!!!! superimposed over the action as it sparked and smoked and eventually exploded. I'd seen promos for it.

Rick Parker continued: "Marling paid Bernie to set up a show there—a thousand bucks to use the sound system and everything."

I remembered the missing speakers. "Why the hell did Peter Marling want Bernie to produce this show?"

Rick shrugged. "You got me. I only saw him when he dropped by the club. I think he might be planning a cable special or something. Maybe he's doing community service and rather than pick up trash on the highway he decided to host comedy shows in prisons."

My list of questions was growing longer than my list of answers. I tried to fill in the blanks as best as I could.

"What were you in for?"

"I sold pot in a school zone," Rick said. "Ended up at Ojai. God, what a mess that place was."

"How?"

"Supposed to be minimum security. What the hell were hard cases like Whiteside and Agar doing there? Douglas fell short of his inmate quota, so they ship a couple dozen violent offenders in from county jail and look what happens."

"What do you know about them?" I asked.

"Whiteside's a bad seed. Agar is like a blank slate. He just does whatever Whiteside tells him to do. I don't know how they ended up together at the same prison. But right now I'll bet they don't want that tape to end up on national TV."

"Why?"

"Maybe it shows something they don't want people to see."

"Too late," I said. "It's going to air next month."

"Not if they can help it," Rick said. "I remember back in Ojai some big tough biker dude shorted Whiteside on some cigarettes. Just to show how nobody's supposed to fuck with him, Whiteside had Agar stick an icepick in the biker's ear and twirl it around. Didn't kill the guy right away but scrambled his brains so bad he walked around the yard funny for an hour and then fell over twitching, blood coming out of his nose and mouth. Died of a brain hemorrhage. Guards came running. You know what Whiteside did while he watched? He laughed. He laughed so hard tears came out of his eyes."

"You think those two killed Bernie?"

"I can't think of anyone else who would want that tape that bad."

"You know where it is?"

"If they killed Bernie to get it, maybe Whiteside and Agar have it now."

"Think they'll leave town now?"

"No," Rick said. "There's still one loose end to clean up."

"What's that?"

"You, Kincaid. The news reports refer to a witness."

"I didn't see who killed Bernie."

"News reports didn't say that."

"News reports didn't say my name, either."

"That's probably why I found you still alive," Rick said. "Whiteside'll find out who you are by hanging around the comedy clubs. He thinks he's really funny. He thinks he's going to make it big."

"He's crazy."

"Yeah, he is."

I pointed to the bandages on my head. "One thing makes no sense. Someone hit me over the head and nearly split my skull. Why didn't they finish the job?"

Rick shrugged. "Maybe they heard sirens. Maybe they thought you were dead before you hit the ground. Maybe it wasn't them who hit you on the head. Maybe it wasn't them who killed Bernie. What I spent three days walking across town to tell you is that these fuckers are on the loose, and they'll do whatever they feel like doing until they get caught."

FOURTEEN

I woke up the next morning to find Rick Parker had gone. On my couch where he had fallen asleep after we were done talking was a note:

COUSIN IN CANADA, it read. GONE TO VISIT.

I checked my kitchen. He'd made himself breakfast, and taken lunch to go. When I put on my pants I checked my wallet. Twenty dollars was missing, but twenty was still there. Thieves and their honor.

I called Gilmore at the Ocean Park Police Department and told him I wanted to see him. I was going to tell him everything Rick Parker had told me last night, and maybe he could tell me if Rick Parker had been telling the truth or if he had been lying his head off.

"He was lying his head off," Gilmore said.

"What makes you think so?"

"You really think this guy walked across town to tell you you're in danger?"

"No," I said.

"Well, see, that's a lie right there."

"Then why did he come see me?"

Talking to Gilmore required a bit more self-control these days, now that I had seen Tim Scofield's impression of him. It was a little hard not to crack up at the soft monotone, the department store dummy posture, the unmoving facial expressions.

"Sounds to me like he wanted to pick your brain," Gilmore said. "Kind of like what you came here to do to me." He looked at the wall clock above his desk at the Ocean Park Police Department Homicide Division. "I have another appointment in five minutes."

"What was he lying to me about?" I asked.

"Rick Parker didn't do time for selling pot in a school zone," Gilmore said. "He did it as an accomplice to armed robbery, acting as the driver for two other guys while they robbed a savings and loan. Want to know who the other two guys were? Johnny Whiteside and Sam Agar. And he was in prison a lot longer than eighteen months. He was just the first one to get out."

I still didn't say anything.

"You should have called me," he said.

"Didn't want to wake you up at two in the morning."

"Comes with the job."

"What was I supposed to do?" I asked. "Tie him to my couch and wait until the Ocean Park Police from across town show up at my door?"

He shrugged. "He was wanted for questioning. He'd violated parole. I had a warrant out for his arrest."

"I didn't know that," I said. "He was Whiteside and Agar's driver?"

Gilmore nodded. "He fingered them at their trial. Got himself a deal. I'm sure when Whiteside and Agar showed up at Ojai while he was there, it made him more than a little nervous."

"So maybe they worked out some kind of deal of their own?"

"Maybe," Gilmore said.

"Like helping them escape once he got out."

He nodded.

"So Ricky had been playing me and Bernie like a couple of harps," I said.

"Bernie seemed to throw them for a loop when he decided to sell that tape," Gilmore said. "Now they seem to want it back. I don't know why we keep saying 'they.' Johnny Whiteside was probably the one who gave Agar and Rick Parker their marching orders."

"Bernie have any family?" I asked.

"An ex-wife," Gilmore said. "One son. Max."

"Know where they are?"

"I know where they might be today," Gilmore said.

"Where?"

"The Belmont Pier."

"Belmont? Down in Long Beach?"

Gilmore nodded.

"What's going on down there?"

"Bernie Coleman's memorial service," Gilmore said. "His body is still being held by the coroner's office."

"What time?"

"Two o'clock."

I looked at my watch. It was almost one.

I stood to leave. "You going?"

Gilmore looked down at his desk. "No. I've got work to do here."

Belmont Shores is what most people mean when they refer to the "nice part" of Long Beach. It's peaceful and residential and full of restaurants and shops. I go there for a day by the water when I've had enough of Hollywood and need to breathe some ocean air. It's my favorite beach in L.A. County. Since I started going to Long Beach, Santa Monica seems crowded and has dirty sand.

One of Belmont's landmarks is its pier. Stretching out into the water, it isn't jammed with carnival rides and restaurants like its more famous Santa Monica counterpart. It's a fishing pier instead of a tourist attraction, with fishermen dangling poles over the side, lingering to clean their catch in sinks.

At the base of the pier is the Belmont Brewing Company, a restaurant with a fantastic view of the sea and sky and the *Queen Mary* docked at Long Beach Harbor. Inside the restaurant is a brewery, and the BBC—as it is known among locals—makes four beers of its own and keeps them all on tap and in bottles to go. I'd gotten to the pier early and taken a walk around. I didn't see any group of people that looked like mourners, so I got a good seat at the bar and ordered an iced tea. No beer. Doctor's orders.

I waited and at two o'clock exactly the only three people dressed in more than shorts and T-shirts walked up from the parking lot. One was a man about Bernie's age, in a suit and tie. A member of the local clergy. One step behind was a guy closer to my age, a little younger, going soft around the middle and pink at the edges, with sandy blond hair and wearing sunglasses. The son? Behind him was a woman in a flowered sundress with great legs who looked like she'd rather be somewhere else.

I left my iced tea on the bar and headed out to trail them, maintaining a respectful distance as the threesome walked the length of the pier, not speaking to anyone or each other. It was the middle of a weekday, so the fishing crowd was thin. There were radios on and children playing. Some of the men stopped to turn and look at the woman's tanned calves. I couldn't blame them. I did some looking myself. I figured she was the son's wife. Bernie's daughter-in-law.

At the end of the pier, facing the ocean, the minister took out a Bible and read aloud from the Twenty-third Psalm. The fishermen with their kids and their radios and their fresh-cut bait, standing in puddles of fish guts in their stained T-shirts and torn jeans took off their caps and quieted the children and turned off the radios.

The minister finished reading the psalm and closed his book.

"Bernard Stephen Coleman," he said to the sea and sky, "we commend your spirit to the sea. May you rest eternally in the hands of God."

He stepped back. The son stepped forward to put his hands on the railing, looking out, his back hunched in grief. The minister gripped a hand on his shoulder and whispered something into his ear. The other man shook his head. The minister squeezed his shoulder and stepped back, shaking the hand of the good-looking woman. She nodded and the minister left. One by one, the fishermen picked up their poles and started talking, the radios coming back on, the normal daily business of living resuming. Death isn't the end, and it isn't the beginning. It's a pause button.

The man's shoulders began to shake, and the other men turned their backs, giving him the privacy grown men need when they weep for their fathers. The woman lit a cigarette and left. I watched her walk away. She hadn't said one word to her husband.

After a minute the man's shoulders stopped shaking and he got a handkerchief out to dry his eyes and then he put the lid back on the urn and turned to go. His face was slack and moist. He saw me standing there and nodded at me once before he saw I was wearing a Flugelhorn's T-shirt under a denim jacket. I'd dressed for the occasion.

He stopped in his tracks. "Who are you?" he asked.

"Biff Kincaid," I said. I extended my hand. "Came to pay my respects."

He took it. "Thank you."

"I hope I'm not intruding," I said.

"Not now," he said. He looked over his shoulder. "It's over."

"Are you Max?"

He nodded. "You a comedian?"

"I am."

Max looked around him. "Big turnout, huh?"

"Maybe it was what he wanted," I said. "You drink beer?"

He put a hand on his middle. "Too much."

"Could you use one now?"

"God, yes."

"Then I'm buying."

FIFTEEN

We sat out on the patio of the BBC, a pitcher of the Top Sail ale between us. We clinked our full glasses together and he drank while I looked at the rollerbladers. I saw one woman with long tan legs and that started me talking.

"Your friend," I asked.

"Who?" Max said.

"The woman," I said. "In the sundress. I didn't mean to exclude her from our little wake here. I hope she's all right."

"She's fine."

"May I ask who she is?"

"Leslie," he said. "My wife. For another fourteen days."

"Ah."

He pointed at balconies that overlooked the beach bike path. "She lives in one of those condos there," he said.

"It's expensive enough just to park in the metered lot," I said. "God knows what the rent is."

Max snorted. "She's not paying it," he said. "Her new sugar daddy is." He drank and set his glass down. "That was one of our problems. Irreconcilable checkbooks."

"I'm sorry."

"I never could figure out why she married me anyway," Max said. "Sure as hell wasn't for my money."

"How did you meet?"

"At my job," he said. "I'm a dog groomer. She had a poodle. Diamond, she called him. I was the only dog groomer Diamond didn't try to bite. And I made house calls. I let her float on credit because I had a little crush on her. One day I showed up and she had a few bottles of champagne waiting for me. I woke up with her in a Las Vegas hotel the next day, a marriage license on the nightstand. She didn't remember it and neither did I. Too bad. The one time we made love, and I don't remember it."

"How long ago was that?"

"Three months. We would have had the marriage annulled before, but she's been out of town. She likes casinos. She likes men who can fly her first class."

"Nice of her to come to your father's ceremony, though."

"He's not my father," Max said. "At least, that's what he used to say."

I shook my head. "I don't follow."

"I was adopted," Max said. "He didn't tell me until I was twenty-five."

I waited. My glass was still full. His was half-empty.

"We got into an argument. I can't even remember what over. He thought I wasn't doing something right and I said 'like father, like son.' It was something I used to say just to piss him off, and I didn't know why it made him so mad whenever I said it. This time, though, he came back with 'I'm not your real father.' At first I thought he was joking. But for a guy who worked in comedy clubs most of his life, he didn't kid around much."

"So that's how you found out?"

Max nodded. He adjusted his sunglasses. "Yeah. I kept waiting for him to tell me more or tell me it wasn't true or apologize for not telling me sooner, but he just said it was time I found out. I kept asking him for details and he told me to ask my mother. They were divorced by then so I went to her and asked her if I was adopted and she said yes and she looked at me kind of peculiarly and said something like 'I just thought you always knew.'"

"Where is your mother now?"

"Ellen?" he said with exaggerated diction. "Ellen Alexander? That's what she calls herself. I don't know. I called her office.

She sells real estate on the Palos Verdes Peninsula now. Makes more money than Bernie and I ever did put together. She runs these little ads in the local papers with her airbrushed headshot next to million-dollar properties. She looks good for fifty. She has what she always wanted now, what Bernie could never give her, and that's money. Amazing how many women want that out of a man. Not love. Not understanding. Just cash. That they love. That they understand."

He drained his glass. I refilled it for him and left mine untouched. I had the feeling Max was going to do the drinking for both of us.

"Not you, though," he said. "You're a handsome guy. My wife would like you." He ran a hand along his jaw. "You got that look."

"I missed out on the tan."

"Irish, right? With a name like Kincaid." He loosened his tie. "At least you got a name. I haven't been able to find out who my birth parents were. Bernie and Ellen knew a doctor who had a patient who was eighteen years old and pregnant. Now, thirty-five years later, the doctor's dead. So's the nurse. The adoption was illegal. So I have absolutely no idea who I am or where I came from. I am a man adrift."

His attention was drawn by a passerby. I looked around for a blonde on rollerblades, but instead he was watching a man tie up his golden retriever to a tree. "Hey, there's Ginger," Max said, his voice softened with tender recognition. He was suddenly smiling.

"Who's Ginger?"

"The dog. The golden retriever. I groom her."

"Ah." I looked. Ginger watched as her master went into the bar, picked up an order to go, and untied her, her tail wagging at his reappearance. They walked away. "She's beautiful," I said.

Max's eyes never left her until she was out of sight. "She's a *good girl*," he said in baby talk.

"Did you want to go say hello?"

"When I've been crying in my beer? No, thanks. Ginger wouldn't mind but her owner might decide it was time to find a new dog groomer. See, that's why I like animals, Biff. People stink. Animals . . . they let you know what they're thinking."

Someone from another table was listening in on our conversation, glancing our way. I leaned in close, inspiring a level of confidentiality and hoping to bring the volume down.

"When was the last time you spoke to your fath—to Bernie?"

Max set his beer glass down with a rap on the table. "About a week ago."

"What was the occasion?"

"He said he was going to pay me back some money he owed me."

"How much money was this?"

"Ten thousand dollars." He looked at the pitcher. The beer was approaching low tide. "Everything I had."

"When did you make this loan?"

He laughed. "My wife keeps wanting to know *why*," he said, "because I didn't really have it. I took a loan out from a bank on my business—my van, the tools of my trade, my list of regular clients, which included the loan officer at the bank—and had fallen behind on the payments. I'd even, uh . . ." He chuckled. "I'd even put my stuff in storage and closed up shop so to speak, living out of my van."

"That what you're doing now?"

"See that white van? Over there, parked under the tree? On the other side it has a sign that says 'Groom and Go.' That's where I lay my head at night."

"Looks big enough."

"It's not bad. If I get up in the middle of the night, I pee off the pier." He shook his head and chuckled. "Can't believe I'm doing this. I got a job, I got a business, but I guess I'm homeless."

"Why did you loan Bernie the money?"

"He called me up and said 'I need help, son.' He'd never called me 'son' before. And I just did it. He was so happy when I showed up with the money. It was like we meant something to each other after all. Or I meant something to him. We even hugged. Isn't that pathetic?" He drained his glass again. "Then I couldn't get him on the phone again."

"When was this?"

"Two months ago," Max said.

"Did he ever say anything about paying you back?"

"A week ago. Called out of the blue. Said he was going to pay

92

me back . . ." He looked at his watch to get the date. "Today. All ten grand. Said he would have it in his hand." He looked at me. "Did he?"

"I think so, yeah."

"So he wasn't lying." His shoulders slumped forward. He ran his hands over his face. He was drunk. He'd guzzled three glasses of ale to my none and the pitcher was almost empty. His good clean white shirt was coming out of his pants. He'd gained some weight since he'd bought his suit. It had been too long since his last haircut. He was overweight, lonely and sad, but I don't judge men too harshly on the day they say farewell to the only father they knew.

"Someone robbed him when they killed him," I said. "The money's missing."

Max nodded. "Ten grand, yeah."

"He owed me a few bucks, too."

Max raised his head and looked at me blearily. "But that's all he owed you, right?"

I didn't know what to say to that without sounding like I didn't know what I was talking about. "I've got to get back up to L.A. before the traffic sets in," I said.

Max reached into his back pocket and pulled out his wallet.

"I got the check," I said.

"Wanna give you my card," Max said. He fished out a small paper rectangle. He turned it over to write on the back. "Most afternoons I'm here, at Belmont Shores Dog and Cat Grooming, on Second Street." He handed it to me. "Lemme know if you find out anything."

"And I'll give you one of mine," I said. "Keep me posted." I looked at the card. It read Max Colton. I looked up.

"My name's not Coleman any more," he said. "After Bernie and Ellen told me the truth, I changed my last name from Coleman to Colton. Max Colton. I told Bernie and he didn't even try to stop me. All he said was he wasn't going to pay for it, because it cost like a couple of hundred bucks. Here I was, the adopted son of a man and woman who couldn't stand each other and as far as I could tell, didn't like me too much either."

I pocketed the card. "Where'd you get Colton?"

"I picked it out of the phone book." He looked up at me through his sunglasses smeared with tears. I moved my beer glass into his hand and he took it. "So who am I, huh? You know why they had to adopt a kid, Bernie and Ellen? They quit having sex. I think adopting me was one of the many futile attempts to try to fix a marriage that just plain wasn't supposed to happen. Like mine. And I was handy because my real parents already decided I was a big boo-boo on their part. So . . ." He leaned forward to whisper. "Here's the secret."

I could smell beer on his breath. "What?"

"I'm . . . not . . . supposed . . . to . . . be . . . here." He leaned back, grinning behind his sunglasses like Jack Nicholson. "I'm a *mistake*."

He drained the last of the ale. The very pretty waitress stopped by and dropped off the check.

I thanked her. Max looked away.

When she left Max leaned forward again. "I'm sorry, but I'm a little short right now."

"No problem." I held up the check. "I got it."

"What I meant was . . . I could really use another drink."

"On its way," I said. I stood up. "After all, you don't have to drive anywhere, do you?"

He shook his head. "Van's right there."

"You like that Top Sail?"

"Sure."

"I'll have her bring you one." I shook his hand. "Nice meeting you, Max."

"You too, Biff." He let my hand go. "Thanks for coming."

I held up a hand in farewell. On my way out of the restaurant I found our waitress and gave her three times what the check was worth. I told her my friend needed another pitcher, but give it to him one glass at a time, each glass clean and cold, and to smile and see how he was doing. If he wanted something to eat, give him that, too. Let him sit there for an hour. When he was done, tell him his bill was taken care of by a friend of his father's. Get him a bottle to go when it's time to leave. Keep the change.

She was young and pretty and tan and her face was clear of lines and sorrows. "Is he all right?" She looked beyond me to where Max was sitting.

"He will be by then," I said.

SIXTEEN

I walked to my car.

I heard a voice in the air: "Excuse me."

I looked up. On one of the balconies on one of the condos above the metered parking lot by the pier was Leslie Colton. She had doffed her sundress and was now wearing cutoffs that were slit up the thigh and a hot pink bikini top that looked painted on. She'd been going to the gym instead of the plastic surgeon. I could see muscles in her stomach. She stood in the sea breeze and looked down at me.

"What did you talk to my husband about?"

I stood back from my car so she could see my T-shirt with the Flugelhorn's logo. "I'm a comedian," I said. "I knew his father."

She brought a cigarette to her mouth and sucked it slowly. "I think I've seen you."

"Where?"

She pointed at my T-shirt. "There."

"I was a regular."

"You were funny."

"Thanks."

"I think you were the funniest comedian I saw that night."

"Thanks again."

"Definitely the cutest," she said.

"Comedians aren't known for their looks," I said. I adjusted my beret. "It's not a fashion show."

"I think I wrote your name down on a napkin," she said. "Biff . . . Kincaid, right?"

"Right."

"I have a good memory for names," she said. "I almost sent you a little note."

"What'd it say?"

"It was my phone number," she said. "What did my husband tell you?"

"That you two are getting a divorce," I said.

"More like an annulment." A small ball of white fur nuzzled at her ankle, licked her toe and looked at me with bright black eyes. Diamond. She reached down and picked him up in her arms. "We don't even live together anymore."

"I know."

She put Diamond inside and closed the sliding glass door. "If we did, I'd be sitting in his dog grooming van wondering where my next shower was coming from," she said. "What fun would that be?"

"I have to get back up to L.A.," I said. "Something on your mind, Mrs. Colton?"

"Just wondered if Bernie had left us anything in his will," she said. "Maybe you're the one to give us the good news."

"Bernie died broke," I said. "He owed his son ten thousand dollars. He was going to pay it back but someone killed him and took the money."

"Aren't you the little detective."

"Only when it comes to the obvious."

"You find any clues down here in Belmont Shores?"

"Only about how sad a day it is."

She shifted her weight from one hip to the other, like the pendulum slowly swinging on a grandfather clock. "Maybe you haven't done a thorough search of the premises."

"I learned all I'm going to know."

"Sure you don't want to come up here and check out any loose ends?" she said.

"Max says you've got a roommate," I said, "and I'm not talking about Diamond."

Leslie stubbed out her cigarette with her sandal. "Kevin? He's in San Diego all week. He's in pharmaceutical sales. Makes a lot of money. Company car." She tilted her head back toward the living room. "Company condo."

"Takes good care of you, I imagine."

"He's forty-eight. I'm twenty-seven. How good care do you think he can take of me? About like my drunk fat hubby you just left. Give Kevin a heart attack to give me what I need." She pushed her shoulders together and arched her back. The hot pink bikini top moved in kind. "Why don't I buzz you in and you come on up? Comfort me in my time of sorrow."

"I don't think that's a good idea," I said.

"Why don't you let me have an hour to change your mind," she said.

"Why don't you go to hell," I said, and got in my car and drove back home.

I didn't have a spot, but I cruised the comedy clubs in Hollywood that night, the headshots of Sam Agar and Johnny Whiteside tucked under my arm. From what I'd learned, Whiteside would be the one looking for stage time, but Agar would stand out in a crowd.

I hit pay dirt at the Comedy Store. Working the door in the Original Room was Spike Olson. He was tall and Swedish with blond hair and big teeth and a horsey face. A good kid, only twenty-five years old, six months in town from Minnesota. He was on duty every Sunday for Potluck night, when anyone who signed up got three minutes onstage.

"I think I seen him at one of the open mikes around town," Spike said, when I showed him the picture of Johnny Whiteside. "I ain't sure."

"What about this guy?" I showed him the picture of Sam Agar.

"Yeah." Spike nodded, much more certain. "He was here. Just last Sunday."

"He with anybody?" I asked. "Because I think these two would be together."

"Kincaid, Potluck goes to two in the morning," Spike said. "I don't watch every act. Why don't you come down this Sunday, see if this guy turns up?"

"I just might do that," I said. We were standing in the hallway in back of the Original Room, between the bar and the back patio. I heard a roar from down the hallway. "What's going on in there?" I said, nodding toward the Main Room.

"Peter Marling's here."

"He is?" I said. I put the headshots of Whiteside and Agar away.

Spike nodded. "Got all his people here. Doing a showcase for one of the movie studios. Not enough he's got a sitcom coming out. Wants to be a movie star."

"His manager here?" I said. "Gary Ross?"

Spike grinned. "Wouldn't be much of a manager if he wasn't. I seated his table."

"Point him out to me."

We went into the back of the Main Room. Only the back row of tables was empty. The rest of the four hundred seats were taken. The Main Room at the Comedy Store was like a Vegas showroom, with a huge polished stage, someone working the lights and the sound, gauzy curtains hanging over a glowing neon Comedy Store logo.

Before the Comedy Store was the Comedy Store, it was a night club called Ciro's where Bogart and Bacall had a booth, Count Basie and Duke Ellington played, and Martin and Lewis cavorted on- and offstage. It was like playing a historical landmark where they served drinks. It was the Alamo of show business.

Peter Marling was on that stage when I walked in. He stood in the spotlight, an open trunk behind him, holding up a remote control in one hand and a car alarm key chain in the other. "See?" he was saying. "You use one of these to find your car, right?" He was dressed the same way as his TV character in the publicity stills I'd seen: sweater vest, khakis, white dress shirt with no tie. He was still in his on-camera makeup, although it looked natural under the bright stage lights. He'd been shooting his show today. "Your car's a lot bigger than a remote control. So, ladies and gentleman, I introduce to you the remote remote— for those times when you can't find the most valuable gadget you have." He walked over to where a stool was set and placed the remote control on it, then walked back, aimed and clicked the alarm button on the key chain and when the remote control chirped and flashed a smaller light, the audience cheered.

Now that was comedy.

Marling reached into his trunk for his next gag. It was a cellular phone attached to a headset with a plastic hand, arm and sleeve already glued to it. "Try this next time you're driving," Marling said, "and you want the guy in the next lane to let you in." He put the mocked-up headset on and picked up a steering wheel to pretend he was driving. He angled his body behind the trunk, using its open lid as a car door. A wave of laughter rippled through the audience. It did indeed look as though he were driving with one hand and talking on a cell phone with the other, holding a mock conversation.

"Uh-huh . . . yeah . . . uh-huh . . ." Suddenly he swung his other real arm over the lid of the trunk, pointing at the audience. "HEY, DO YOU MIND IF I GO AHEAD OF YOU?!" The sight gag of him having three arms led to another eruption of laughter and applause.

And so he went. Glasses glued to coasters, shirts with hangers sewn into the back, chairs with five legs . . . all of it came out of Marling's magical trunk to amuse and delight the crowd. Nothing about politics, relationships or anything having to do with real life as people lived it. And this guy had a TV show. If this was what you had to do to get a sitcom these days, I was going to stick with the road.

I got a flyer for the show in the Belly Room upstairs and flipped it over, using a pen from my pocket to write a note to Marling's manager that consisted of a single word: OJAI.

I snagged a waitress and slipped her five bucks to take it to Ross's table along with their next order. I stood in the back and watched as he got the note, read it, and excused himself from the table.

Gary Ross came walking out, dressed in a dark lightweight suit, younger than me or Marling, his black curly hair cut short around his head, his round face perpetually red. He moved quickly and with purpose. He was the business side of the business, and wanted everyone to know it just by looking at him.

He came out into the lobby of the Main Room, the note in his hand. His eyes darted around behind oval frames until he found me.

He held up the note in question, looking at me over his glasses like a schoolteacher.

I nodded.

He tore the note in half, then quarters, and then eighths before letting the pieces flutter to the floor. I watched him do it.

"Who the hell are you to drag me out here when my client is onstage in front of two dozen movie producers?" His voice was already loud. A born yeller.

"Biff Kincaid," I said. I didn't shake hands or move from where I was standing. "I'm a comedian."

"Who cares?" he said, and turned to go.

"Why did Peter Marling finance a comedy show up at the Ojai Correctional Facility?"

That stopped him.

"I don't know what you're talking about," Ross said, but he turned back around to face me.

"Three months ago," I said. "He hired Bernie Coleman to put on a show there. During the show one inmate pretended to stab another and they both escaped. The whole thing was caught on tape. Bernie sold the video to a TV show and now Bernie Coleman's dead."

"So what the fuck are you saying?" His voice rose in volume, filling the space. The doorman glanced our way. "That I killed Bernie Coleman? Look, I'll do anything to get what I want out of people but I haven't murdered anybody yet."

"You didn't want Bernie Coleman to sell that tape."

"I was protecting my client," Ross said. He was gesturing now, adding arm waves and finger jabs to his high-decibel speech. "You know—my client who has the hottest network sitcom ready to debut in six weeks? And who's about to make his first movie deal? He makes me more in commissions in one week than you'll see all year doing road gigs and picking up weekend spots around town." He looked me up and down and found me lacking. He snorted in disdain. "I don't have the time to argue bullshit with some open-miker no one's ever heard of or ever will."

For the second time he turned to go and for the second time I stopped him.

"Marling went on, didn't he?" I said.

Ross stopped but he didn't turn around. "I'm done with you, man," he said to the wall.

"Marling went onstage at Ojai, didn't he?" I said. "That's what's on the tape."

Ross started to pivot around slowly, as if he was on a turntable.

"What did you hear?" Ross asked. He wasn't yelling now.

"I heard that Bernie's only stipulation was that the emcee be cut out of the raw tape of the performance," I said. "At first, I thought it was himself that Bernie was editing out of the show, but no. Now I think it was Peter Marling. But that's what's got you so nervous: that Peter Marling did something that might blow your precious movie and TV deals."

"I didn't know the show was going to be taped," Ross said. "Neither did Peter."

"You know what I think?" I said. "I don't think you knew there was a show. I think Peter Marling did this behind your back."

"He got hustled by Bernie Coleman."

"Your client was the one who came to Bernie," I said.

"Peter didn't know Bernie," Ross said. "He never played that shithole club of his."

"Then how did they meet?"

"Through a contact of Bernie's," Ross said, "when Peter was looking for a house. But the show was a mistake on Peter's part. He lets his charitable nature get the best of him. Bernie Coleman was hustling him for a few extra bucks so he wouldn't have to close his lousy club."

"That why you threatened Bernie?" I said. "So loudly a witness overheard what you said?"

"I yell all day long," Ross said. "It's the only way people hear you in this stinking town."

"You said you were going to kill him if he didn't hand over the tape of the Ojai show," I said.

Ross swallowed. His face looked like a dry napkin. He sure was keeping quiet now.

"You tell the police that?"

"Not yet," I said. "But you watch who you call an open-miker."

And then it was my turn to walk away.

SEVENTEEN

I got home that night to find a limousine in front of my home. I live in an apartment complex at the end of a cul-de-sac in a canyon. It's not easy to fit a limousine back in there, and when it has been idling for some time it is bound to draw attention. It certainly got mine.

After I parked in the back and walked around front, the driver got out. She was six feet tall, with long brown hair and wore a small velvet cap.

"Biff Kincaid?" she asked in a throaty voice.

"That's me."

"My name is Melody. Mister Kyle Matthews would like to know if you would join him for a late supper at Dan Tana's."

I was a little hungry. Also, I don't get limousines sent to my door every day, and Dan Tana's has the best New York steak in town. It was only ten o'clock. Most evenings I wouldn't have gotten offstage yet.

Melody held the door open for me. There was Guinness already stocked in the back, and the radio was set to jazz station KLON. Someone had been reading my mail. When she got back in the car she made a phone call to leave a message that she'd picked me up.

I passed on the pint but listened to Oscar Peterson as I looked out the window at the city I lived in. Through tinted glass, even the homeless people looked glamorous. Melody didn't say much. I didn't either. She'd just spent the last hour and a half of her life sitting in this oversize moving van dressed like a chauffeur waiting for some moron to come home and then drive him to dinner just so he'd be impressed.

Dan Tana's is on the cusp of Beverly Hills, right where West Hollywood runs out and the real money begins. The maître d' wears a tuxedo and the waiters wear dinner jackets. It's got a great bar and padded booths to sit in. It's my kind of place. I just don't make their kind of money.

Kyle Matthews already had a booth. He was waiting for me. He was wearing an orange beret for some reason, and glasses tinted yellow. His shirt had a sixties flower power design to it and over it he wore a sheepskin vest. He kind of looked like Sonny Bono. This guy was weird.

He stood to greet me. "You like it?" he asked.

"Like what?"

"The beret!" he said. He took it off and handed it to me to look at. "I liked yours so much I decided to get one of my own!"

We sat back down. Whenever he moved too fast or spoke too loudly, people looked at him, wondering who the hell was this idiot. Maybe that was what he wanted. I'd seen this before in behind-the-scenes movers and shakers who envied the spotlight a little too much. They tried to make themselves into characters, personalities, usually by affecting certain kinds of clothes or accessories as a trademark.

"I love this place," Matthews said. "Order the New York steak. You almost don't need a knife."

"Thanks for the nice ride," I said.

"The car is yours until midnight," he said.

The waiter brought me a fresh Guinness. I was afraid it was going to go to waste. "What's this all about?" I asked.

"Sharon told me what you've been up to," Matthew said. "I mean, she's told me what she wanted me to hear. I don't want you to think she's been spying on you or anything."

"I don't."

"She likes you. Every guy in the office has made a play for her. Rich guys. Guys with connections in the business. Then suddenly in comes this redheaded two-bit comedian and he's got her sliding off her seat."

"You watch your mouth about her."

"Sure. No problem." He put his hands up in the air to indicate no harm, no foul. "Jesus Christ, put that look away, will you? You'll hurt somebody with it." He lifted his drink and looked at me over the glass, trying to cover his discomfort with a quirky little smile in his pink pudgy face. "Kincaid—Irish, right? You guys go around blowing up school buses in England, I can only imagine what you're like about your women."

I looked at my Guinness. It had settled. I didn't touch it. "Do you have some kind of point," I said, "or did you bring me here to show me that you're as bad a conversationalist as you are a dresser?"

He was nipping at his drink and it nearly came out his nose. He didn't reply right away.

"Otherwise," I said, "I'll get a cab home and hit the In-N-Out Burger on Sunset on the way because then at least I won't have to put up with the ridiculous nonsense coming out of your mouth."

Kyle wiped his chin with a napkin. He was choking and laughing at the same time. "I like you, Biff."

"Feeling's mutual. I like me, too."

"You say what's on your mind, don't you?"

"I'm paid to."

He set his drink down and dabbed at the sheepskin vest. "Sharon tells me you're running around, looking for the tape Bernie Coleman shot up at Ojai."

"I'm trying to find who has the original," I said.

"You think that's what he was killed over?" Kyle asked. "Maybe by those two cons that escaped?"

"I don't know."

"Johnny Whiteside and Sam Agar," Kyle said. He picked up his drink again. It was some kind of orange concoction in a highball glass with a cherry on top. A Tequila Sunrise? A Tom Collins? "A couple of bad hombres. They look pretty mean, and they're meaner than they look."

"I wouldn't put it past them," I said.

"Well, I'm not saying that they did kill Bernie Coleman, or

107

that they didn't." He used his hands to gesture. He enjoyed having control of the story now. "All I am saying is that if they did kill him for the original tape, they came up empty-handed."

"Why?"

"Because I know who has it," he said. "You can stop looking."

"Who?"

"Me." He swirled his drink and took a little sip.

The waiter came and took our order. New York steak. Fettucine Alfredo on the side. Caesar salad. I'd been to this restaurant half a dozen times, usually on someone else's tab. I'd never had anything else. I asked for an iced tea. Guinness might not go well with a concussion.

The waiter left. Matthews sat back against the padded leather of the booth, eyeing me with confidence. This was why he had brought me here—to regain the upper hand.

"You," I said.

Kyle shrugged. He was pleased with himself.

"How did you get it?"

"Bernie Coleman."

"Sharon told me that he bumped it up from VHS to digital Beta in a bay with only him and an editor."

At the word *editor,* Kyle broke into a big smile. "And I paid that editor and an engineer a thousand bucks cash in advance to make the switch," he said. "The tape was out of Bernie's sight for five minutes while we did the bump up. Bernie didn't know shit about postproduction, so while we futzed with the digital in front of his eyes I had an engineer in the back pop the top off the tape—the one with Bernie's handwritten label—and put it on a blank cassette. The original got the cover of the blank cassette. He never checked! He trusted us!" Kyle chuckled. Even he found it a laughable concept.

His face grew serious. "Of course, ten days later he was dead and that's a terrible thing, but it was totally unnecessary from the standpoint of whoever killed him. If Bernie had spotted the switch I would have said oops and gotten the original back to him, but otherwise I was planning on telling him to bring the original back for a quick fix, there was a glitch on our tape, and switch it right back after I'd made a copy for myself. He might have been a little pissed, but I was going to give him the limo-

and-steak treatment to make up for it. No harm done and who cares?"

The salads came. "Why did you do it in the first place?"

"Because I was dying of curiosity," Kyle said. He leaned across the table between us. No joking here, no goofball tactics. "I had to see what was on that tape that Bernie Coleman didn't want anyone else to see. And do you know what it was?"

"Peter Marling doing stand-up," I said.

He blinked at me and sat back. "How did you know that?"

"Because Gary Ross, Peter Marling's manager, was after that tape as well. He threatened to kill Bernie if he didn't give it to him. Maybe Bernie wanted to. Maybe it was a bargaining tactic in the last minutes of his life. But when the tape was popped into the VCR in Bernie's office—well, what do you know? It's a blank. Think Bernie was able to talk his way out of that one? Doesn't seem like it now, does it?" I pointed at him with my salad fork. "Your curiosity might have killed that club owner."

Kyle blinked some more. He reached for his drink, looked into it and then set it down again. "I . . . I didn't think of that."

"He's dead," I said. "Isn't anything you can do about it."

"All that was on that tape was Peter Marling emceeing the show," Kyle said. "I mean, what was the big deal?"

"Did you watch it all?"

"Yeah. He does some prison material that the inmates think is funny, but I couldn't air it because I didn't have a release on him. If I mentioned it, it would have been one line in my show. What did it have to do with anything?"

"I don't know yet," I said. "What about the riot after the stabbing? Did you watch all of that?"

"Yeah."

"Was there some stuff on there Bernie didn't want you to see?"

"Yeah, but I figured it was the hard-core stuff. There was a guard who got beaten up pretty badly and one of the inmates gets raped by five guys on a cafeteria table. He screams bloody murder, let me tell you."

"Anything else?"

"What do you mean?"

"Anything else that might have shown how Whiteside and Agar escaped?" I said. "Because nobody seems to know."

Kyle shook his head. "No. Not that I can think of."

"Can I see it?"

"What?"

"The original tape?"

"Sure," Kyle said. "I bumped it up to digital even before I looked at it." Our steaks arrived and he didn't touch his. "I swear to God, if I thought it was going to cause Bernie those kinds of problems, I never would have done it. Okay, maybe I would have done it but I would have gotten him the tape back a lot sooner."

"And maybe he would have been dead anyway," I said. "Maybe he was killed over the money you paid him and this had nothing to do with the tape. But I want to find out."

He looked down at his food and was suddenly hungry. He picked up his knife and fork. I followed suit. The steak was better than I remembered.

"When can I see that tape?" I asked.

"I'll get it to Sharon," he said. "She can show it to you."

"When is she editing again?"

"Tonight," Kyle said. "I can take you there after dinner."

"Okay."

"Now that brings me to an interesting point, Biff. See, you asked me for something and I gave it to you. Now it's my turn to ask you for something in return."

"And what's that?"

"An hour of your time," he said, "to sit for our cameras, and tell us what you know about the death of Bernie Coleman."

"Not much."

"So is that a yes?"

"No. That is a no."

"Now, come on, Biff, you're asking me to show you this tape, which is highly confidential material, but you're not—"

"Do you want me to have Detective Gilmore declare it as evidence? Maybe I can see it that way."

Kyle waved his knife and fork in the air to dismiss such a thought. "I'll tell you what," he said. "Watch the tape. It's forty-five minutes in all. I'll give it to Sharon to show you. She might be pissed because she didn't know I had it either, but that's TV, you know?"

We went back to our food.

"But do me one favor, will you?" he asked.

"What's that?"

"Think it over," he said. "Will you at least think over the possibility of doing an interview?"

"I have thought it over."

"We'll pay you," Kyle said "Five thousand bucks. Cash American, wired into your checking account, whatever you want."

"I make my money on the road," I said. "Not in town."

"How about as a donation to your favorite charity?"

"I don't have one."

"Pick a worthy cause. A suffering individual. Hell, give it to the bums in Hollywood, I don't care."

"The answer is still no."

"Okay." He held his fingers up in mock surrender. "Look at the tape. Anything beyond that is open to negotiation. Fair?"

I wasn't sure what we were agreeing on, but it sounded good. "Fair."

"How's the steak?"

"One of the best I've ever had in my life, if not the best," I said.

"Good. So now you know you can trust me about one thing: food. So now I want to know if I can trust you about something."

"What's that?"

"Those jugs of Sharon's," he asked. "Are they real? I mean, there's a betting pool at work. I got fifty bucks they are."

EIGHTEEN

After dinner, Kyle Matthews told Melody my ride was over and tipped her a hundred bucks. We got in his Ferrari and sped across town to the GUN studios. There, he signed me in past the guard post and opened up a locked filing cabinet in his office. Out of it he withdrew a bulky blue tape. "This is the digital Beta copy," he said. "The original I keep locked up in a safe-deposit box off site. You understand."

"Of course." I looked at the tape. I hadn't seen anything like it before. "Can't play this in my VCR at home, can I?"

Kyle shook his head. "You'll need an editing suite. Sharon's got one until two in the morning every night this week. You can play it there. Freeze-frame, fast-forward, do whatever you want to it. If the editor squawks, wondering who you are and what this is for, tell him to charge me an hour of overtime. Those guys make all the money in this business, I swear to God."

He steered me toward the editing facilities in the building behind his offices and turned me loose on the upper floor before vanishing in a roar of Italian automotive engineering.

I walked in. There was a row of open doors, rooms dimmed to levels of light for television watching, from which bursts of sound emanated at different intervals. I poked my head into three rooms until I found Sharon sitting at the editing console and pushing buttons.

She did a double take when she saw me. "Biff?"

"Hi," I said. "Sorry to bother you—"

"I left a message for you at home earlier," she said. "Kyle was looking for you."

"He found me." I took a seat in one of the chairs at the back of the room. "He took me to dinner and dropped me off here." I looked around the editing suite. On the half dozen monitors positioned around the console were images of the prison riot, Whiteside and Agar's takeover robbery, stills of Bernie Coleman and moving video of prison life at Ojai. "Your editor on a break?"

"I sent him home early so I could practice editing and do revisions at the same time. Maybe work on my reporter reel."

"I thought this story was in the can," I said.

Sharon sighed. "The Kyle Matthews school of video production," she said. "If he didn't do it, it wasn't done right, so why not do it all over again? He's prone to bouts of last-minute rewriting and reshooting, which—on my part—leads to lots of unpaid overtime. So did you get the limo at the house with the foxy-looking driver and the New York steak at Dan Tana's?"

"Yeah," I said. "And here I was feeling so special."

"It's his standard schmooze tactic," she said. "What did he want?"

"He wants me to do an interview about what I saw regarding the death of Bernie Coleman."

She brightened. She was dressed like a cat burglar, wearing black from head to toe, with black jeans and a black turtleneck. Her blond hair fell about her shoulders naturally. She was wearing contacts instead of glasses. She looked beautiful. "Are you going to do it?"

"No."

"You know, we pay for interviews."

"That's what Bernie told me."

"You're the closest thing there is to an eyewitness."

"That's why I'm cooperating with the police."

"It'd be good exposure."

"Yeah. Let the killer know who to take out next."

"We'll shoot you onstage at Flugelhorn's," she said. "Even include some of your comedy act."

"The first letter is 'n,' I said. "The second letter is 'o.' "

"Maybe some casting director or agent will see you in it and make you a star." Even she couldn't say that with a straight face.

"And maybe I can wash their car while they think about it," I said. "I'm not an actor."

She scooted her chair away from the console and toward me, until our knees were almost touching. "What if I told you that if you don't do the interview, I might lose my job?"

"Then I'd say you have excellent grounds for a lawsuit against your boss."

She burst out laughing. "First time that line hasn't worked all year."

"Heard it before," I said. "Sorry to disappoint you."

"You're far from disappointing."

She reached out with one hand and put it on the back of my neck, giving me a one-handed massage. It was the first time she had touched me. I leaned into it, like a cat. "Kyle won't stop trying, though."

"He'll keep getting the same answer."

"He thinks he has the silver tongue of show business and will probably offer you more money."

"I'll probably turn it down."

She grinned. "Probably?"

"Well, how much money are we talking about?"

She put both hands on my neck, rubbing away, still facing me. I was wondering if I was going to have to leave a tip. "Look at what he paid Bernie. We started at five hundred dollars and ended up paying him fifteen grand."

"Kyle's got a nice expense account, doesn't he?"

"It's the network that gives it to him. This series has shown fourteen percent ratings growth in the last quarter. We're closing the gap on our nearest competitor. Demographics show that men aged eighteen to thirty-four are being served up on a silver platter during the commercial breaks."

I put my hand up on her neck, and started rubbing in return. She tilted her head to one side and moaned. "So they can be programmed into thinking they need a new car or aren't getting a close enough shave?" I said.

"You left out light beer and bad action movies."

"I've been known to avoid both."

"Well, you don't need them," she murmured, turning her mouth to kiss the open palm of my hand. "No room for improvement here."

I leaned forward, my hand sliding up the back of her neck. Our chairs slid toward each other and just as her mouth opened, the case of the digital tape I'd been holding in my lap slid forward and gently hit her on the knee.

She looked down. "Whoa," she said. "Is that a Digi-Beta or are you just glad to see me?"

I laughed. "Both."

She picked it up and looked at it. "It's unnumbered."

"What?"

She showed me. "There's no number on the side. All of our tapes for broadcast use are numbered so they can be tracked by our tape library." She opened it up. "Is it a blank?"

"No," I said. "Kyle gave it to me."

She read aloud what was printed inside, on the label on the face of the tape: "Bernie Coleman video."

"That's Kyle's handwriting," she said. She edged away from me. "What is this?"

I told her.

"And he kept this from me?" Her brow furrowed in disappointment.

"He probably didn't want you to feel you were part of some subterfuge," I said.

"Theft is more like it," she said. She looked at me. "Did he say anything about editing this into the segments he's already got me recutting?"

"No," I said. "This is just for us to look at."

"You mean you," she said, turning away from me. She slid her chair toward the console. "He wants that interview bad." She slid the tape in and rewound it. The images blurred into small video squares that sped by too fast for the human eye to detect.

"I think I already know what's on there that Bernie didn't want to air," I said. "Peter Marling not only was at the show up at

Ojai, but he also went onstage, serving as host and emcee."

"That's interesting." She set the tape going, adjusted the volume and sat back to watch. "Well, now I don't feel so bad."

"About what?"

"The stuff I haven't told Kyle." She turned her head to look at me. "Or you."

"Like what?"

"Let's watch this first."

The video opened with thirty seconds of wild audio and a static shot of a restless crowd as Bernie focused his camera on the stage. The shot went suddenly wide, to encompass the cafeteria of Ojai Correctional Facility, showing how the tables had been taken out and extra chairs brought in. The prisoners were seated, guards patrolling the perimeter. The stage was set with a microphone in a stand and two trunk-sized speakers.

The camera zoomed in to focus on the mike stand, then pulled out to find a comfortable performance shot that would include the comedian from the waist up. The camera moved back and forth, in a practice tracking shot.

Then the tape shut off.

The camera resumed taping sometime later as a voice over the loudspeaker I recognized as Warden Douglas's announced that this was the start of the comedy night and here was their special surprise guest, from *The Marling Show* soon to be seen on a major network, Peter Marling!

The crowd erupted. The camera pulled back to catch the standing ovation as Marling walked onstage, his arms held high. It took a minute and a half for the applause, cheers and whistles to die down.

"Is he famous?" Sharon said.

"Not yet," I said. "They just don't get too much entertainment where they live."

Marling took the mike out of the stand and started talking. No props. No gimmicks. Just material.

"Skip to the stabbing," I said. "We'll watch Marling's act later. I think I know what we're looking for."

Sharon fast-forwarded through Marling's act and the three inmates and their five-minute routines. When Whiteside's image came on screen she slowed, hitting the PAUSE button just as Agar jumped on stage and thrust a knife at Whiteside's abdomen.

"Go back," I said. "Let's see the attack in slow motion."

"How slow?"

"Half speed."

We watched it play out at half speed. It was still too quick. "Half again as slow," I said.

We watched the attack replay, at an even slower pace. "See?" I said. I got up out of my chair and walked to the editing console to point at one of the monitors. "The knife goes into the handle. It's a prop. Whiteside bursts the blood bag himself when he clutches his stomach."

"All smoke and mirrors," Sharon said.

"One big fakeroo," I said. "But it's a good one. It's a professional job. These guys had help, and not just on the blood bag and the collapsing knife."

"From who?"

"Who do you think?" I said. "Who have we seen that's capable of making this quality special effects?"

In response, she rewound the tape back twenty minutes, stopping it on a frame of Peter Marling. "Him."

"He's a prop comic," I said. "He knows how to build things. He works on a TV show. He can get a studio department to make him anything he can't make himself." I tapped the screen. "The stabbing was rigged to look as real as possible. Marling travels with a trunkful of physical gags. Most likely the fake knife and the blood bag came from the same place as the rubber chicken and the arrow through the head."

"Let's watch the rest of it. Normal speed."

"Aye-aye, Captain."

At normal speed, the audio kicked in and we could hear the wild shouts, roaring voices and random screams as pandemonium ensued. Guards rushed the stage, prisoners rushed the guards. Chaos reigned. The demon was out of the box.

The camera was taken off of the tripod in a frantic effort to follow the action. The lens jerked wildly, catching haphazard bits of action. It focused on small pockets of violence, recording for posterity brutal sudden beatings, savage brawls and copycat stabbings. That went on for a few minutes and then the video image cut off. End of tape. Bernie Coleman had decided to pack up his equipment and get the hell out of there.

"Jesus Christ," Sharon said. "That was awful."

"Wait a minute," I said. "Go back."

"To where?"

"The start of the riot. Let's look at it half speed."

"Okay." She rewound the tape. "You know, I feel like I'm working on one of those wild animal shows."

"You are."

We watched. A guard got dragged off the stage by inmates and kicked on the floor in a circle. One inmate was thrown up against a wall and used for punching practice. Others started running for the hallways in groups of ten or more. The prison break was on.

"See what I'm looking for?" I asked.

"No. I . . . this is kind of hard for me to watch. I never get used to this stuff."

"It's not exactly my idea of family entertainment, either," I said. "But see what he's doing, though?"

"Who?"

"Bernie Coleman. Do you see how he's shooting this?"

She was getting tired of guessing games. "Tell me what you mean."

"He's shooting everything in sight . . ."

"Don't get me wrong, it's some great footage."

". . . except the stage."

Sharon kept watching, her eyes searching the video monitors for an answer. "What?"

"Bernie's not shooting the stage," I said. "Matter of fact, he's avoiding it. It's like he knew someone might be looking at this videotape later."

"I didn't notice that."

"You're not a comedian," I said. "Okay. Go back. Look. There. He screwed up. He showed what was onstage but he jerked his camera away, looking for something else."

Sharon rewound the tape ten seconds back. The camera pulled back into a wide shot that showed all of the lunchroom and a portion of the downstage area.

"See? Watch that. He knows he's not supposed to shoot the

stage. Freeze that shot, though. Let's see what was going on." I was still standing next to her. "Look at that. See that pair of legs there? He's only visible from the chest down, but the waist is stained with fake blood. That's Johnny Whiteside."

"Uh-huh."

"Look at what he's doing."

"He's walking."

"Exactly. He's still acting like he's stabbed, but he's staggering forward. We only see him for like two steps. Run it back in slow motion so we can see it."

Sharon did so. "I don't get it," she said.

"Look where he's walking. He's moving toward the front of the stage."

"I still don't get it."

"He's going for the speaker," I said. "And look. There's Agar. He's going for the other speaker. These men were supposed to be grappling in a life-and-death struggle and now they're going their separate ways?" There was a better shot of Agar farther on. An unknown inmate jumped onstage and rushed him and Agar knocked him aside as if he were a shirt hanging on a clothesline.

"Go to twenty-four minutes and thirty seconds."

She looked up at me and smiled slightly. "Calling out time codes? You catch on quick."

"I've done this before," I said.

"When?"

"A couple of times."

"Okay, man of mystery," she said. "Twenty-four minutes and thirty seconds."

"Okay. Back and slow it down to a frame a second."

The camera pulled out and a completely static shot of the entire lunchroom and stage was visible. Most of the shot was blurred by the zooming effect, but there were a few frames that showed everything I needed to see.

"This is just twenty seconds later," I said. "And we can see the entire cafeteria, stage and all. So where are Whiteside and Agar?"

Sharon's eyes searched the images as they clicked by slowly, like separate still photographs. "I don't see them."

"Exactly," I said. "They disappeared." I pointed to the side of the stage. "They should be here, but they're not. They're not in the crowd and they're not onstage."

"Where'd they go?"

"They're still there," I said. "You just can't see them." I tapped the screen. "This is why they caught all of the other inmates who tried to escape except them. And this is why they wouldn't want anyone else to get their hands on this tape. And by they, I don't just mean Whiteside and Agar."

"So where did they go?"

I sat down. "Inside the speakers," I said. "They're hollow. Peter Marling, Bernie Coleman and Rick Parker brought them in empty, and when they hauled them out, inside were Johnny Whiteside and Sam Agar."

"And that's how they escaped?"

"I told you Marling built things or could have them built. He's a prop comic. That's like being a magician." I waved my hands in the air. "Presto, chango, al-a-kazaam. He made them disappear. The only evidence left was this tape . . ." I pointed at the screen. "And those speakers. Bernie's murderer could very well have been after them, too."

"So why did Peter Marling arrange to have two killers freed from jail?"

"Maybe he had a job for them to do."

NINETEEN

I woke up the next morning around noon, looking out at a view of Farmer's Market from about ten stories up. It took me a moment to remember where I was.

I turned over in bed. Sharon Temple's blond hair spilled out over the pillow, her face turned away from me. She looked as though she had been dropped out of a plane. A fellow late sleeper.

Gently, so as not to wake her, I turned over again and looked out at Farmer's Market. Sharon had an apartment in Park La Brea, a housing complex in the middle of Los Angeles that stretched several city blocks. I had rarely been inside it, but drove past it at least once a week. I'd never awakened inside its gates before. This was a first.

Sharon and I had packed it up in the edit bay around midnight and headed for Tom Bergin's, my favorite Irish pub in Los Angeles County. It was the first time I ever drank iced tea there, that's for sure. We'd edged closer and closer in our wood-backed booth and by the time last call was announced we'd started making out like teenagers at a drive-in.

Bergin's isn't far from Park La Brea and by the time we got past the commendably stone-faced security guard it was after two in the morning. We didn't wait to get to the front door. Riding in the elevator on the way, shirts started to come out of pants, belts were fumbled loose, and fabric was being pulled tight against skin flushing red. We fell through the door and onto the couch.

Now it was the end of morning, the start of the afternoon, a new day. I looked out at the city from ten stories up. From there, it looked almost livable.

"Good . . ."

I turned over. Sharon was stretching like a cat, her eyes still closed, her fists clenched, her arms straightened so rigidly they bent back at the elbows. She let everything go in a rush of air and collapsed.

". . . morning," she said.

"Good morning to you," I said.

Her eyes opened and blinked. They were clear and blue and slightly unfocused. She couldn't see without her glasses. I stuck my face close to hers.

"Here I am," I said.

"Hi there." She wrapped her arms around my neck and gave me a dry-lipped smooch. "How's my midnight lover?"

"He's awake."

One hand left my neck and traveled downward under the sheet. "Oh, yes, he is."

"That's a natural reflex," I said. "Happens every morning."

She gave me a squeeze and a stroke, rolling over on top of me. "Well, let's take advantage of it while we can, shall we?"

"As you wish, madam."

There are several restaurants in L.A. that serve breakfast all day, but my favorite is Dupar's in Farmer's Market. There they have the best pancakes in the world, especially if you order them with the melted butter on top. Combined with a few poached eggs, I think all of the nutritional requirements for the day are met.

"Oh my God these are good," Sharon said. "I can't believe I live right across the street from this place and I never come here."

"Dupar's?"

"Farmer's Market."

"You've never been to Farmer's Market?"

She shook her head and sipped coffee. "First time."

"Today?"

She nodded and smiled.

"I feel honored."

"Can we walk around afterward? It seems like there's a lot here."

"There is," I said. "If you like fruit, there's great fruit stands. Do you like Cajun food?"

"Love it."

"There's the Gumbo Pot. There's the Italian place right across from the Gumbo Pot. Besides Dupar's, Kokomo's makes a great breakfast. One place sells nothing but hot sauce. There's barbecue, Chinese food, sushi, ice cream, a few open-air bars that sell great beer."

"You mean that motor oil I saw everyone drinking at Bergin's last night?"

"That's Guinness," I said. "But here they have Newcastle Brown Ale, Sierra Nevada, Mackeson's . . . all on tap. And that's just in the central area. Across the parking lot is a bookstore and a row of shops and Antique Alley."

"What do they have in Antique Alley?"

"A lot of old collectibles, and memorabilia. It's where I bought my Green Hornet lunch box."

"Your what?"

"My prize possession," I said. "My Green Hornet lunch box. I got a corporate gig once for these developers who were turning part of Orange County into a condo hive and they paid me like five thousand bucks for one night's worth of work. I came up here to celebrate and get something nice for myself and commemorate the occasion. It was the most money I'd ever made in one night in my life. So I went into Antique Alley and bought a Green Hornet lunch box. One of the metal kind I used to take to school with me."

"I always wanted one of Charlie's Angels," she said. "Cheryl Ladd was my favorite."

"I don't know if she's on the lunch box, though. I think it's Farrah Fawcett."

"But what's a Green Hornet? Is that a kind of car or something?"

I shook my head. "He was on television," I said. "A costumed crimefighter."

"Like Batman?"

"In spirit," I said. "Not in execution. There was a radio show, two film serials and a television series in the sixties. The Batman series was played for laughs. There was no funny business about the Green Hornet."

"What did he do?"

"By day he was Britt Reid, publisher of the *Daily Sentinel*, a newspaper." I dropped my voice to sound like a radio announcer. "At night, he and his chauffeur Kato dressed up and cruised the streets in a 1966 Imperial they called the Black Beauty."

"Fighting crime?"

"In their own way. The catch was that the criminals thought the Green Hornet was one of them. The police thought he was bad, too. Only the district attorney knew his true purpose and real identity. He led the police to the scene of the crime because they were hoping to catch him, but in the end he delivered other criminals into their hands. Sometimes people ask me if I always wanted to be a comedian. I tell them the first thing I wanted to be was the Green Hornet."

Sharon finished her breakfast and sat back. She was wearing prescription sunglasses. I couldn't see her eyes too well, but her mouth was curved gently upward in a smile. "So if you're the Green Hornet, does that make me Kato?"

"In the movie serials, Kato was played by Keye Luke."

"Who's that?"

"He was on *Kung Fu*."

"I remember that show. Who was he?"

"One of the masters who taught Grasshopper."

"And on the TV show?"

"Kato was played by Bruce Lee."

Her eyebrows went up. "Kato kicked some ass, didn't he?"

"They both did," I said.

"Well, then." She lifted her hands. The fingers were straight, and the thumbs tucked. "I am ready, Green Hornet," she said in a low guttural voice. "Let us get in the Black Beauty and ride to protect our city from evildoers."

I laughed. She made a few knifelike movements with her hands going "hiyah, hiyah" and I laughed again.

The Palos Verdes Peninsula is south of Los Angeles, between Redondo Beach and San Pedro. It sticks out into the bay like Jay Leno's chin, and parked on that precious expanse of real estate is some of the priciest property in the county. I saw a bumper sticker on a silver Jaguar down there once that read: WEALTH HAPPENS.

Ellen Alexander, Bernie Coleman's ex-wife, worked at Peninsula Properties, a real estate firm. It was on Crenshaw, a street that went in a straight line through metropolitan L.A., even cutting through Inglewood, but south of the 405 began snaking through hills and trees by the sea. I drove up and into Rolling Hills and found Peninsula Properties in a shopping mall. I'd phoned first to talk to Ellen Alexander and was told she was showing a property. I lied and said I was supposed to join them. I got directions to a house just across from Del Cerro Park.

I headed up Crenshaw, through wide lanes that banked lazily through housing developments that were priced according to their position on the incline. I liked Belmont Shores, but this was real money. I passed stables. The bus stops were built like little houses, with wooden eaves to keep the rain off. The traffic was light and the air was sweet. A different life.

Del Cerro Park was at the top of the hill, where Crenshaw ended in a small patch of green that looked as though it met the sky. I parked and got out, walking up to the crest of the hill and looking over the cliff's edge. There was a gull's-eye view of the Pacific, homes below with trees and trails. The water stretched in front of me to the horizon.

I turned away from the ocean and scanned the surrounding houses, looking for a yard sign that read Peninsula Properties. One was staked just next to the park at a Spanish-style stucco house, white with a red clay tile roof. I waited and watched from the park. If I had to be on stakeout, I couldn't have picked a more scenic spot.

The front door opened and three people came out, a tall thin Asian man with jet-black hair and thick glasses and an Asian woman of the same age, being led by a taller woman in her late forties wearing a beige business suit and carrying a black three-ringed binder. Ellen Alexander.

She and the Asian couple shook hands and parted company, the couple getting into their car and Ellen hers. She had parked next to me and as she opened her car door I called to her by her first name.

She looked up. She had an intelligent face with features so strong they bordered on masculine. She was six feet tall, with wide shoulders and broad hips. The suit was expensive, and she wore a string of pearls around her neck, but those were the most feminine aspects of her appearance. She looked like she used to be a man.

I walked toward her, repeating her name. "I'm Biff Kincaid," I said. "I called your office."

She was not one to be caught off guard. I noticed she had a key chain that was a vial of pepper spray. "Did we have an appointment?" Her voice was low and full.

"No," I said. I kept a respectful distance of ten feet and didn't close it. "I'm not here to see you about a house. I'm a comedian. I knew Bernie Coleman. Your husband."

"Ex," she said. "Ex-husband."

"Does it matter?" I said. "He's dead."

"So I've heard. I didn't go to his funeral."

"I did. That's where I got your name. From your son, Max."

"Adopted," she said. "He's not my real son."

And I thought I'd met some cold people in show business. "That's very clear to him."

"I have another appointment, Mr. . . . Kink? Is that it?"

"Kincaid," I said. "Most people have trouble with the Biff part."

"Well, I have another appointment, Biff or Kincaid or whoever you are."

"Can I wait for you here?"

"I won't be back."

"Can we meet at your office?"

She sighed, rolled her eyes and shut her car door from the

outside. "Look, what's this about?" She was not a pretty or pleasant person, but neither was she weak or stupid. She didn't move property on the Peninsula by wasting time on niceties.

"Before your ex-husband was murdered, he had put on a show up at a private prison north of Los Angeles. The Ojai Correctional Facility."

"So?"

"So that prison show was hosted by a comedian named Peter Marling. I think the two of them met through you."

She knew the name. "I showed Peter a house," she said. "Two months ago." She looked around. "Not far from here."

"Did he buy it?"

She snorted. "I think he needs his TV show to run a few more years before he can afford to buy this far up the hill. He ended up looking at condos on Palos Verdes Drive." She turned back to me. "But in the course of our conversation he told me he was a comedian and I told him about Bernie's club."

"Did he seem interested?"

"Very. He had just moved out here. The guy's been on the road for the last five years doing colleges and concerts. He hadn't heard of Flugelhorn's. I gave him the number of the club. I thought he was just looking for a place to perform locally, maybe put on a special event. I didn't know he was looking to do a comedy show up at a prison."

"I don't know when or where or why he got the idea," I said. "I only know the consequences."

"Consequences?"

I told her about the escape of Johnny Whiteside and Sam Agar, the videotape and how I was the one who found Bernie stabbed. "That's why I'm wearing this," I said, indicating my beret. "I think I surprised the killer and they conked me on the head."

"And you've been trying to find out why?"

I nodded.

She chuckled and walked toward me. "Let's sit," she said. "I want to smoke."

We found a bench looking out at the clouds and the water and the undeveloped land. She lit a cigarette and blew smoke. "You been poking around at this ever since Bernie got killed, huh?"

"Yes."

She chuckled again. "Anybody ask why a comedian is playing detective?"

"A few."

"Yeah, well, I won't." A third chuckle. "I know what you guys are like. Punchy bastards who'd take on a charging rhino if he interrupted your best bit."

"Thank you."

"Everyone thinks it's all laughs and good times, but . . ." Another smoky exhale and a shake of the head. "I had my fill of it. Twenty years, Bernie and I shared a two-bedroom, one-bath apartment in Santa Monica with no air-conditioning. The kid made it even cozier. That's how I got interested in real estate, I think, wandering around looking at houses, wishing I could live there. Only took two decades to realize it wasn't going to happen on what we made out of the club."

I let her talk.

"He started as a doorman when Mel Sikorsky owned the club, and then moved up to booker and then showroom manager. Bernie had bigger dreams than just a club all along. He was going to represent comics, he was going to produce sitcoms, we were going to move to Malibu . . ." She shook her head. "That's why I'm such a hard-ass now, working all the time. Too many Christmases with no presents under the tree. Just a bunch of promises. Everything went toward buying the club when Mel retired. We would have done better buying savings bonds."

Smoke. Blow.

"I remember when we got the kid, I thought well, now this is what a family is, this is what my life is supposed to be like. I kept waiting for happiness to come. But I realized I was trying to do what made other people happy, not what I wanted to do. Do you know what I mean?"

"I know exactly what you mean," I said.

"I bet you do," she said. "You ever tried anything besides comedy?"

"I tried."

She shook her head. "Comedy. Toughest racket there is. Not surprised it killed Bernie. It sure as hell wasn't doing him any good. I told him not to buy that club from Mel. I told him to quit

130

showbiz and get into the stock market or computers or fixing up houses . . . something that was going to grow. But no, there wasn't enough excitement in that stuff for him, I guess, or anything else. That's when I knew if I wanted enough money for a house, a new car, even retirement, I was going to have to earn it myself. So at forty-one I ditched the husband and the kid and went back on the job market. That was five years ago."

"When was the last time you saw or spoke to Bernie?"

"Two months ago," she said.

"What was the occasion?"

"He called me."

"About?"

"He wanted money."

"A loan?"

"That's what he called it," she said. "I knew I'd never see it again."

"How much did he want?"

"Ten thousand dollars."

"And you said no?"

"You're damn right I said no. You know how many times I asked him for money? For new clothes? Wear the old ones. Can we fix the car? Ride the bus. Can I go see my mother who's sick? He spent that money on bringing in a headliner who'd done the *Tonight Show*. There was never enough money. To hell with him. He said if he didn't get the money he was going to have to close the club. I said good."

She had worked herself up a little bit and took time to calm down, stubbing out her cigarette on the side of the park bench. "I felt bad afterward a little bit so I called him back and said look, I met this comedian while showing him a house and he's supposed to be hot shit with this new TV series coming out, he's looking to find a local club to do a special event, maybe you and he could work something out, like he takes the door, you take the bar. I had no idea if Peter Marling was a draw or not. I don't pay attention to that crap anymore."

"And that was it?"

"That was it. I gave him Peter's number. I gave Peter his number. Two months later, Bernie's dead. End of story."

"No, I don't think it is," I said.

She reapplied her lipstick, looking in a compact mirror. It didn't improve anything. She still looked like a man in drag. She snapped the compact shut and smirked at me. "You going to catch Bernie's killer? Like one of the Hardy Boys?"

"I'm going to do something."

"I'll bet you will. You know who you remind me of?"

"No."

"You ever hear of a comedian named Mike Gallahan? Red-head like you?"

"Sure. Did a week in Florida with him."

"I met him when he was twenty-three and just off the bus from Chicago. Bernie used to let him sleep in the basement at the club in exchange for sweeping up the place. He was all full of piss and vinegar and a few other things. Walked around like he knew something you didn't. He used to smile and wink at me and call me 'Mrs. C,' like he was the Fonz or something. I gained some weight in the last twenty years but back then I wore my skirts a little higher, my blouses a little tighter—sometimes just for him. One night I went back to the club to get something I'd left and he was bedding down and Bernie was on the road doing a show and . . ." She smiled and looked down at the grass. "Mike Gallahan."

"He's dead now," I said.

"I know he's dead," she said. "Car accident on his way to a gig, I heard. I thought he was going to make it big. I thought he was one of those who had it all."

She didn't say anything. I had the feeling a lot of comedians reminded her of Mike Gallahan.

"Do you still talk to Peter Marling?"

"We just closed escrow with him," she said. "He bought one of the condos I showed him."

"I'd like to speak to him."

"Doesn't he have a manager?"

"Already met his manager," I said. "I don't think he's interested in helping me."

"So why should I?"

I shrugged. "Because I did a week in Florida with Mike Gallahan."

She looked at me, then back out at the water and down at her lap. She fumbled in her purse and brought out an appointment book. "He just got the keys to the condo this week. Want me to let you know the address?"

"Please."

She handed me a folded sheet of paper. "This was the flyer I used. I don't know if he's moved in yet. Here's his old home number in the meantime." She read it aloud and I had to borrow a pen and paper to write it down. Some detective I was turning out to be.

"Thanks," I said.

We stood. "Don't mention it," she said.

"Sorry if I made you late for your next appointment."

"It's with a shrink." She took one last look around at the million-dollar scenery. "Remember how I said I thought all of this would make me happy? It hasn't."

We started walking back to our cars.

"You comics, though, at least you have your time onstage. That's what Mike used to say. 'At least I have a show tonight.' That's where he was happiest, he said."

I nodded. The week I'd spent with Mike Gallahan he'd screwed three strippers and gotten heckled off the stage the second show Friday because he was drunk. "Thanks for your time," I said. "And the information."

I got in my car and drove away. In the rearview mirror I saw Ellen Alexander light a cigarette and leave her car parked to look out at the panorama of the park. She decided to let her shrink sit and wait. She liked it better here.

TWENTY

When I got home I tried calling Peter Marling. The phone rang four times, and then a machine picked up and a recorded voice said, "I'm not here," followed by a tone. Now that was friendly.

The number was in the 310 area code, with the prefix of 826. Brentwood. Information had no listing for him, and therefore no address.

But the Comedy Store . . .

I swung by and hung out and bullshitted the comics I knew that were working in the office and after I'd hung out long enough I finally learned that Marling's home address was on Darlington. I got back in my car and took Sunset all the way through Beverly Hills, the turns curving and banking as the glittery Strip gave way to mansions and trees.

I found Marling's apartment in a luxury complex and parked down the block. The building had a sign out front that boasted of a pool, a private gym, maid service and twenty-four-hour security. The latest uniformed shift worker had yet to see me.

There was a button panel outside with a directory of names. I found Marling's and pressed it. It rang the phone inside the apartment.

This time it was answered by a male voice. "Hello?"

"Peter Marling?"

"No."

"Is this Peter Marling's residence?"

"No, not anymore."

"Is this . . . ?" I read off Marling's number.

"No, that's his voice mail."

"I see. Peter moved out?"

"Yeah, who's this?" He was getting tired of talking to me.

"My name's Biff Kincaid and I—"

"Kincaid?" He recognized the name. "You a comic?"

"Yeah."

"Kincaid, it's Larry Sharp."

I had no idea who that was. I put a convincing amount of recognition into my voice. I guess he was another comedian. "Larry, hi."

"What are you looking for Marling for?"

"It's kind of a long story," I said. "I was in the neighborhood and I—"

"You're downstairs?"

"Yeah."

"I'm in 703," Larry Sharp said, and the door to my left buzzed open.

I went inside and took the elevator upstairs. The security guard eyed me without curiosity or menace. Maybe he had been hoping I was trouble. Maybe he wished a little trouble would come his way soon.

The door to 703 was already open and Larry Sharp was standing in the doorway. I recognized him now. He was a little taller than me, skinny, with jet-black hair and sunken cheeks, cool blue eyes and given to leather jackets and T-shirts and other pseudo-Brando biker gear. He affected the air of an underground comic, smoking cigarettes onstage even after the ban, talking about death and disease and saying the f-word a lot.

"Kincaid, you asshole, what are you doing looking for Peter Marling?" He gave me a handshake that turned into an awkward hug.

"Just in the neighborhood," I said. "Thought I'd say hi."

He let me into the living room. It had a balcony and a bar and a big-screen TV. It was at least a two-bedroom place. These guys were living high. I had to learn to write funnier material.

We sat on a leather couch. "I didn't know you guys were friends," Larry said.

"We knew each other through Bernie Coleman."

"Bernie, yeah, too bad. Heard a comic found him when he was still alive and the killer knocked the comic out before he made his getaway."

"Guess who that comic was."

"Who?"

I took my beret off and put it on the coffee table to show him the bandages.

"You?"

I nodded.

"Wow." His eyes widened. "And he was still alive?"

"For a little bit."

"How'd they do it? I mean, was he shot or . . ."

"Stabbed," I said. I clenched a fist and touched it to my ribs. "In the chest. I called 911 and then I got knocked out."

"You know who hit you on the head?"

"No."

"The cops on this?"

"Oh, yeah."

"They got any suspects yet?"

"If they do," I said, "they're not telling me."

"Wow. Coleman, that cheap bastard. I couldn't afford to play his club, he paid so little."

"Wish I could say the same," I said. I looked around at the spacious apartment and new furnishings. "Things must be going well."

"Yeah, if only I can find another roommate. Can't afford this place all by myself."

"What happened with Peter?"

Larry snorted and got up to go to the bar. "Want a beer?"

"Sure."

He got out two cans of Miller Lite. I must have been mistaken. For a minute there I thought he offered me a beer.

He opened his and sipped it. I let mine sit.

"How long you been in L.A.?" he asked me.

"Long enough."

"And you're still working the road . . ."

"Some."

". . . going on auditions . . ."

"A few."

". . . getting spots at the clubs . . ."

"Sure."

"Getting by?"

"A little better than getting by."

He sighed. "I been in this town five stinking years since I moved out from Boston. I never got used to it. I never liked it. I never . . . I just never got L.A., you know? I mean Boston's a town. It's a city. It's got character. It's got people. But L.A., it's all just cars and freeways and traffic and bullshit."

"Can't argue with you there."

"I mean, I been here five years and I feel like I'm still trying to get settled in, you know?"

I nodded. I wanted him to just keep talking.

"But Marling gets spotted at the Just for Laughs Festival in Montreal and bang! He gets signed by Gary Ross. Ross persuades him to move to L.A. Even sets him up with me, because I'm also a client of his—supposedly. I mean, I'd had a holding deal at Fox, a development deal at NBC, a pilot at WB . . . it's all come down to a big fat nothing. My money's running out, I'm gonna have to go back on the road, Ross knows I need a roommate because I'd been using that second bedroom as an office and so he introduces me to Marling. I think yeah, okay, another comic, on the road most of the time, we'll never see each other but he'll help with half the rent. So he moves in and within a month, bang! He's got a series deal at ABC. Not a development, holding or a pilot. A series with a thirteen-episode commitment. After they shoot the pilot the network schedules it for a mid-season replacement. He gets on Leno. Letterman. Conan. I'm living with this guy, going what the hell? What happened to me? When Ross calls here, it's to give Peter a message. Meanwhile I haven't had an audition or a meeting or nothing for six weeks. I try to talk to Ross about what's going on, he thinks I should hit the road again, work on my material. Put together a one-man show. Well, thanks a lot! Some manager he turned out to be! You're supposed to get me *off* the road, you jerk."

He slugged back his beer. I took the opportunity to look

around the apartment. Through an open door I could see a pile of clothes and books. Marling's room?

"So when did Marling move out?"

"He's still moving. He bought a condo down in the Palisades. No, not the Palisades. The Peninsula. Rancho Palos Verdes."

I played dumb. "So he's moving down there?"

"Yeah."

"When was the last time you saw him?"

"He's getting the keys today, so he took a load of stuff down this morning. Coming back to get the rest of it tomorrow."

"How long did you guys live together?"

"Three months. As long as he's been in L.A."

"He's only been in town three months?"

Larry nodded. "And he's already got a series. You know what I heard? I heard *Class Dismissed* or whatever the hell they're calling it this week was originally developed for Jim Post."

Post was a comedian from England. "And what happened?"

Larry was almost giggling. "They saw his act. Can you believe it? They just heard he was hot and signed him to a series after seeing him in some BBC thing, but they'd never seen his act."

"Neither have I."

"He comes out in drag!" Larry burst into laughter, almost spilling his fresh beer. "He does his whole act as a woman! Calls himself Miss Mayfield, the Queen's social secretary or something. He went onstage at the Brea Improv dressed as a woman in front of all these network executives and they dropped their teeth. Then he does all this royal family humor that nobody on this side of the Atlantic gets and when he gets offstage, still in his women's clothing, they fire his ass!" Larry cackled with delight. "So they're stuck with a crew, a script and a pilot to shoot, but no star. That's when they found Marling." He wiped his eyes. "But first they made sure they saw his act before they signed him." He chuckled some more.

"That's funny." I wondered how long I could sit there and pretend to drink beer and wait for Peter Marling. "How's it been?"

"How's what been?"

"Living with Marling."

"He's a strange guy. He's a different cat." The first can of suds was gone. He went to get another. He could have had mine. "He's real into his new show. He brings his scripts in envelopes and reads them in his room with the door closed like they're missile plans or something. Doesn't want to talk about it, never invited me to the set and he sure as hell isn't interested in getting me on it. He never wants to share a ride with me to the clubs. It's like having a roommate is something he's doing for as short a time as possible."

"Any bad habits?"

"Doesn't smoke, doesn't drink, doesn't get high. At least not around me. I don't trust people who don't have any vices, do you, Kincaid?"

I shrugged. "I don't trust people who don't trust people," I said. "Sounds like he's one of those."

"Yeah." He finished his second beer. "Yeah, I see what you mean." He got up and quickly got a third brewski. The alcohol was loosening his tongue. Good. "There's, uh, something else, too."

"What's that?"

"He's into a strange kind of self-help. He's got books and tapes on how to change your life that he's always listening to. Not the motivational stuff you see on TV. This is different. This is . . ." He sat up straighter and looked in the direction of Marling's bedroom, then over to me with a funny little smile. "I was going to say it'd be better to show you, and then I was going to say too bad I can't, and then I realized, well, who's to stop us?" He stood up, bold with beer. "Let's take a look."

I followed him to the bedroom. There were about a dozen boxes left, some taped shut, some still open, with clothes piled in a corner. The rest of the room had been stripped bare, as if it was ready for repainting.

"He left some stuff . . ." Larry said, walking around the boxes. He nudged one with his foot. The cardboard flaps had been taped shut. "I don't know what's in here." He bent down and opened up another. "Socks." He went to the next one. "Towels. Ah. Here." He bent down on one knee and opened up a box. "Books." He started picking them out and handing them to me. "You can see by the titles . . . *How to Bend Others to Your Will*. Nice, huh? *The Lessons of War. The Principles of Revenge. Masters of World*

Power. A History of Torture. Jesus Christ, this guy is nuts. Holy shit, look at this." He handed me a black book with a pentagram on it. "What the hell is this?"

I took it and flipped it open, scanning through it briefly, turning to the title page. "It's a Satanic Bible."

"It's a what?"

"Look." I turned the title page to him. "And look at this." I turned to the next page. "That's the sign of the inverted cross."

"I never seen one of those before," Larry said. "A Satanic Bible. Have you?"

"Yeah, I've known a few comics who were into that." I closed it and handed it back to him. "They think it'll get them ahead in show business."

"How?"

"By working their will on the world. He have any candles in there?"

Larry dropped the black book back into the box and rooted around. "Candles? What for?"

"I'm wondering if he practices magic offstage as well as on."

Larry stopped rummaging and reached into the box and pulled out two candles, one red and one black, tall and in glass containers, but instead of pictures of saints these had angular designs on them. The red one had a drawing of a human face, a cartoon of a woman with masculine features and short hair, oversize earrings dangling from her earlobes. The eyes and mouth were cut out so the red tinged light of the candle would show through. It was grinning.

"That's . . ." Larry cleared his throat. "That's Jim Post. The comedian I was just telling you about. That's what he looks like in drag, when he does Miss Mayfield."

I took the candle from him. "Uh-huh."

"What's that for?" Larry asked. "Why would Marling paste a drawing of him on a candle?"

"I think to focus his thoughts," I said. "To pray to it." I handed the candle back to him.

"Oh man," Larry said. "Oh, man." He put the candle back in the box.

"Anything else in there?"

Larry held up a glass cylinder. Inside was a miniature wooden coffin, painted black, a red crucifix painted on it upside down. "What the hell do you think this is for?"

"I would imagine it's some kind of voodoo doll."

Larry opened up the top of the cylinder and shook out the coffin. It was held shut by a piece of string that tied the hinged lid down on one side. He untied the string and opened it up.

Inside was a doll, sewn together from satin and stuffing. The face was made of paper, cut out of a black-and-white photograph, the eyes pierced with pins to hold it in place, a strand of black hair taped to the back. Larry held it up and turned it back and forth in the light.

"I wonder who that is," Larry said.

I took it from him and studied it. The photograph was grainy, the paper colored yellow. It had been cut out from a brochure, one that I had seen many times before. Otherwise, I wouldn't have recognized it.

"It's Bernie Coleman," I said.

"What did Marling do?" Larry asked. "Put a voodoo curse on him?"

"He wanted Bernie in his power," I said.

"Well, it worked," Larry said.

"No," I said. "Actually, it didn't."

"What the hell are you guys doing?"

I turned around.

Peter Marling was standing in the doorway of the bedroom. He looked the way he did when I saw him onstage—tall, receding curly hair, bulging eyes, built like a scarecrow and hawklike nose.

In his hand he had a gun. A .38 revolver. He could hurt someone with that thing if he wasn't careful.

Larry slowly started to rise up from his kneeling position, his hands floating in the air. "Hi, Peter," he said. "I thought you weren't coming back until tomorrow."

"I came back today."

"We were just looking around."

"I repeat," Marling said, the bumbling schoolteacher he played onstage and TV screen having been replaced by a cool-eyed character who seemed quit comfortable holding a gun on

142

people, "what the hell are you doing in my room?" He shifted his gaze and the gun to me. "And who the hell are you, anyway?"

"Biff Kincaid."

He cocked his head. "I've heard your name before."

"I'm a comedian."

"No, I mean I've heard you're poking around into my business."

"Gary Ross must have told you."

"Wait a minute," Larry said to me. "You talked to Ross?"

"Shut up," Marling said. To me, he said: "Move that box over to me with your foot. Slowly. Keep your hands out of your pockets."

I did as he told me, but he had said nothing about keeping quiet. "What else is in there, Marling? Who else did you make voodoo dolls of?"

"Shut up."

"I mean, the one on Bernie Coleman worked. Or did it? He sold the tape of your prison show to TV. He wasn't supposed to do that. Your voodoo that you do didn't do so well that time, did it?"

"I have no idea what you're talking about," Marling said. The box was close enough that he could reach it. He bent down to pick it up. I stepped back to let him. The only weapon I had was my mouth, and I used it.

"I think you're one of those comics who'll do anything to get ahead. Steal a joke? Fine. Worship the Dark One? Okay. Whack a club owner? No problem."

"I didn't kill Bernie Coleman," Marling said, backing out the door.

"Doesn't seem to have done you any good if you did," I said. "All it's done is get me on your case. What I want to know is what are you up to now? You got a series shooting, money coming in, you're about to be rich and famous, maybe even just for a little while. You could lose it all, and never get it back. So what's your plan?" I paused, then I hit him with my trump card. "Why did you spring Johnny Whiteside and Sam Agar from jail?"

He was a cool customer, I'd give him that. Not a blink, not a flinch at the sound of those two names. Instead, as he was edging toward the apartment door, he caught sight of my beret on the coffee table. He tossed the box out into the hallway and picked up my hat.

"You like it?" I said. "You can have it. My gift to you."

Marling put the beret down and reached inside and pinched something out of the lining, holding it up to the light to see.

"No," he said. "This is all I need."

I saw what he was looking at: two strands of my red hair.

He closed his fist around them and smiled at me for the first time. "Your picture I can get easy," he said.

In spite of myself I felt a small cold worm along the back of my neck.

"Peter," Larry said, his tough guy voice gone high and dry, "what about the rest of your stuff?"

"Burn it," Marling said, still looking at me. "Give it to Goodwill. I don't care."

Then he closed the door and locked it and he was gone.

I walked to the coffee table and picked up my beret. There were strands of hair still sticking inside the band.

Larry Sharp was instantly at my side. "What do you think he meant by that?" he asked. "Taking your hair and getting your picture?"

"I don't know."

"Think he's going to make a voodoo doll of you?" Larry asked.

I put my beret back on. It felt funny, like it now belonged to someone else. "I've probably given him reason to do so."

"Man, that's creepy. I mean, I was raised Catholic, praying to the saints and Jesus, but just the thought of someone using black magic scares the hell out of me. That's some stuff you shouldn't mess around with."

TWENTY-ONE

That night I hit the open mikes.

Open mikes were the underground part of the comedy scene in L.A. They sprang up in coffeehouses, restaurants, bars and nightclubs, put together by the desperate souls who couldn't find stage time at any of the comedy clubs. All that's needed is a microphone and a speaker, and I've been to open mikes that didn't even have those. Stage lights, a sound system, hell, even a stage were all optional. Such fly-by-nights were sometimes operated by fellow comedians who just wanted to give themselves and their friends an extra workout space. Others were operated on a shoestring by untalented despots who went on for twenty minutes at a time between acts. Some were packed every night they were in business. Others were operated under strict rules that each comic had to bring at least two people. Some had a sign-up list that was law. Others only put you up if you were a friend of the host or a good-looking woman. There was a regular crowd of stragglers that went from open mike to open mike, cadging five minutes here and three minutes there, a nomadic tribe of wanna-bes and fringe players. I'd known open mikes that ran for years, printed flyers, got listed in the *Weekly* and drew regulars from the Comedy Store and the Improv. I hit them myself when I didn't have a spot at any of the clubs. Others operated for only a few weeks in places I was afraid to park my car, throwing comedians up in front of drunks and empty chairs, sometimes at lunchtime or happy hour when it was still daylight outside, places that offered no hope or haven, just the knowledge that whatever dream you were chasing had become something closer to a nightmare.

If Johnny Whiteside was in L.A. and he was doing comedy, it would be at the open mikes. Spike Olson at the Comedy Store thought he had spotted Whiteside at one of them. I called Olson back and got a list of half a dozen open mikes he frequented himself. I looked up a few more in the *Weekly* and that night I went looking for trouble.

I started at a biker bar in Hollywood and worked my way up and down the Boulevard and the Strip, then Highland and La Brea. I didn't sign up. I didn't ask for stage time. I said I was checking the scene out and showed the headshots of Whiteside and Agar to the emcee and asked if he or she had seen them. I got a lot of shaking heads and puzzled frowns when I showed Whiteside's, but Agar got a few nods. I think he was easier to recognize. He had been seen in the audience or out in the parking lot. He never said anything. He just waited.

I found them just after midnight.

There was a hotel on the east end of Pico, down toward Vermont. An open mike had been set up in the bar. Its usual clientele consisted of confused tourists and foreign low-end businessmen who didn't speak much English. A paper flyer stuck to the door identified it as High-Octane Comedy. The emcee was named Dave French and he'd recognized me when I walked in and hustled over to meet me. Onstage a squat overweight man of about fifty was doing a bit about the various stains he found in his wife's underwear. He looked like a talking bowling pin.

"Kincaid," Dave asked, "you want to go on next? The crowd's not much, but you can do fifteen if you want."

I looked around. There were maybe three tables with people at them, occupied mostly by comics. It had been a long time since anyone had laughed. The act onstage was struggling between silences. "Sure," I said, "but there's something else I wanted to ask you."

"What's that?"

I reached into my pocket for the headshots and then the bathroom door opened and Johnny Whiteside stepped out and sat down at a table. My search was over.

I let the headshots stay in my pocket next to my real purpose. "When do I get the light?"

"Two minutes," Dave said.

"Good," I said. "Am I bumping anyone?"

"Don't worry about it." He looked at a stop watch. "I'm giving this guy the light and then I'll get you on and you can get out of here. You have to get to the Store?"

"Not until later."

Dave wrote my name on the list and set it on a table next to a lit candle. Then he took the candle and waved it in the air as a signal to the act onstage to get off. Dave set the candle down and walked over to Whiteside to whisper something in his ear. It gave me a reason to take a long look at the man I had been searching for.

Whiteside had dyed his hair platinum white and let it grow longer than his prison haircut, sticking something in it to make it stick up from his head stiffly. His face was crusted with acne scars. Furrows and ridges ran along his cheeks and neck like the canals of Mars. He had an earring in one ear. He was wearing a black T-shirt tight across his chest and biceps, faded jeans that must have been waiting for him when he got out of prison, and stomping-weight work boots.

When Dave was finished whispering to him, Whiteside turned and looked at me with his bullet-colored eyes. I pretended to be watching the act onstage wrap up. I guess Dave had said something to him about the change in the lineup and I guess he didn't like it. Well, Johnny Boy, you're going to like it even less after I get offstage.

Dave didn't even bother asking for another round of applause for the last act. I guess he figured he was lucky to get the first one.

"Coming to the stage right now is a very special guest. He's an actual professional comedian, tours the road and I think he's even been on TV a couple of times. He's a regular at the Comedy Store and a very funny man. We're glad he decided to stop by tonight, please welcome Biff Kincaid."

I shook hands with Dave as I stepped onstage and by the time my hand touched the microphone I had my first bit ready to go. I stripped my material down to just the essentials and kept it to one-two combinations: setup, punch line. Setup, punch line. Dave said I could have fifteen minutes but I was going to probably do less. I treated it like a TV showcase, showing the best of what I had, making the dozen or so people there laugh as hard as I could. It was all the more impressive because the atmosphere had been so dead up to that point.

Within three minutes I had people laughing and pointing. All idle conversation in the back of the room had stopped. People were coming in from the lobby outside wanting to see what the commotion was. I waved them in, using a bit I had developed on the road about not having anything to do after a movie.

The only person in the room not laughing was Johnny Whiteside.

He sat in his chair with his arms folded, smoking a cigarette in defiance of the local laws. I had a bit for that but I didn't use it. I left him alone. I didn't work anyone else in the crowd at all. Once you sat down, you were safe.

I bailed at eight minutes, before I even got the light. I left to cheers, applause, whistles and a "yeah!" from the back of the room. Whiteside lit another cigarette. Follow that, buddy.

As I walked to the back of the room, I got congratulations from the other comedians and some of the audience members. The ultimate accolade was that there were now more people in the room when I left the stage than when I got on. I had brought people in.

Dave got back onstage. "Biff Kincaid," he said again. "Thanks for dropping by. You're welcome anytime, Biff."

Whiteside leaned forward, his elbows on his knees. He snuffed out his cigarette even though it was only half-smoked.

"Coming to the stage right now, it's his second time here at High Octane Comedy, please welcome back, Jack Whitehall."

A new name to go with the new look. Whiteside stood and walked up onstage. He and Dave did not shake hands. Whiteside turned around in the spotlight. He had all the stage presence of a police sketch.

"How about another hand for what's-his-faggot," he said. His voice was dry and whispery, like a cowboy villain.

I didn't know if he was talking about Dave or me, so I let it slide. All right, tough guy, I said to myself. Let's see how badly you want to be a comedian.

His eyes found me. "I knew a redhead once," he said. "We called him red ass, 'cause his ass was always sore. From being a butt bitch."

No laughs. Dead silence. Must have killed them on Cell Block D, though.

Whiteside continued with his cavalcade of comedy. Women were sluts and whores, gays were faggots, Mexicans were spics and blacks were . . . well, it's a word I don't use. On- or offstage. Even as a joke.

People got up and walked out. Whiteside taunted them, saying he ought to come kick their asses. At five minutes, Dave gave him the light. Whiteside ignored it. More people left. Comedians began to study their notes. At ten minutes Dave gave him the light and Whiteside told him if he saw that light again he was going to stick it up his ass so far his hair would be on fire.

Whiteside did twenty-three minutes before he left the stage. Dave had to cut the mike and the lights to get him off. Whiteside treated it like a joke and walked off, bumping Dave so hard along the way Dave went tripping into the wall. The schoolyard bully decided he would try to be funny.

Whiteside went to the bar and ordered a drink as Dave quickly got another comedian onstage. Other drinkers moved away from him at the bar. The bartender was Asian, and apparently didn't like Whiteside's jokes about gooks taking over L.A. Whatever Whiteside was having, they were out of. He was cut off.

Whiteside leaned across the bar, reaching an arm out to grab the bartender. Dave quickly came to the rescue, telling Whiteside he had to leave. Whiteside turned and shoved Dave aside again, this time sending Dave into a barstool.

If Johnny was looking for a fight, I knew I would make a great target.

I got up and walked out to the parking lot outside. Sure enough, Whiteside followed in less than two minutes.

I went to my car first and unlocked the trunk. Inside was a .38 revolver, empty. Using a speed loader I quickly filled the chambers with hollow points, clicked the cylinder shut and put it in the pocket of the Dodgers jacket I was wearing, my hands resting lightly in the pockets. I retraced my steps so it looked like I was taking my time heading to my car. I didn't want him to know which automobile was mine after we were done dancing.

It was after midnight and the lot was dark. I couldn't see behind or between every car, so I kept to open ground.

"Hey."

I heard Whiteside behind me.

I pocketed my car keys and turned around. "Yeah?" I said.

"Don't walk away from me." He stood on the sidewalk just between the hotel and the parking lot. There was no one else in sight.

"I didn't know that I was," I said, and walked away from him.

I could hear his boots as he stepped off the sidewalk and headed toward me. When he was about ten feet away, I turned around again, slowly, my posture not anticipating a problem, but my hands were loose and ready at my sides.

He stopped. "Why'd you do that in there?"

"Do what?" I asked.

"Bump me, you asshole." This close his facial scars were so pronounced they looked white under the lamplight. It looked like he was wearing a mask made of someone else's skin.

I shrugged. "What's the matter? Couldn't follow me?"

I noticed that a small mountainous shadow stepped under the sole overhead light. Sam Agar. I hadn't seen him in the bar when I was on, and he was hard to miss. He had been here in the lot. Waiting.

"Listen, shithead," Whiteside said, his voice as dry and soft as a snake's rattle, "I'm new at this, but I know I don't like people taking my stage time."

"Yeah? Well, other comics don't like you walking the crowd," I said. I turned away.

"I'm not done with you, partner," he said, and caught me by the shoulder and spun me around. The big surprise for him was that instead of looking at my face or my fist, he was looking down the barrel of my .38.

"Don't touch me," I said. I looked at Agar but kept the gun

150

on Whiteside, who had stepped back. "You. Shamu. Stay where you are or your boss gets a free nose job."

"You don't know who you're fucking with, man," Whiteside said.

"Yeah, I do." I pulled the hammer back on the .38. "An unarmed man." I let him look at the gun some more. "Now are we cool, or do we need to discuss this further?"

"We're cool, man. We're cool as can be."

I looked at him over the barrel for a few seconds and then I uncocked the hammer and lowered the gun, pocketing it. "Sorry," I said. "Just ever since I got back on the street I've been a little jumpy."

Whiteside's eyes went back to my face now that the gun was out of sight. "You did time?"

I nodded. "Eighteen months."

"Where?"

"Alameda State."

Whiteside grinned. It was the first time I'd seen his teeth. They were gray and small.

"Alameda," he said. "I did mine at Ojai. Hey, let's go back inside. Let me buy you a drink."

"Don't know if the bar's still open," I said.

"Oh, it will be. For us."

We started walking back toward the hotel. "Thought I saw you and the bartender have a few words."

"Hell, we're old friends," he said. "That's just the way we say hello."

TWENTY-TWO

Agar got us a couple of beers from the bar. No one argued with him. Instead, they made room. He was too big to squeeze between barstools, so he picked them up, two at a time in each hand, and set them aside.

He brought Whiteside and me two bottles of suds and then sat at the next table by himself, looking at nothing. He looked like a flesh-and-blood version of the Michelin man, somone made from the same strength and resiliency as automobile tires. No introductions were made, and Whiteside never spoke to him directly. He just let Agar overhear his conversation and anticipate his needs. Even though it was obvious the bar was closing, no one bothered us.

What Whiteside wanted to talk about was comedy.

"How long you been doing this?" Whiteside asked.

"Now, now," I said. "A lady never tells her age."

Whiteside sipped his beer and grinned. More gray teeth. It was an unsettling expression. It was like watching a wolf smile at a deer. If you were the deer.

"Ten years," I said.

"And how long you been on the outside?" he asked.

"Three months."

He nodded. I was completely faking my identity as an ex-con.

I had no idea if my answers were mollifying him or not.

"How'd you pick it back up again?"

"Tapes."

"What kind of tapes?"

"Tapes of my act. That's why every comic needs to tape himself," I said. "It's better than handwritten notes. Best way to write and edit material while you're performing, and the best way to get back up to speed when you've laid off for a while."

"I started on the inside," Whiteside said. "At Ojai. They had an amateur night there, about once a week. This stuff is all new to me."

"I can tell."

The wolf grin. "How's that?"

"You're not used to people bumping you," I said. "Here in L.A., it happens all the time. Wait until you go to the Comedy Store and one of the hotshots there decides he needs to go onstage for an hour."

"So it ain't that big a deal, huh?"

"It's allowable bad form," I said. "Usually practiced by those whose stars don't shine as brightly as they once did. Personally, I don't like to do it. I didn't know I was bumping anybody."

"What were you doing down here, anyway," he asked, "if you been at it for ten years?"

"Stage time is stage time."

"Why don't you go to one of the big clubs?"

"I've been in jail," I said. "Didn't do my reputation any good. I was gone for a year and a half total. I'm working my way back. I had better luck getting booked out on the road. Stage time's a lot easier out there. You get to do a lot longer and you can grow and develop. You might want to think about trying it."

"You trying to get rid of me?"

Jesus, was everything a challenge to this guy? "No," I said. "I've just seen some guys find a part of the country where they're welcome, like Florida or Seattle, and move there and build up a following. They don't shoot TV sitcoms there and you might never become a star, but you can make a living at it. There's some acting jobs lying around. Pick up some corporate work. At least you're doing comedy."

Whiteside nodded. "I might do that. I got some business to take care of here first."

"How long you planning on being in town?"

"You sure ask a lot of questions."

"No, what I meant was . . ."

"I sit you down, buy you a beer . . ."

"All I was trying to say . . ."

"Now you're getting all in my business."

Agar's eyes shifted to me. It was like having a rhino catch your scent and wondering when it was going to charge and exactly what you were going to be able to do about it if it did.

"My point was . . ."

"Don't point at me."

I looked down. My index finger was stretched out between us. I curled it back.

"If I can finish my sentence . . ."

"Don't raise your voice to me."

I had figured out part of what made Whiteside a criminal. He had the quickest temper of anyone I had met in a long time.

"I know more places where you can go up," I said.

He didn't say anything. I took that as encouragement.

"I can help you get up."

Silence. He drank some beer.

"To make up for bumping you tonight."

He lit a cigarette and dropped the match on the floor. I had to move my foot so it didn't land on it. It was like I was no longer there.

"And you can go on before me," I said.

He turned and grinned. "That sounds good. Where?"

I drove home, taking a long route up over into the Valley and back through Lake Hollywood, twisting and turning among the canyon roads, driving in full view of the Hollywood sign, before I finally made my way down Beachwood Canyon. I just wanted to make sure I wasn't being followed.

I'd blurted out the name of a place in Studio City I knew of, on Lankershim, the Tomato Grill. They had an open mike there every Tuesday, or at least they did last time I drove by it. Ron

155

Coffee ran it, a comedian I knew from playing the Comedy Store in La Jolla. Now I had to find his name, call him, and ask if I could get Whiteside on stage there. I'd suggested we meet there Tuesday at nine.

My real goal was to get Whiteside someplace where I could have the police arrest him. I had better call Gilmore first thing tomorrow.

When I got home I locked up my car and kept the .38 on me as I walked up to my apartment, looking both ways before unlocking the front door and sliding a chair in front after bolting it shut. I sat the gun down on the kitchen table after checking every room and closet.

It had been some night.

I still didn't know if Whiteside had bought my cover story about being an ex-con or not. After spending an hour with him, it was difficult to know exactly what was going on inside that feverish brain of his. It was like talking to a cougar.

After I'd named the time and place for Tuesday's open mike, we'd talked a little bit more about the road. He wanted to know what the clubs were like. How you got paid. If there were women after the show. What would they do for you.

He could have sat and drank and smoked all night if I had let him, but I yawned and excused myself and left. He followed me to the parking lot, and as much as I tried to avoid it, walked me to my car. As I backed out, I saw him check my license number. Damn.

I got in bed and lay awake in the dark and wondered just who I had met that night, what I was up against.

The phone rang. Once, twice, three times. I let the machine get it.

My outgoing message played out, and then the beep sounded. "Hey, Biff."

It was Whiteside's voice. There was a slightly blurred quality to his voice, as if he was calling from a mobile phone.

"Just wanted to say it was nice meeting you tonight, man. Sleep tight." He laughed, and then he hung up.

"Making a voodoo doll of someone doesn't mean you killed them," Gilmore said. It was the next day, Friday, and we were talking on the phone.

"I know."

"And as evidence, it won't hold up in court. I don't think it would even be admitted."

"I guess I knew that, too."

"And then you go and pretend to be an ex-con so you can sit and have a beer with Johnny Whiteside? You got guts, Kincaid," Gilmore said. "I'll give you that."

"Some days I think I have more guts than brains," I said.

"You're lucky to walk away with both," Gilmore said. "The warden up at Ojai told me Whiteside used to get the younger inmates to carry his cigarettes for him."

"He didn't ask me to do that."

"He used to have them carry his cigarettes up their asses. Said it kept them from getting stale."

"Oh."

"This guy's a stone killer, Kincaid. That's probably why someone sprung him. Next time you see him, you drop some quarters and you call me or the LAPD and get out of there. He's an escaped con and to be considered armed and extremely dangerous."

I accepted the scolding tone of his voice.

"Now you give me the name and number of the emcee, and any other comedians you knew on the bill. I want to see if they have any more information on him."

I did so.

"So you're meeting him this Tuesday night?"

"That's the plan."

"We'll be there."

"He's changed his look. Dyed his hair competely white. And he calls himself Jack Whitehall now."

"I can't believe he broke out of prison just to do stand-up comedy."

"He didn't break out of prison alone," I said. "He had help from Peter Marling. And Whiteside mentioned he had other business in town."

"Did he say what it was?"

"No."

Silence.

"Well," Gilmore sighed. "Maybe he wants to eliminate the closest thing there was to a witness to the crime."

"You mean . . . what do you mean?"

"You thought you were the one looking for Whiteside," Gilmore said. "Maybe he was looking for you. You're the loose end he's been looking to tie up."

"No," I said. "Marling just met me yesterday. If he needs Whiteside and Agar, I think that's to kill someone else. Just need to figure out who."

"Why don't I ask him," Gilmore said.

TWENTY-THREE

"Global United Network."

"Sharon Temple, please."

"Is she with a production office?"

"She works for Kyle Matthews on *Eyewitness Crime*."

"Hold, please."

Hold . . . hold . . . hold . . .

"Kyle Matthews's office."

"I'm looking for Sharon Temple."

"She's in editing."

"Can you ring me through to her bay?"

"Let me see . . . where's she scheduled? . . . hold, please."

Hold . . . hold . . . hold . . .

"Scheduling."

"I'm trying to find Sharon Temple."

"Is she editing today?"

"I believe so."

"Do you know what bay?"

"Let me check . . . that's edit bay 13."

"Can you transfer me?"

"Hold, please."

Hold . . . hold . . . hold . . .

"Edit 13."

"Sharon?"

"Yes."

"It's Biff."

"Hey, stranger. Where've you been?"

"Busy."

"Out riding in the Black Beauty? Keeping Gotham City safe?"

"Right car, wrong city. You're thinking of Batman."

"Sorry."

"It's not an insult."

"Well, guess what?"

"What?"

"Last night I had to sleep allllll by myself."

"You did?"

"Yes . . . Karen's laughing."

"Who's Karen?"

"She's my editor. We were having girl talk before."

"And what did you tell her?"

"Girl things."

"About me?"

"Yes, sir." I heard a muffled voice and Sharon laughed, and said, "Shut *up*."

"Is that her?"

"Yeah. She wanted to know if there were any more like you back home."

"No, I think I'm about it."

"So what's up?"

I told her about my encounter with Peter Marling. "And I met Johnny Whiteside last night."

"You . . . you what?"

I told her my story.

"Biff, that's dangerous."

"You sound like Detective Gilmore."

"Well, someone needs to talk some sense into your head."

"You're both getting through, believe me. Whiteside's going to meet me Tuesday night at the Tomato Grill for an open mike and Gilmore and the LAPD are going to be there to greet him."

"That's four days away," she said. "He could be in Mexico by that time easy."

"That's why I need your help."

"Did you notice at the end of the segment we're going to air that it says if you have seen this man contact the police? It doesn't say sit down and have a beer with him and pretend you went to prison, too."

"I know," I said. "But—"

"Jesus Christ, you think you really are some kind of superhero, don't you?"

"I wanted to find out as much as I could."

"By how? Pulling a gun on him? How do you know he didn't have one, too?"

"Sharon, I'll admit what I did was a little foolish," I said. "But now I'm just trying to get him into police custody. Tuesday night, if not sooner."

"I like the sooner part."

"Well, that's where I need your help."

"Uh-huh." She sounded thrilled.

"Whiteside said he was here to conduct some unfinished business," I said. "I'm wondering if that's tying up some loose ends in the form of some people he may have dealt with in the past."

"Uh-huh."

"One of those people is Rick Parker. I think he might be the link between Whiteside and Marling. He may have met Whiteside while he was in jail at Ojai and then run into Marling bartending at Flugelhorn's."

"Uh-huh."

"And since you dealt with him, I was wondering if you had a home address or phone number for him."

"I thought you said he skipped town."

"That's what he told me," I said. "I'd like to see if I can find out where he is."

"What are you going to do? Break into his place?"

"I just want to see what I can find out," I said. "Talk to his neighbors."

She sighed. "Let me look in my book here."

I waited.

She read me a phone number and an address. "That's in Venice," she said. "Did he live there?"

"I think so."

"I never went there," she said. "You know where that is?"

"I think it's right off Abbot Kinney."

"Are you going to go down there?"

"Just to see what's up."

Pause.

"When am I going to see you again?" she asked.

"How about tonight?" I said.

"Sure."

"You're not working?"

"No, I'm off at six. How about you?"

"I've got a spot at the Store around ten," I said. "But after that . . ."

"How about even before that?"

"That sounds even better."

"You want to meet for drinks? Or dinner?" she asked.

"How about both at Bergin's?" I said.

"Great. See you there—when?"

"Say around seven?"

"Got it," she said. "I've got to get back to work."

So did I. I hung up.

I drove down to Venice through an adding machine of freeways: 101, 405, 90. The air was cool and the traffic clear as I exited the Marina freeway and made the turns onto Washington and then Abbot Kinney. Rick Parker lived on Crest Street. The neighborhood was borderline funky, and I'm not sure how long a shelf life my car stereo would have there on a Saturday night. I parked in a back lot, fed the meter quarters until it burped, and rounded the corner to scope out Rick Parker's apartment.

It wasn't there.

The address was for a coffee shop called Coffee and Copies, advertising photocopies and cappuccinos under the same roof. In the storefront window it also advertised mailboxes and voice mail. Ah-ha.

I went in and bought a double latte and a pastry from the coffee bar and as I eased a dollar into the tip jar I told the guy behind the counter I was looking for someone who was supposed to live in this building.

"Who's that?" he asked. He had long seventies hair, three

piercings in one ear, and a scruffy beard. He looked like a modern version of Shaggy in the old Scooby Doo cartoons. This wasn't Kinko's.

I gave him a rough description. "Rick Parker," I said. "He's a bartender at a comedy club."

"I know him," he said. "I mean, I know who he is."

"Seen him around lately?"

"Not in the last couple of days. Usually comes in during my shift for coffee and a muffin. I know he works late, so he's a regular. I give him free refills, he gives me tickets to the comedy club. Flugelhorn's, right?"

"He have a mailbox here?"

Shaggy nodded. "I think I saw him pick up mail a couple of times."

"That's how I got this address," I said. I said nothing about Bernie Coleman's murder. "But you haven't seen him much lately?"

"No. The cops were here looking for him, though."

"Ocean Park cops?"

"I didn't notice. Cops are cops to me."

"They come in here?"

"Yeah."

"They talk to you?"

"I don't talk to cops." He looked at me. "You a cop?"

"No," I said. "I'm a comedian. I knew Rick from Flugelhorn's."

"Why are you looking for him?"

"I think he might have left town."

"Well, if he did, he didn't take his car, that's for sure."

"He has a car?" I'd seen him take the bus home from Flugelhorn's.

"Yeah. Doesn't run."

"How do you know that?"

" 'Cause it's parked on the same street where I park. Clearwater." He pointed. "Just a block up and to your right. He has an old cream-colored Galaxie. It's been sitting there a while. He told me the distributor went out on it and he was waiting to get enough money to fix it. The street sweepers ticketed it last week,

163

and it still hasn't moved so I don't know how long before they're going to boot it."

He had another customer so I left him alone. I took my coffee to go and went walking up Crest Street toward Clearwater.

I found Rick's car still there. I walked around it slowly, looking at the interior through the windows streaked with the dust from dried morning mist. There was a blanket and a pillow wadded up in the backseat. If Rick got his mail at Coffee and Copies, I think I found where he lived—in his car. The Galaxie was big enough to sleep in. I felt in the wheel well of each of the four tires until I found a magnetic key holder. I used it to open the car and crawled inside.

There was a musty smell to the air inside, as if no one had rolled down the windows in a week. There was the stink of food gone bad. I used the key to try to turn the engine but the battery was dead and the dash lights glowed feebly. I unlocked all of the doors and opened them up so the sea air could wash away the various odors.

I started searching the car, doing the glove compartment first. The car did, in fact, belong to Rick, but the registration was expired and he didn't have any proof of liability insurance, a no-no in California. What he did have was a big ticket for not having such insurance and therefore the reason why he had lost his license and why he didn't drive. Add to that being on probation from having just left prison and the risks were too great for Rick to get behind the wheel with expired tags. It explained why he took the bus home from Flugelhorn's. That and a bad distributor.

I searched the backseat. I found fast-food wrappers and small cartons of spoiled milk. There were dirty socks and underwear, a toothbrush and toothpaste. Some hand washer and bottled water. The blanket and pillow. A roll of toilet paper and an empty Baggie. Rick Parker had been a man down on his luck.

In the map pocket of the backseat was where Rick kept his mail. He had a letter from the cousin in Canada, asking him to come visit when he got a break. A notice that his driver's license had been revoked. A bill from a storage company: U-Store.

I opened up the storage bill. It was for a facility within walking distance, across the Venice border in the Marina. He was over-due for a payment on a twelve-foot-by-twelve-foot storage space. If he did not pay, his access would be limited until he paid the outstanding balance of sixty-five dollars. The notice was dated three weeks ago. Stapled to it was a receipt from last week. Rick had ponied up the cash.

I copied down the name and address of the storage place and the number of the unit. Before I locked the car I checked the trunk. Rick had used it as his closet. There were clean clothes: jeans, T-shirts, socks, a second pair of well-worn shoes, under-wear and detergent. I began to get the feeling that Rick might not have left town yet. I felt underneath his wardrobe and found the spare tire compartment, but no spare tire. I lifted the clothes out and laid them on the curb carefully, and then lifted up the trunk compartment. There was no jack and no spare tire, but there was some blue waterproof canvas wrapped around some-thing the size of a couple of hardcover books.

I took the package out of the spare tire compartment and care-fully unwrapped it. Inside it was a small metal box with a tiny lock. I broke the lock open on the bumper and lifted the lid.

Inside was a videocassette marked OJAI PRISON SHOW. I took it out and looked at it. Bernie's original tape, now blank after Kyle Matthews had switched it with a dummy copy. Carefully guarded and protected, maybe even killed for, but totally, un-knowingly worthless.

Rattling around in the bottom of the box was a padlock key. Since my next stop was the storage unit he rented, I put it in my pocket.

I closed up Rick's car, putting the car key back in the wheel well, and walked back to my own. I drove to the storage place on Washington Boulevard.

I parked a block away and walked to the U-Store on Wash-ington. The guy behind the counter in the front office was on the phone, trying to get a friend of his to agree to a band practice. No, dude, you gotta come. We need a bass player.

He didn't ask for ID. I nodded at him like I already knew him, and scribbled Rick's name into the register as if I'd been there a dozen times before. I walked past the front counter toward a separate building in the back, where there was a freight elevator and very few customers.

Rick's unit was number 183. I fitted the key I'd found in the trunk of the Galaxie to the lock and it popped open. I opened the door and reached inside to find a light switch. I pulled the metal chain my fingers found and a single bare bulb at the top of the unit turned on, glowing feeble yellow light around the tall confines of the space.

The door had a nasty habit of swinging shut automatically, so I propped it open with a wad of scrap paper before looking around. The space was empty, except for what looked like two large wooden boxes, each as big as a refrigerator, set at odd angles to each other, the fronts covered with fine black nylon mesh.

The speakers from Flugelhorn's.

I circled each of them, inspecting their construction. Their backs were made of plywood, two doors set in place like a kitchen cupboard, held in place by brass hinges on the edges and joined together by a small hasp, the hasps closed by a small brass padlock. Each was large enough to accommodate a man, and the man did not have to be small. The doors were designed to swing outward easily and noiselessly, with a minimum of space needed. Someone could open them up, step inside and close the panels behind them. Without looking, I was certain there were internal locks so that the occupant could seal himself in and therefore easily escape detection. Very clever.

I put my hands on one speaker and applied my weight. It slid across the floor with little effort. I tried the other one.

It didn't budge. Inside it was something heavy.

With icy fingers, I fumbled at the hasp holding the panels in place. There was something pressing on it from the inside, something that kept the lock from turning. The plywood construction and small locks wouldn't have been able to keep anyone of moderate strength inside against their will. Any occupant would have to be a willing passenger, or no longer able to resist confinement.

The small brass lock wouldn't give. I wedged it using the padlock key and gave it a good couple of kicks. The noise echoed in the hallways of the storage space, but as far as I could tell I was the only one on this floor. I didn't care.

The lock broke, and I freed the hasp. I opened the panels to the back of the speaker, and that was how I found the body of Rick Parker.

TWENTY-FOUR

I stumbled back against the back wall of the storage space, slamming into it with all my weight. The impact jarred the door loose, and it began to slowly swing shut. The thought of being trapped in there with a dead body snapped me out of my initial shock, and I scrambled forward, shoving the door back open and lurching out into the hallway.

My heart was beating fast and my mouth felt dry. I could still see a three-quarter profile of Rick's corpse, the head tucked into the knees at an angle both unnatural and stiff, as if he was a ventriloquist's dummy stuffed into a trunk for the next performance. Although it wasn't exactly my idea of a new ride at Disneyland, I went back inside the space to take another look.

He had been stabbed in the chest. The knife handle stuck out from his rib cage and fitted between his knees. There was a lot of blood down the front of his chest, and it had pooled at the bottom of the speaker cabinet. The wood had been lined with foam padding for passenger comfort. As it soaked up the blood, the padding had turned from a light cream to a crusty, almost chocolate brown stain.

This was a matter for the police. I closed the storage space up and walked down to the front counter. The counter dude was still trying to get a bass player to show up for band practice. He pointed to a pay phone. I picked it up and first thought about dialing 911, but then I realized there was nothing anybody could do if they got here any more quickly, so I dug Detective Gilmore's number out of my wallet and called him.

When I got off the phone the counter dude was shaking his head and paging through ads in the *Recycler*. He looked up at me and with an earnest concern he asked me if I knew any bass players who could handle kick-ass rock and roll. I said, no, I didn't, and then I told him there was a dead body upstairs.

Gilmore listened as I recounted the events that led to my discovery of Rick Parker's body.

"Where's this tape?" Gilmore asked.

"In my car."

"I need to see it."

"I'll go get it."

The storage space had turned into a crime scene. There were at least a dozen uniformed officers and lab technicians working away.

I walked past the yellow tape and out to my RX-7. I retrieved the tape I'd gotten from Rick Parker's car and gave it to him.

"Thanks," Gilmore said. "You still on for that gig with Whiteside Tuesday night?"

I nodded.

"We'll be there. You get any more bright ideas, you run them by me first—okay?"

I nodded again.

Gilmore fixed me with his dead-eye gaze. "And you see Peter Marling, you tell him it's not a real bright idea to keep ducking my calls. I still need to talk to him."

"So you think Whiteside and Agar have more on their minds than just getting stage time?"

Sharon Temple and I were sitting in a wooden booth at Tom Bergin's. There were three parts to Bergin's, and I had yet to decide which was my favorite. There was the horseshoe-shaped bar, a middle section by the kitchen entrance, which had a few wooden booths where dinner was served, and a back dining room, elegantly laid out. I was having a Bergin Burger. Sharon was having the Cobb salad.

It was she who had asked the question of me. I took a moment to chew and swallow. "Yes," I said finally.

"Another murder?"

"Maybe," I said. "I don't think those guys are out to clean anyone's house."

"You think someone arranged their escape?"

"You should see these speakers," I said. "They were custom-made, to accommodate someone of Agar's size. Rick Parker hauled them in empty to Ojai prison, and hauled 'em right back out."

"Why weren't they stopped?"

"They were inspected going into the prison," I said. "Not going out. There was a riot going on. My guess is that Rick Parker went back for them as soon as the riot was quelled—hours or maybe even a day later."

"And how does Peter Marling fit into all of this?"

"Maybe he bankrolled the whole operation," I said.

"Why?"

"It wouldn't have happened without him," I said. "I think he's the one who set Whiteside and Agar free."

"How did they meet?" she asked. "How did he know who they were?"

"I don't know."

"Who are they supposed to kill?"

"I don't know that yet, either," I said.

Sharon looked at me, ate some more of her salad, sipped some wine, then reached into her canvas carryall that doubled as a briefcase and pulled out a small manila folder. "I think I do."

I reached for the folder. "What's this?"

"Some research."

"When did you do this?"

"I didn't," she said. "We have a researcher on staff and I just give him topics and he scours the Academy library and the Internet and he comes up with all the information he can. I take a look at it and ask him to chase down anything interesting."

I opened the file. "What did you find?"

"Take a look."

There were half a dozen photocopied articles from the trade papers, highlighted in yellow marker, each of them having to do with *Class Dismissed*. The most recent one was dated three months ago, announcing Marling's signing on as the lead character in the new sitcom. Representation was listed as Gary Ross, manager, and Sylvia Henn as agent for the Marsh Agency.

"So?" I said. "Comedian becomes star of his own sitcom."

"Read the next page."

The next page was a clipping from the pilot show credits that had run that week in *Variety*. Peter Marling was not listed as executive producer, but Gary Ross was.

"So Gary Ross got himself executive producer credit, but not his client," I said.

Sharon nodded. "Therefore, when *Class Dismissed* does sell to syndication, who makes all the money?"

"Ross," I said.

"And what's Marling left with?"

"His salary and residuals," I said. "I'm sure his salary is . . ."

"Twenty thousand a week," she said.

"That's . . . more money than I ever made in a month."

"Same here," Sharon said. "More money than a lot of people make in a year. But that's just this year. Before he was making two thousand a week. I'm sure it sounded good to someone who was doing the road as a comedian."

"He was a big hit at colleges," I said.

"But twenty grand a week is chicken feed on a hit sitcom. If *Class Dismissed* goes to a hundred episodes, this syndication deal is going to be worth millions. Anyone with producer credit is going to clear eight figures, maybe nine. And none of it is going into Peter Marling's pocket. He may not have known that when he first came to Hollywood, but I'm sure he's found out by now."

"So you think Marling might have hired Whiteside and Agar to kill off Gary Ross?"

"I'm not the one playing detective," she said. "I just brought you some information you might find interesting. I've worked in TV long enough to know that the producers make the real money, not the people in front of the camera, and they make it through syndication sales when they're selling a show that's already been made and now can rerun forever. A lot of times they'll eat production costs in hopes of being able to recoup a profit in syndication. It's called deficit financing. And when those deals are being made and everyone smells money, it's like a hemophiliac going swimming in a shark tank. People get excited. They get crazy. They start feeding off each other."

"Enough to kill for it?"

"We are talking millions, Biff. The last sitcom to sell to syndication that had as good a pilot testing as *Class Dismissed* was *Pip and Squeak*. You ever see it?"

"Once." Pip was a cat. Squeak was a dog. The show was animated, with a lot of fire hydrant and litterbox jokes. "It looked like it was for kids."

"It sold for three million an episode in syndication," she said. "There were a hundred shows, and the producers each walked away with a hundred million. They had bought the concept from a college kid in Texas for fifty grand outright. He sued for a piece of the profits. He didn't get shit. The actors who did the voices got bonuses equal to a week's salary. You know what that was? Five thousand dollars. One of the principals quit the show over it."

"What happened?"

"He was replaced by a new guy who was even cheaper." She leaned forward. "We are talking big money, Biff. Enough to make a person wealthy for the rest of his or her life. You think people aren't willing to kill for that you haven't been living in this town long enough."

TWENTY-FIVE

I spent the night in Sharon's apartment in Park La Brea, and the rest of the weekend in her life. We drove up to Santa Barbara in my RX-7, toured the wineries with me as designated driver and her as an increasingly inebriated passenger.

We stayed at a hotel just a few blocks from the beach and when we stumbled through the door at sunset, golden light streamed in through the windows as we ran to the bed.

Talking in the dark, she told me about herself. Her home. Her family. School. Boyfriends. Dreams. Desires. Fears. Losses. Gains.

We drove back the next day. We rolled the windows down and let the sea air buffet around inside the car. We sped along Highway 1, my one hand in both of hers.

Sunday night we got a pizza and ate in, watching TV and looking out her window at the lights of L.A. after we had both gotten naked. I fell asleep with the city's glow to my right, her head resting on my left shoulder.

Monday morning we had breakfast at Farmer's Market, then went our separate ways. Bye, honey. See you after work. I could get used to this.

I went home and called Gary Ross's office.

"Ross Entertainment."

"My name is Biff Kincaid. May I speak to Gary Ross, please."

No response. I got about halfway through the last word in my sentence before I was put on hold. I got "pluh" out and by the time I got to the "ease" part I wasn't talking to anyone. Being put on hold can be like getting phone probation; you're this far from being hung up on, mister. You'd better behave.

After ninety seconds, the same person answered the phone. Again.

"Ross Entertainment."

"I'm still Biff Kincaid," I said, "and I'd still like to speak to Gary Ross."

I got to the "r" in "Gary" before I was put on hold again with no notice. Hollywood etiquette. After five years in the business, most people have the manners of a can opener.

"Gary Ross's office." A different female voice. "This is Lenore."

"May I speak to Gary Ross, please?"

"May I ask what this is regarding?"

May I ask that you not ask? "My name is Biff Kincaid . . ."

"Uh-huh."

"I'm a comedian."

"Uh-huh . . ."

"And I'm calling regarding—"

"Could you hold, please?"

I held some more. I should add that I don't hold well. Maybe I'd be farther along in my comedy career if I entertained myself better while on the phone with no one to talk to.

"Yes?" Lenore was back.

"I wanted to talk to Gary Ross about seeing if any of his clients were interested in performing at a charity function."

"Which charity?"

"It's to benefit the Ojai Correctional Facility." That ought to get his attention. "May I speak to him, please?"

"Mr. Ross is in a meeting at the moment," Lenore said. There was enough frosting in her voice to ice a birthday cake. "May I take a message?"

I left my number and put her on permanent hold: I hung up.

I paged through the batch of research Sharon had given me. One of the more recent articles was from an issue of *Show Busi-*

ness Weekly, a glossy magazine aimed at the treadmill market. A lot of their editorials focused on celebrity clothes, homes and hair, but this was an in-depth look at the business called "The Uncivil War Between Agents and Managers."

> Twenty million a film. Five million an episode. One million a night. The money is bigger than ever for top stars of movies, music and television . . .

The article started out naming the latest quotes to hit the trades for the biggest names in front of the camera and asking how these figures got so high. The answer, the reporter theorized, lay not in the demands of the entertainer, but those who represented him. (Mention was made of women's lower salaries, and referred the reader to another article by the same writer on that subject.)

> On their way up the ladder, actors, singers and comedians acquire a phalanx of representation, an entourage of agents, managers, attorneys and publicists—not to mention trainers, assistants, drivers, hairstylists and script doctors—that Elvis would envy. Being a movie star pays better than ever before, but it's also expensive—especially when it comes to paying the gross percentages staked out by all of those who play a part in getting the big deals done . . .

The writer concentrated his first several paragraphs on the movie business. Halfway through the focus shifted to television dramas and then sitcoms. Peter Marling's name came up in passing because Gary Ross was having a hard time hanging on to his client, not from poaching threats from other managers, but one of Marling's own agents—the very people Ross was supposed to be working with in advancing his client's career—had started talking.

> Quite possibly the most ambitious agent under thirty in the highly lucrative world of stand-up-comics-turned-sitcom stars is Sylvia Henn of the Marsh Agency. Younger than many of her clients, with the dark good looks of a soap opera diva but

the rapid-fire speech of a track announcer, "Mother" Henn presides over a brood of comic talent that includes Sam Prather, Jack Iman, Scott Grover, Peter Marling, and Karen Fuller.

"When the client gets screwed, I get screwed," Sylvia says in her office with a power view of Sunset and Doheny. There is a sign on her desk, similar to Truman's "The Buck Stops Here," except this one reads "I'm Not Your Mother." (Her nickname is short for the common twelve-letter epithet.) She speaks between phone calls piped directly into the headset she wears to negotiate breaking deals. "The managers in this town aren't interested in their clients anymore. They're only interested in padding their own portfolios with producer credits. If the client is on drugs, put him in rehab. If they've got marriage problems, get 'em a new girlfriend. Whatever it takes to get the hundred episodes for a syndication deal. The managers get in bed with the producers and start thinking like them and pretty soon they're sitting on the other side of the fence, trying to talk their clients into bad projects so they can become executive producers."

One of the managers Henn has had acrimonious relations with in the past—and present—is Gary Ross, whose hottest new client right now is Peter Marling of *Class Dismissed*, a sitcom set to debut on ABC this spring as a mid-season replacement. But Ross's stable includes at least one other Henn client, and several up and comers that he is grooming for success. He says that agents complaining about managers getting producer credit on their clients' shows is like "the day player complaining about the size of the dressing room." Ross has his own office on the Sunset Strip ("a knife's throw away from the Marsh Agency") and his schedule has little time for anything but business. (This reporter was granted five minutes that Ross timed on his watch.)

An intense driven man in his thirties whose vocal volume control seems to have been glued to loud, Gary Ross paces the length of his office as he expounds on the sad state of affairs between managers and agents.

According to Ross the manager's role is to "get his client career opportunities. I see the big picture. It's a matching of talent and timing." Ross thinks that it is unfair that a manager will work with a client every day for years and see their work belittled by an agent who signed them two weeks ago. "I've worked with agents who are downright rude to their clients. A client will book an under-five part—his first SAG job, let's say—and instead of congratulating them, the agent will say 'What are you—an extra? We don't handle extras. Is this all you want to do?' They only look at the check they're getting next week. I look at the under-five part as something that's going to take a comedian who's used to working nightclubs on the road, and get him—or her—in front of the camera, on a set, working with actors and directors. I represent these people because I've seen them do their acts live—which a lot of agents don't do—and know they have a certain quality, a presence. A theatrical agent only looks at two things: a headshot and a check."

Then why does Ross deal with agents at all? Simple. He has to. Legally, managers cannot get clients work. Only agents, licensed and bonded by the state and franchised by the actors' guilds, can book talent on jobs. But the manager's role has increased in importance over the last several years, with even novice talent getting signed at comedy festivals and clubs around New York and Los Angeles. As such, it has proved even more nettlesome to agents who often are forced to deal with managers as baggage rather than assets. And it's not just agents who are feeling the squeeze; producers are complaining as well.

"I booked a comedian for a pilot," says Jeff Lewis, producer of a network sitcom pilot, "and within an hour of breaking the news to the comic's theatrical agent I get a call from his manager saying 'I need to be executive producer or the deal is off.' My response is 'First of all, who are you, because I've only been dealing with the agent up until now, and if you're a producer, how about helping me bring this pilot in under a million rather than trying to get your name on it when I know all you'll do on the set is clean out the craft services table the one day you're there?' "

And it isn't just the on-camera talent that has managers, it's the powerful writers and producers themselves who are getting signed by Gary Ross and other heavy hitters in the TV and film business. Mike Stanfield is . . .

That was the last mention of Gary Ross. I read the rest of the article, but its emphasis was on how some stand-up comedians who didn't become stars of their own series after a failed pilot or two were often making even more money and acquiring even more clout by going behind the camera and launching their careers as writers and producers with the help of the managers who tried to get them famous as a "face."

I read a few more articles about Gary Ross. Most of them were limited to trade blurbs announcing the signing or transfer of a client. Except for his one bow shot at agents in *Show Business Weekly*, he seemed to keep a low profile. I looked for comedy names I recognized as his clients. About six months ago Ross had signed Barry Norton, a comedian I knew from the road, to work on *Class Dismissed* as a writer/producer. I'd played Canada with Barry, in Winnipeg to be exact, and we had spent Friday through Saturday with a few of the local ladies who showed us the sights, including their own. It had been a few years ago, but I liked to think of it as a bonding experience. We were furthering the cause of international relations. Who knew what that could mean in terms of a free trade agreement?

I looked in my card file. I still had his number from when he had been working the road, imprinted on a business card that read "Barry Norton, Comedy Contender." His logo was a pair of boxing gloves underneath his name. Barry had been a Golden Gloves competitor in his youth.

I picked up the phone and dialed. If he was making sitcom money now, he had most likely moved to a better neighborhood. I hadn't talked to him in years, but he was someone that might be able to get me a little closer to Gary Ross's office.

The line rang only once before being picked up.

"Hi, this is Barry Norton."

I'd reached his voice mail.

"You're thinking you've reached my voice mail. And you know what? You're right."

I looked at the card again to see if I'd written a home number on the back. Blank.

"You know why? Because our relationship hasn't developed to the point where I feel I can trust you with my home phone number. Otherwise, obviously, you'd be calling me there."

I smiled to myself. Barry's voice still had a tinge of the East Coast to it. He was from Philly. I think we had stopped our revelry in the Great White North—or at least he had—to watch a Flyers highlight reel.

"So, maybe this is the first step toward a new understanding between us, a heightening of trust, if you will." His tough guy accent made his formal phrasing sound all the more comical. "Think of this not as leaving a message, but as building a bridge between peoples."

Beep.

"Barry, it's Biff Kincaid and yes, I want something. I'll just come out and say it. I mean it's Hollywood. Why mess around?" I left my number and hung up just as I was getting another call.

I clicked over to the other line. "Hello?"

"Biff?"

I didn't recognize the voice. "Yeah?"

"Hi."

"Hi."

"You know who this is?"

"No."

"Just wanted to make sure we were still on for tomorrow night."

I held the phone in both hands as I realized I was talking to Johnny Whiteside.

"Sure," I said. "We're still on."

"Good. I'm looking forward to it."

I heard him drag on a cigarette and exhale. A TV was on in the background. I could hear it. Sports.

"I catch you at a bad time?" he asked.

"No," I said. "Not at all."

"So I'll see you tomorrow night?"

"Absolutely."

"Where is this place again?"

"The Tomato Grill," I said. "On Lankershim in North Holly-wood."

"I'll find it," he said. "After all, I found you, didn't I?"

"I'm not that tough to find."

He chuckled. "No, you're not. All I had to do was call information."

"If something comes up," I said, "how do I get ahold of you? I have the feeling your number's unlisted."

Another chuckle.

"Nothing's going to come up. You'll see to that."

"What if the show's canceled?"

"That's why I was calling," he said. "I wanted to make sure it wasn't."

"But I don't book the room," I said. "The restaurant manager may decide not to have comedy that night. I mean, that happens."

"He'll change his mind." Another drag on the cigarette. "I know you'll take care of it. See, Biff, I want you to be my manager. All the big stars have them before they hit it big. You seem to know the ropes. I need someone who's going to look after my career, help me develop and make decisions. I think you're the right person for that job."

"Thanks, but I just do my own thing."

Silence.

"I'm not in the management side of the business," I said. "I'm just a comic. Like you."

"Gee, Biff, you're going to hurt my feelings, you keep talking like that," Whiteside said.

"I don't mean to," I said. "Just telling you the way I see it."

"So was I."

"Let's talk about it tomorrow night," I said.

"Let's do that," Whiteside said. "Let's have a nice long talk. I like to look in a person's eyes when he talks about my future."

Then he hung up.

TWENTY-SIX

"He called you at home?"

"Just . . ." I looked at my watch. "Eight hours ago."

Since then I'd reported in to Gilmore, done a spot at the Store and now I was closing down Tom Bergin's with Sharon Temple again.

"Biff, this is getting dangerous."

"I like to think it was already dangerous."

"I mean, this Whiteside character has focused on you for some reason."

"Probably because I went out of my way to attract his attention."

"But if he's a violent felon and he's into this black magic voodoo like Peter Marling . . ." She set her drink aside and shook her head, taking off her cat's-eye glasses and putting the heels of her hands against her forehead. "Why do I always end up with men like this?"

"Men like what?"

She took the heels of her hands away from her forehead. They left red marks. "Adrenaline junkies. Envelope pushers. Guys who can't seem to live a normal life."

"Stand-up comedy seems like a normal life to me."

"The last three men I've dated were a cop, a fireman and now a comedian." She ticked them off on her fingers, then threw her hands up in the air. "There must be something about me that's drawn to them."

"Maybe it's because they work the same hours you do."

"So now here you're going on what might as well be a drug bust or a fire call tomorrow night, and I'll spend the night worrying. Again." She rubbed her forehead and neck.

"I'll call you as soon as it's over."

"All *right*."

It sounded like she had heard that one before.

"And then it's done."

"I hope so."

"So do I." She kept rubbing her neck.

"I can do that for you."

"Yeah, let's get out of here."

Back at her place, I had her take her clothes off and lie facedown on her bed on a towel. I took my clothes off—it was only fair—and started rubbing the small of her back with some massage oil we picked up at a twenty-four-hour pharmacy. I had heated it in her microwave.

"Oh, that feels good," she moaned into her pillow. "Where did you learn how to do that?"

"Practice," I said. I moved up her spine, a vertebra at a time.

"You have the magic fingers."

"You didn't know that by now?"

"I'm sorry I got mad earlier."

"Was that mad?"

"I mean, comparing you to other men in my life."

"A cop and a fireman? I didn't take it as an insult."

"This was in New York," she sighed. "The cop was Irish, like you. And the fireman was Italian. And married."

"And the relationship didn't work out? There's a shock."

She laughed into her pillow. "He told me he loved me."

"See, you should stick with us Irish guys."

She went up on one elbow to look at me. "You ever been married?"

"No."

"Ever been in love?"

"I will be if I spend much more time with you."

"I meant before me," she said. "You'll have to forgive me. I have a reporter's curiosity."

"Not to mention the good looks."

She rolled over on her back and ran her arms up mine. I guess the shoulder massage was over. Time to work on the front. "Wasn't there ever one special woman who you still think about, who you wished it had worked out with, who when the phone rings in the middle of the night you hope and wonder if it's her calling?"

I puddled massage oil on her stomach and started spreading it with my fingers. "Not anymore," I said.

"What happened?"

My hands moved up her body, slick and slow and strong, and she closed her eyes. She forgot the question just as I remembered the answer.

The next day, Barry Norton returned my call.

"Kincaid. What the hell do you want?" he demanded.

There was a slightly tinny tone to his voice. "You calling me on your cell phone?" I asked.

"Yeah. I'm on the lot."

"Listen to you. The lot. Mister Hollywood."

"And get this, I'm in my convertible."

"I got a favor I want to ask you."

His voice went flat. "What's that?"

"Don't worry. It doesn't mean I want to show you a script or get a job as a writer."

"Oh, good. That's about ninety percent of the favors I'm asked these days."

"You're still working on *Class Dismissed?*"

"Yeah. Just made me story editor. The pilot tested through the roof with women eighteen through thirty-four. The network's show order is now up to thirteen episodes."

"You still have Gary Ross as a manager?"

"Yeah."

"Good. I need to talk to Gary Ross."

"About what?"

"I think someone might be trying to kill him."

"What? What'd you say?"

"I said I think someone might be trying to kill him."

"Kincaid, you're breaking up here on the cell phone. I don't know if you can still hear me . . ."

"I can hear you."

". . . but if you can meet me for lunch at Jerry's Deli in the Seinfeld booth."

"Be glad to."

There was a burst of static, and then silence.

Barry had me meet him at Jerry's Deli in Studio City for lunch. We took the Seinfeld booth, so named because the cast of *Seinfeld* used to meet there after taping. It was marked with a commemorative plaque. Barry and I caught up on old times over sandwiches so big they almost hid the plate.

"So you're still doing stand-up?" Barry asked.

"Sure," I said.

"Still doing the road?"

"Absolutely."

"How's the money out there these days?"

"Not as good for some," I said. "Better for others."

"You doing okay?"

"Sure," I said. "What—you worried about me?"

"No, just—" He shrugged. "Can't do stand-up forever."

Barry Norton was a short and stocky guy, who favored baseball caps since he started losing his black hair. He had a thick lower jaw and lips that—along with a heavy beard—made him look like a caveman. He had icy blue eyes and small ears. He had thick arms and a muscular chest. He'd been working out since I'd last seen him. He wore a sweatshirt with the sleeves cut off at the shoulders and gym shorts.

"Yes, you can," I said. "It's not like I'm playing professional hockey."

"When I heard you called I wondered if you had finally decided to hang up your microphone and get into TV writing."

"Not yet."

"You don't have any spec scripts to show?"

"No."

"Got a manager?"

"No."

"Got a booking agent?"

"No."

"Theatrical agent?"

"No."

"Commercial?"

"No," I said. "I got three weeks in Florida coming up, is what I got."

"Working for who?"

"The Laugh Bin, The Comedy Cove, and Gilligan's Isle."

"Gilligan's is fun," Barry said. "I played there."

"So how about you?"

Barry poured mustard directly onto his plate and dipped his sandwich into it after every bite. "I got started in this business about two years ago. Wrote a couple of spec scripts. Led to some freelance assignments. Joined the Guild. Made a few bucks."

"How'd you hook up with Gary Ross?"

"Worked on a show with Larry Grey. You know Larry?"

"Comic," I said. "Out of Michigan, right?"

"Yeah, Detroit. So I showed them to him and he passed them on to his manager."

"Gary Ross?"

"Yeah. So Ross shows them to Peter Marling and Marling's in development on his show and they just happen to be looking for writers. Larry gets signed up and so do I. Only problem is, I don't have an agent. Next thing I know, I'm getting a call from Sylvia Henn. She comes down to the set, has lunch with me, wears a really short skirt, acts like she's hot for me, calling me at home right before I went to bed, sending me tickets to ball games . . . I mean, this woman is relentless. Turns out she's doing the same to every other writer on the show. You know why? Because the pilot caught some buzz, and it was written by a bunch of low-wage comics looking to get off the road. She figures if she signs us all up now, she'll be making bank when the show's a hit. Well, that's exactly what happens. In the meantime, I'd signed a deal with Ross giving away fifteen percent, and when I tell him about Sylvia Henn, his input is exactly this."

He sat back in his chair and acted like he was on the phone.

" 'She's a good agent.' " Barry sat forward in his chair. "That's all he does. So I sign with her and when she asks if I have a manager I tell her and she just laughs and says 'How about a manager that'll work for you?' I bring in my agreement with Ross, she looks at it and shakes her head. 'Thank God commissions are tax deductible,' is what she says. When I get back from her office Ross wants to know every word of the conversation. I get the feeling I'm dealing with a couple of kids fighting in the school playground during recess, but I don't say anything because I know it's my big break."

"Sounds like they have a history," I said.

"I don't know what's going on with them and I don't care," Barry said. "All I know is that I'm paying Ross fifteen percent, Henn ten and a lawyer five. That's thirty percent of my gross I'm giving away, Ross gets the biggest piece, and I spend all my time talking to Sylvia and the lawyer. Ross hasn't done shit for me since."

"Marling's his big client, I guess."

"Yeah." Barry shrugged. "He's done that for me. Made the show a hit by concentrating on Marling as a star. But when my agreement's up in six months I'm not renewing. I'm going with Sylvia Henn."

"What do you mean you're going with Sylvia?" I said. "I thought you were already with her?"

"Oops." Barry made a sheepish grin as he finished his sandwich and started to work on his pickle. "Secret's out." He leaned forward across the table. "Sylvia's quitting the agency business. She's getting into management herself. Her assistant is going to take her place at the Marsh Agency. Alan."

"I think I talked to Alan on the phone."

"The two of them . . . I don't know what they've got planned. But Sylvia's going to take all the clients she has from Ross and go into management and production herself. All that stuff she says about how she hates managers? She hates the money they're making. She's tired of watching Ross get rich off syndication deals for their clients as executive producer while she's stuck with just ten percent. She's going to raid Ross's stable. And he can't stand it. He's trying to stop the tide from turning, but I don't know if he can. He's got a lot of clients coming due who aren't renewing."

"What about Marling?"

Barry laughed. "Marling's going to be the first to bail. You read about the syndication deal for his show? You know what he gets if the show goes to a hundred episodes? Residuals. You know what Ross gets? Millions. That's because he's got executive producer credit. He's put his own needs ahead of his client's and his client's tired of it. Marling can't wait to dump Ross. His agreement runs out in just a couple of months. Ross is in there, negotiating away, trying to keep him, but it may be too late. Sylvia Henn is talking a mighty sweet deal."

"How so?"

Barry grinned. "She's cutting her commission," he said. "Only taking five percent. I tell you, Ross is desperate and Henn smells blood. It's two sharks in a tank. Each would do just about anything to get the other out of the picture."

"What do you mean by anything?"

"I don't know," he said. "What's your interest in this, anyway? Ross want to sign you up as a client so don't you want him dead."

I shook my head. I told him the whole story, beginning to end, all the names, dates, places and crimes.

"So that's what happened to Bernie Coleman," Barry said. "I thought it was a robbery, but someone deliberately put the ice in his drink, huh?"

I nodded. "Now I'm wondering about these two killers for hire, Whiteside and Agar. Who set them free? Who are they working for?"

Barry blinked and reached for his water. His pickle had gone dry in his mouth. "You, uh . . ." He cleared his throat. "You think it might be Sylvia Henn? Out to whack Ross?"

"Or vice versa. That surprise you."

"Nothing these people do would surprise me. What would surprise me would be to find out they haven't killed anyone already. But don't you think you'd better leave all this to the cops?"

"You sound like this woman I'm dating."

"No, but I mean, shouldn't they be, uh . . ."

"The ones talking to you instead?"

Barry nodded.

"They know criminals, but they don't know comedy," I said. "I'll let 'em know everything I find out."

Barry nodded. "Well, I can set up meetings for you. Who do you want to talk to?" he asked. "Ross or Henn?"

"Both."

TWENTY-SEVEN

I said thank you, good night, and stepped offstage. As the emcee came back on, I made my way to the back of the Tomato Grill. A jazz club that hosted live music, the Grill's stage easily adapted every Tuesday night to stand-up comedy. One mike instead of five, a quick sound check, and you were ready to go. That's one of the things I liked about stand-up. You didn't travel with a group or heavy equipment. If you showed up alone, you had a show.

I threaded my way through the tables, taking nods and winks from the fifty or so patrons in the audience. It was a good night, with a bigger crowd than usual. I think about ten of them were undercover police officers. If that was the case, then they were good laughers, better than industry. Entertainment people just sat there and said nothing, waiting for their phones to ring.

The comics were hanging out in the back by the bar, trading gossip and cashing in drink tickets the manager had passed out for a free beer from the bartender. There were two bartenders on duty this Tuesday night. Normally there was only one. Besides the regular 'tender, there was a bar back, who was busy getting beer out of the cooler, pouring ice and washing dishes—a square-jawed blockhead with shoulders like a middleweight. I caught him with my eye and handed him my drink ticket.

He pulled out a bottled Guinness and slid it across the bar to me. "Where are they, Kincaid?" Gilmore asked.

"I don't know," I said. "Could I have a glass?"

Gilmore got a glass from the shelf and poured stout into it. "I've got cops on the corner, on the parking lot, in the audience, on the roof but I don't have anyone for them to arrest."

"I could throw a brick through a window."

He looked at me like he'd like to throw me through a window instead. "This is a lot of overtime, and I'm responsible for it."

"Thanks," I said, and dropped a dollar bill on the bar.

Gilmore took the dollar and put it in the tip jar. "This comes out of my department budget, which is stretched thin as it is. I don't come up with some arrests, I start to look like an idiot."

"What do you want me to do?" I said. "Call them at home and offer 'em a ride to the club?"

"I think I'm going to start letting my men go," he said. "They only committed to a four-hour shift. Me, I'm stuck here until midnight, counting straws and folding napkins."

I could tell he wasn't happy with me. I put another dollar in the tip jar and walked away.

I stood in the back of the room and scanned the backs of heads. The emcee was bringing another act onstage. I had been there since 7 P.M., before Gilmore and his crew had arrived. I'd staked the place out on my own, taking only bathroom and burger breaks, and I hadn't seen Whiteside or Agar anywhere.

I dropped coins into the pay phone by the bar and checked my answering machine for the fourth time that hour. No messages.

I walked out front and stood, looking up and down Lankershim, watching the cars go by, and realized that I wasn't as smart as I thought I was. Evil people were often clever as well. That's what made them especially dangerous, when combined with an utter lack of conscience, a ruthless sense of will and a playful delight in seeing random victims bleed, suffer and die.

My luck didn't improve the following day.

The Marsh Agency was on Sunset Boulevard, near Doheny. Parking was either expensive or impossible, so I chose expensive, putting my car in the lot below the building at the rate of something like two dollars every fifteen minutes.

I walked in like I knew what I was doing and where I was going because I'd been there before. I'd called ahead and made sure I knew what floor the Marsh Agency was on so I wouldn't have to stop and look at the building directory, the sure sign of a newcomer and a way to get noticed by the building security.

I took the elevator up to the eleventh floor and stepped out into hushed splendor: new carpet, new wallpaper, new art, new chairs and a receptionist that looked like she hadn't been around that long herself.

"Can I help you, sir?" she asked. She said it with as much enthusiasm as if I had approached her with a speculum in one hand and a patient's smock in the other.

"I have an appointment with Sylvia Henn," I said.

If she ever decided to quit answering phones, she could have easily made a living modeling makeup products. She had cheekbones that looked like they had been sculpted out of ice, and would hold up under the exaggeration and scrutiny offered by print, billboard and computer advertising. Her skin was as smooth and flawless as sanded pine. "And your name?" she asked.

"Biff Kincaid."

"Did you say . . . Biff?"

"Yes. It's a nickname. For Brian Francis." I gave her my best smile that said have-I-got-a-surprise-for-you-in-*this*-box-of-Crackerjacks.

It made no impression on her whatsoever. Maybe I should get my teeth cleaned. "Please have a seat and someone will be with you."

I took a seat. I picked up a magazine. It was thick and large and glossy and one I had seen only on the newsstands, called *L.A. Elite.* On the cover was an aged producer standing in front of his Beverly Hills mansion with five pedigreed boxers on leashes. The cover blurb read "Harry Falcon and the Power of Style." Oh, great. Another periodical flaunting wealth and success in a city where people sold fruit on corners and lived out of shopping carts. Just what the restless populace needs.

I opened it up. It turned out Harry Falcon had produced thirty-two one-hour dramas for network television in the last twenty-five years, eleven of which had been top ten hits and I think if you added up all of the time I'd spent sampling his wares you would have had the length of an early Beatles tune. The article was the product of a very expensive publicist. It made him sound like a patriarch of the arts, rather than someone who recycled plot lines via memos and focus groups and would air child pornography if it would get him a rating.

I skimmed the article. He was a Marsh Agency client.

"Mr. Kincaid?"

I looked up into the face of a man a few years younger than me, but far better dressed. I had come in khakis and a polo shirt, the better to show off the bulging biceps I'd spent hours sculpting at the gym just like Ah-nold. He wore a black silk shirt, black pants and far more hair products than I could fit on my bathroom counter. He had a lean foxlike face and sallow skin. At first glance, I knew I'd rather be me than him.

"I'm Alan," he said, and extended his hand.

"Biff," I said, and shook as I stood.

He put his hands together like a Buddhist acolyte and I knew some kind of explanation was coming. "I'm afraid Sylvia got pulled into a last-minute meeting regarding a client in contract negotiations," he said. "Is there something I could help you with?"

"Sure," I said. "I just need an answer to a simple question."

"What's that?"

"When is she planning leaving her job here to become a manager with you taking her place?"

He looked as though I'd slapped him with my glove and mentioned something about pistols at dawn. "Let's go into a conference room," he said.

It took three tries but we found an empty one. "Okay," he said, taking a seat at the head of a table and making sure he was sitting by a phone in case he needed to summon someone quickly. "Who are you?"

"Biff Kincaid."

"That means nothing to me."

"It will in five minutes," I said. "I have a way of making a lasting impression."

"Are you a comedian?"

"Gee, how'd you guess?"

"I'll have to see how you got on Sylvia's appointment calendar."

"You put me there," I said, "because Barry Norton asked you to. I knew him from the road."

"Barry shouldn't have done that."

"Comedians," I said. "We stick together. What can you do?"

"And what did you want to talk to Sylvia about?"

"I already told you," I said. "You haven't been paying attention."

"She has no plans to leave the agency," Alan said. "I have no intention of taking her place."

"You think you're clued into what really goes on in your boss's head?" I said. "You flatter yourself, Alan." I leaned forward and put my elbows on the table, a gesture that caused him to move back in his chair. "You want to know why I'm here? I'll tell you. You want to call security, that's fine. I'll go peacefully. But here's what I see from where I sit.

"A few months ago Peter Marling did a show at the Ojai Correctional Facility. That's a private prison, not a state or federal one. The show was produced by Bernie Coleman, who owned a comedy club called Flugelhorn's."

"I've been there," Alan said.

"During the show, two convicted murderers escaped. Now they're here in L.A. I think they killed Bernie Coleman to get what they thought was the only existing copy of a videotape of the Ojai show—the one that showed them escaping. Why do I think that? Because I ran into them. One of them—the one that talks—mentioned he had some unfinished business here. To me that means they plan to murder someone else, per a contract. So I'm here to see if your boss is either employing them, which I don't expect her to tell me, or their next target, which I intend to tell her."

I sat back.

Alan picked up the phone and pressed "O." I had told him just enough to let him know that he was in way over his head.

"Deb? It's Alan. Can you ring me through to Bruce's office?

Sylvia's in a meeting there and I need to speak with her immediately."

Sylvia Henn was a looker, I'd give her that.

She dressed in Hollywood power babe style, walking into the room on high heels with a short black leather skirt. The legs were by StairMaster, the blouse by Donna Karan and a few accessories under the skin by a plastic surgeon. She had never been an actress so the implants were for effect, as her strategic dressing allowed intermittent glimpses for saline landscaping. I didn't look. This was L.A., where even the cows have fake boobs.

From the neck up she was all natural, though: full sensuous lips, a dark tint to the skin that made her look slightly Indian, brown liquid eyes that burned with a fierce confidence and thick black hair that tumbled around her shoulders. The under-thirty part had played well in the article, but up close, I could tell the big three-oh was no longer looking her in the face. It was sitting on her shoulder, hitching a ride to work.

"Who are you again?" she said by way of greeting.

"Biff Kincaid."

"What's a Biff Kincaid?"

"It's a comedian," I said.

"What's it doing in my office?"

"Actually, I think we're in a conference room."

"Cut the shit, Red." She moved her head and her eyes flickered to the door. Alan left as quickly and quietly as if he were a ghost.

I laid out the story for her the way I had for Alan. None of the details made any impressions. Her eyes looked into me as though they were searching for stock market tips.

"So you think I hired these hit men?"

"Someone did," I said. "If it wasn't you, then maybe you're one of their targets."

"You threatening me?"

"I'm warning you."

"Why?"

"If someone makes a move on you, you'll know who it was.

Call me, or better yet, call Detective Gilmore at the Ocean Park Police Department."

"Call him yourself."

"Don't know if he'd be so happy to hear from me," I said. "Last night he staked out an open mike in the Valley because I'd arranged to meet Whiteside and Agar there."

"They show?"

I shook my head.

"It's been my experience comedians should stick to being comedians," she said. "And leave the business to the business people."

"This isn't comedy and it isn't business," I said. "This is criminality. I'm trying to keep you from waking up dead. I said all I have to say." I reached into my pocket and pulled out a business card. "I was hoping I could ask you a few questions, but I have the feeling your assistant left here with orders to call building security. Since I'm going to be forcibly escorted out of here within the next ninety seconds, just ask yourself this question when you double lock your doors tonight: Who wants me out of the way?"

I spun the card onto the conference room table like an ace of spades. There was a knock at the door. A hard knock from a big hand.

"Come in," Sylvia Henn said.

I could see Alan behind the two burly security guards, but just barely. One of the guards was so tall he had to stoop to get in through the door. He had a big friendly face on top of a fullback's body. He had a shaved head and light black skin. I pegged him to be six-six, and about two-eighty, and he was only one of a set of two. "How ya'll doing?" he asked softly. His name tag read Clarence.

"I was just leaving," I said. I eased my chair away from the table, keeping my hands on the surface and slowly came to a standing position. "Could you show me the way out?" I asked Clarence. "I think I got a little lost."

"You want us to call the police?" Clarence asked Sylvia.

"No," Sylvia said. "Just get him out of here."

Clarence put his hand on my shoulder and I gave him my-there'll-be-no-trouble-from-me smile and he nodded once. As I turned to go, I saw Sylvia Henn pick up my card, look at it once, tear it in half and drop it in the trash can.

TWENTY-EIGHT

I was wakened in the middle of the night by a shotgun pressed underneath my chin. The sight dug into the fleshy part of my throat just behind my teeth and that's what caused me to open my eyes and see the long dull metal barrel telescoping away from my neck to the stock and trigger that were in the hands of Sam Agar. His fleshy shaved head was bent down, one massive cheek flattened along his mountainous shoulder as he aimed the gun at me. I knew that shotgun. It was mine. I kept it loaded under the bed. It was a bolt action .410. I don't know why Agar was bothering to aim. His finger was on the trigger and the safety was off. If he fired, he'd blow my head off like he was clipping the top off a carrot.

Whiteside's face floated next to Agar's shoulder, his acne scars making his skin look as pockmarked as a lunar landscape.

"Rise and shine, sweetheart," he whispered gently. "Surprised to see me?"

"What do you want?" I said. I spoke slowly and carefully so as not to cause the shotgun barrel any undue movement.

"What we want we already got," Whiteside said, "and that's your ass. To go. With a side order of fries."

"Tell me what you want," I said, "and I'll give it to you."

"Okay," Whiteside said. "I'll have a half dozen screams, three or four please-don't-kill-me's, and ten torn fingernails." He moved the barrel of the shotgun aside with his hand and reached forward and looped a circle of rope around my neck and yanked it tight. "Get out of bed," he snarled, and dragged me onto the floor.

My hands went to the rope, which was biting into my neck. I stumbled to my feet but Whiteside yanked me back down so hard I heard my vertebrae wrench like someone twisting a celery stalk. I sleep in a T-shirt and boxer shorts when the canyon nights are cool so when my knees hit the hardwood floors they had precious little padding. One hand left my throat to brace my fall.

"That's right," Whiteside said. "Good doggy. We're going for a little walk."

He jerked on the rope again and my breath was cut off completely. The circulation to my head wasn't doing much better, either. Large purple splotches started to appear in front of my eyes. I could feel the shotgun barrel jabbing me in the small of the back. There were no lights on in my apartment. I was about eye level with Whiteside's knees.

"Come on, doggy." Whiteside made a little whistling sound. "We're going to the kitchen."

On my hands and knees I crawled, trying to keep pace with him. I rounded the corner to the kitchen and saw he had already taken one of my dining table chairs and planted it in the center of the kitchen, in front of the sink.

Whiteside pulled the rope around my neck hard enough to ram my face into the seat of the chair, forcing my upper lip against my teeth. I could feel blood weeping out. "Oops," Whiteside said, and laughed. "Doggy hit the fire hydrant."

Then he turned me around and pulled me up into the chair by the rope around my neck until I was in a seated position, facing the sink. Agar laid the shotgun aside and held my legs as Whiteside bound my hands to the faucet of the kitchen sink. My ankles were next, tied to the legs of the chair. I was completely immobilized in a matter of thirty seconds. It had been maybe two minutes since I'd wakened. My neck was throbbing from the pressure of the rope. I could hardly breathe, let alone speak.

"Well, he'll never talk that way," Whiteside muttered. I heard a switchblade open and a *snick* as he sliced through the rope just behind my neck. The noose was still around my neck, but cut free it was no longer pulling my head back.

My head lolled forward and I caught my breath as I felt Whiteside run his fingers through my hair. "What a beautiful shade of strawberry blond," he murmured. "It's natural, isn't it?"

"You . . . drag me out of bed . . . to ask . . . me about . . . my hair?"

Whiteside's fingers clenched against my scalp and he yanked my head back by the hair and leaned down into my face, grinning. "No, baby doll, I got you out of bed to have some fun with you."

Agar lumbered behind me. I could hear him opening kitchen drawers, filling a pot with water, turning on gas jets, laying out utensils.

"We're going to play a little game," Whiteside said. His face was so close to mine I could smell the rotten tobacco stench from his smoker's lungs. "It's called 'What Do You Know?' " Agar reappeared with a paper towel in hand that he soaked with clear liquid from a bottle I recognized. Rubbing alcohol. He'd gotten it from under my sink. Using the paper towel, he began to roughly scrub my fingertips. "See? That's to keep everything nice and clean. Avoid the risk of infection. Sam was a medic in the Marines."

I realized the reason my hands were tied over the sink was to catch the blood. "I don't know much, Whitehall."

"The name's Whiteside, and you know it, asshole," he growled. "You had a room full of cops waiting for me last night at the Tomato Grill. You think I didn't see through your jailhouse act from the very beginning? I just played along while I asked myself, why is a comedian trying to get me to think he's a con? I still haven't been able to figure it out, even after you tried to bust me. So I thought I'd come here and ask you while Sam splits your fingernails open one by one and peels them back."

I heard the sound of a knife sharpening. I knew that sound. I had a whetstone, and a set of cooking knives. The stone had come with the knives.

Just to my right was the microwave oven. The time glowed green in the dark. 2:38 A.M. Moonlight came in through the kitchen window in front of me. It was an old-fashioned window with glass slats that rotated open and shut with a crank. Just then they were shut to keep out the cool night air. I could see out of my window and over into my neighbor's yard, set along a hill and divided from my apartment complex by a fence. I strained to see light next door, shadows, anything. On their front doorstep I saw three yellowed newspapers. Out of town. No help there.

I wondered if I was going to die this way.

Time to do some serious talking.

"I know who you are," I said. "Both of you."

The sharpening sound continued. Whiteside looked at me with amused pity.

"I know you broke out of Ojai prison," I said.

The sharpening stopped.

"There is a videotape of that performance."

Agar stepped into my sight, laying a large butcher knife aside. It didn't look good. My heart began to beat faster and more insistently. Agar ran water in the sink and wet a dish towel.

"I know where the tape is," I said.

Agar stuffed the wet dish towel into my mouth. I didn't need to know what the gag was for. I already knew it was to muffle my screams. I don't like pain. I really don't. I worked my head around and spit it out so I could say one more thing before being gagged.

"I know because I'm the one who killed Bernie Coleman," I said.

The gag had fallen on the floor with a wet slap. Agar had bent down to pick it up and put it back in my mouth but Whiteside stopped him with a gesture. Agar was like a robot he controlled.

"You're the one who killed that club owner?" Whiteside asked.

So they hadn't. It was a desperate gamble, but the lie had paid off. I had a momentary stay of execution. I nodded. "Yeah."

"Why?"

"He got in the way."

"Of what?"

"I was working on a deal with Gary Ross."

"What deal?"

So he knew who Ross was. "Simple. I get the tape back from

Bernie Coleman, Ross gives me five grand. Ross knew I was working Flugelhorn's that weekend."

"And?"

"I broke into the club Monday, when I thought the club would be empty." I was making the whole thing up as I went along. I hoped it didn't show. "I started searching the place. I found the tape in the bottom of a file cabinet. But I must have set off an alarm or something because Bernie came back into the club and surprised me. Saw me with the tape in my hand. He had a gun with him. I was carrying a knife to pop the lock on the file cabinet. I made a run for it. He caught me. We struggled over it and . . ." I shrugged. "It was either me or him. I stabbed him once, took the tape and ran."

"Where is it now?"

"I gave it to Ross. If he didn't destroy it, I can get it back. Didn't he tell you?"

"Who, Ross? Tell us what?"

"About the tape," I said.

"What's on this tape?"

"It shows you escaping," I said. "Hiding in the hollow speakers."

Whiteside looked at Agar and nodded. Agar bent down to pick up the gag. They didn't believe me.

"I mean, that's how it worked, isn't it?" I said. "Marling busted you out to do a job, right? Kill Ross or his agent, Sylvia Henn. There's some big deal going down and he wants one or the other of them out of the way, right?"

"It's a good story, Biff," Whiteside said. "You had me going there for a minute. But there's a few details you were missing." Whiteside bent down to whisper in my ear. "Peter Marling didn't break us out of prison to *do* a job for him. He broke us out because we already *did* one."

He backed off so I could see him smirk.

"I don't know what you're talking about," I said.

"Still don't follow? See, we know something about Peter Marling the rest of the world doesn't. We know he doesn't just do magic on stage; he does it off. He thinks he's a shaman. A priest. A holy man. Think the Nielsen families would dig that too much if they found that out? Think that would make a good feature for

TV Guide? America's newest comedy star walks on the dark side."

"He makes voodoo dolls," I said. "I've seen them."

"He make one of you yet? Bad sign. That kind of means you're on his shit list. You know what the funny thing is? He didn't study with anyone else, he didn't go to Haiti and learn it there . . . he got it all from movies and books. Me, I don't believe in any of that crap. You know why? 'Cause I am bad luck. I am voodoo. Peter knows better than to break a promise to me. He got into that black magic ever since . . . well, ever since his first kill. I think taking a human life kind of put him over the edge."

"He's a murderer?"

Whiteside made a sound like a game show bell. Nothing worse than a sadist who thinks he has a sense of humor. "Ding-ding-ding! Yes! He's a murderer! He killed someone and got away with it! He must be able to do magic! He made a human being disappear! And you know how we know? We were there. We supplied the victim."

"Who'd he kill?"

"Gus Fletcher," Whiteside said.

"I never heard of him," I said. "Was he a comedian?"

Whiteside laughed. "Yeah. We helped Peter take care of old Gus. This was about ten years ago, before anyone had ever heard of Peter Marling. Peter owes it all to Gus. Got him started in his comedy career, you might say. Our help was on one condition: that he do us a favor in return. Getting sprung was it. I thought it was time Hollywood had another superstar—namely me." He looked up at Agar and smiled.

"But who was Gus Fletcher?" I asked. "Why did Marling want him dead?"

Agar wadded the gag and jammed it into my mouth so deep I had to breathe through my nose. He wound a strip of adhesive tape around the back of my head and over the gag to hold it in place. I tried to make a sound, but my muffled voice was loud only in my own ears.

Whiteside ignored my question. "There've been a few complications, though. Bernie getting killed was one. You're another. And . . . well . . . we don't like complications."

Whiteside gently cupped my chin and drew his face close to mine, as if he was going to kiss me. "See, now I don't think you killed Bernie Coleman like you said but I do think you've been up to something. You've talked to the police. You've been playing detective. And I want to hear all about it. But, so far, all you've told me were lies. I need the truth. And I believe there's only one way we're going to get to that."

Then I saw something move outside my window. A reflection caught in the eye of a cat or coyote.

"See, Biff, I think you've spent a lot of time chasing down this stupid videotape. There was one thing you failed to consider. I don't give a shit if my face is all over TV. It'll be good exposure for my comedy career. People will know they've seen me, but they won't be able to remember where from and it won't matter. Besides, they'll drop that story for the one on Gus Fletcher. It'll be my deal out of jail: immunity for a turn on the stand fingering Marling. Those TV producers'll like that. I hear the one that came to the prison to interview Warden Douglas is a blond chick that's a real looker. You met her?"

There it was again: a wink from a watching glassy eye. But this time the eye steadied and held, evenly reflecting the moonlight, and that was when I knew it was no eye.

"Sharon . . . Temple? Isn't that her name? Is she as hot-looking as I hear? Maybe when she meets me and gets the big story from me about how America's new sitcom star helped me escape from prison, she'll want to take me out. Have a few drinks. Then let me kiss her good night. Invite me in for coffee." He chuckled. "Of course, some of the women I've been with didn't want that right away. I had to force the issue. Show them what they've been missing."

The reflection came from the telescopic sight of a high-powered rifle. There was a man dressed in black crouched on the other side of my neighbor's fence, taking aim through my kitchen window. Other black shapes moved around him. One of them stuck his face in the moonlight so I could see him clearly.

Gilmore.

Agar stepped forward with the knife in his hand. He took hold of my third finger on my left hand and held it almost straight up, bending it at a painful angle. He held the blade close, almost touching the nail. He wasn't looking at me. He was looking at Whiteside, waiting for the command.

"Time for the fun part, Biff," Whiteside said. "Just want you to know I don't enjoy doing this to a fellow comedian."

I saw one last gambit. I bit back the gag and started to chuckle, turning to look at Whiteside. In the face of torture, I was laughing in Whiteside's face.

He looked at me, puzzled. Things weren't clarified when I talked into my gag. The only word I made sure he could understand was "comedian."

Whiteside made a gesture to Agar and Agar stepped aside. I didn't dare look out the kitchen window again to see if the sharpshooter was still there. Be there, I thought. Please be there now. With medals on.

I kept laughing. I looked at Whiteside and shook my head in amusement.

"What?" he said. "What is it?"

I said something into my gag without making any effort to be understood. This time all he could hear was something that sounded like "stand-up."

He gestured to Agar and Agar loosened my gag. I sneaked a look outside. I saw Gilmore and the sharpshooter still there. They had seen two clean shots at Agar and hadn't taken them. Gilmore made a hand movement. He pointed where Whiteside was standing and then pointed at me. They were waiting for Whiteside, who was leaning up against my kitchen counter and cabinets, out of the line of fire. I had to lure him in. He had to forget Agar and want to put his hands on me himself.

There was only one way to do that: make him angry.

The gag fell around my neck like a kerchief and I could speak, only I didn't. I kept chuckling.

"What's so funny?" Whiteside asked.

"You," I said. "Calling yourself a comedian." I giggled. "You don't have three minutes onstage. Do you really think you have a shot in this town? You can't even cut it on the open-mike scene. The only way you'll walk through the door at the Comedy Store is with a ticket in your hand."

I saw anger flicker in his eyes and I knew I'd found a sore

spot. I pressed. I needed him to come over by me. I needed him to hit me.

"I know I have a ways to go . . ." he said.

I interrupted him. "A ways to go? How about getting the fuck offstage? I'm surprised they even let you up at Ojai. You weren't even the best one I saw on that tape. Let me tell you something, Johnny. I been at this game a lot longer than you, and you don't have enough timing, material or presence to fill a shot glass."

"That audience wasn't any good." Whiteside eased himself away from the kitchen cabinets, but his feet stayed in place. "They were a dead crowd."

"I know enough," I said. "You said you saw through my pretending to be an ex-con? Well, talking to you like a comedian, like you had talent, let me tell you, *that* was acting. You cleared the room the night I saw you. You had walkouts. You couldn't follow me with a bullhorn and a searchlight. The other comics were rolling their eyes and holding their noses when you were onstage."

"Shut up," Whiteside said. He stepped in front of me and took the knife from Agar. His head was peeking around the edge of the window. He needed to be standing right in front of it. "You shut up."

I did not shut up. "You know what you are? You're not a comic. You're what we call a hack."

"I said SHUT UP!" he yelled and stepped in front of the sink. He drew the butcher knife back in an arc and brought it down to slash across my throat.

And then his head exploded.

TWENTY-NINE

The sharpshooter's bullet entered the back of Johnny Whiteside's head. The knife blade meant for my neck sliced into my upper left arm with slight but sudden force. I yelped and jumped in my chair, but with my hands still tied to the kitchen faucet there was little I could do as Whiteside's body flopped onto my shoulders before he slid to the floor.

At the sound of the gunshot Agar had fallen to his knees, and when he saw what happened to Whiteside he rushed to him and put his hands over the wound to Whiteside's head, as though he could somehow stop the bleeding with his fingers.

The police came through the door like an arriving train, a stream of black-clad bodies with guns and vests and helmets, ready to mow down anything that stood in their tracks. I stayed very still, my hands in plain sight, making no sudden moves or sounds, my head up, blood trickling off my hands and shoulder. Some of the cops didn't know if they were there to save or shoot me, and kept shouting for me to get down get on the floor, now, and I kept yelling back, I can't, I can't. Dogs were barking and my neighbors were stumbling out of bed and Agar was howling without words and then someone turned on the lights and the men in helmets rushed around my chair to tackle Agar into a corner. He fought them off and they rushed him again and my kitchen is far too small for that kind of thing.

I felt a tugging on my wrists and saw that Gilmore was sawing away at the bonds that held my hands tied to the kitchen faucet and when the last strand snapped he dragged me out of there as the SWAT team boiled over Agar like ants on a dead mouse. He was grunting and kicking and swinging fists until one of the officers used pepper spray to blind him. He screamed and they bound him like a bucking bull. I heard wood cracking, tile breaking, dishes smashing.

In the living room, Gilmore cut my hands apart and my feet free and I tried to stand and caught myself as I almost fell over.

"You okay?" Gilmore asked.

I nodded. "Fine. Thanks."

Gilmore took his hand off my shoulder. "Sure."

"No, I mean thanks for saving my life."

"Someone had to," he said. "You keep trying to get yourself killed."

"How'd you know to check up on me?"

"After we got stood up at the Tomato Grill I figured they might come after you," he said. "Especially if you kept poking around. And . . ." He looked over his shoulder. "You had a concerned friend who hired an off-duty police officer as private security to tail you. He was the one who saw these two scumbags pull up and work the lock on your front door."

"Friend?" I asked. "What—?"

In the doorway I saw Sharon Temple. She had her hair pulled back, she was dressed in plain black sweats and she had no makeup on. She looked beautiful. "Hi, sweetie," she said. "Did they hurt you?"

Gilmore stepped aside and I went toward Sharon as she closed the distance between us and I held her tight, very tight. "Thank you," I said.

"I just thought . . . you were taking this too far . . ."

"I know . . ."

Her voice caught and she cleared her throat. "I tried to tell you to stop but you wouldn't listen."

"I know," I said. "I'm sorry."

She pulled her face back from my shoulder and wiped a tear

210

from one eye. "I told you I had a thing for dangerous men."

I smiled and touched her face. Her eyes went to the wound on my arm and she took my hand. I winced. "What happened?"

"I almost got a really bad manicure," I said, "courtesy of Sam Agar." I looked behind me. Agar was being dragged out of my kitchen, his arms and legs bound behind him, his face smearing pepper spray onto the tile. It mixed with Whiteside's blood. How was I going to explain this to the maid?

"Paramedics are just outside," Gilmore said. "You might want to have them look at that."

"Paper cut," I said.

Gilmore didn't smile. Sharon tried to.

"What did they want?" Gilmore asked.

"For me to scream," I said.

"Did they say anything?" Gilmore said. "Anything of interest?"

"A bunch of stuff that didn't make sense," I said. "They didn't kill Bernie Coleman."

Gilmore frowned. "They said that?"

"Actually, Whiteside did the talking for that pair," I said. "He claims Marling broke him out of jail because he helped Marling kill someone named Gus Fletcher, and he's the only one who knows it."

Gilmore looked at Whiteside's body. "Not anymore he isn't."

"I'm wondering if after Whiteside escaped Marling decided to cover his tracks, starting with Bernie."

Gilmore turned his attention back to me. "Do yourself a favor, Kincaid. Let it go from here. You've had a little excitement, a narrow escape and you got the pretty girl in the final reel. Get patched up and go home."

"This is my home."

"We can go to my place," Sharon said.

"We'll be here until dawn," Gilmore said. "But if you want to pay me and your girlfriend back for saving your ass, stick to comedy."

"I thought that's what I was doing."

"Can you talk some sense into him?" he said to Sharon.

"I think I'll have about as much luck as these guys did," she said, meaning Whiteside and Agar. "And they were going to use pain."

"I respond much better to pleasure," I said.

"Then we'll try that," she said.

Breakfast at Farmer's Market. I had a gauze pad on my shoulder and rug burns on both knees, but I didn't get those from Whiteside. Sharon was right about one thing: pleasure was very persuasive.

"So if Johnny Whiteside didn't kill Bernie Coleman," she asked, "who did?"

"I don't know," I said.

"Come on, I have a TV segment to wrap." She poked at my good shoulder with her fork. "Take a guess."

"I'm beginning to think the bartender did it," I said.

"Rick Parker? You think Gilmore thinks the same way?"

"I don't know," I said. "Maybe he's trying to find out who killed Rick."

She nodded. "We're going to have to go to air with the mystery unsolved."

"Looks like it," I said. "Unless you can hold it to see if Gilmore arrests anyone."

Sharon shook her head. "I can't do that."

"Why not?"

"I have to have this wrapped by next Friday."

"How come? Wouldn't it make a better story if—"

"There's something I have to tell you," she said.

I swallowed. We were at a café called Kokomo's, sitting at the counter in the open air. I was having the black bean cake and eggs. I needed my protein. I was feeling depleted from the loss of blood and other fluids my body produced.

"Okay," I said.

She looked into her coffee. "I got promoted."

"Congratulations!" I said. "To what?"

"Reporter," she said.

"On-air?" I said. "You're going to be on-air?"

She nodded, smiling. "Been my dream since I was a little girl and saw Barbara Walters on TV."

"That's great!" I smiled and hugged her. "When do you start?"

"Two weeks."

"That's terrific. We'll have to celebrate."

"Yeah, it's been a long time coming," she said. "Shooting stand-ups on the sly, getting editors to cut together my reel, making sure different looks worked okay on camera . . ."

"I think all of your looks work just fine," I said.

". . . sending my tapes out to affiliates, getting feedback, interviewing . . ." She shook her head. "Actually, the pay's not that great to start, but it could get better very soon."

"What network?"

"The Global United Network," she said. "Same one I work for now."

"Channel Twelve?"

"Uh . . ." She looked into her coffee. "Not exactly."

"They're putting you on another station?"

"You could say that." She still wouldn't look at me.

"Sharon, what do you need to tell me?"

"I didn't get hired at the GUN affiliate here in Los Angeles," she said.

"Oh."

"I got hired at one out of town."

"I see."

"Out of state, actually."

"How far out of state?"

"Outside of the continental United States," she said. "KPAL in Anchorage."

"Alaska?"

She nodded.

"Wow," I said. "That's . . . that's far."

"It's cold, too," she said. "In the winter, especially."

"Have you ever been there?"

She nodded. "To interview. About three weeks ago. Before we met."

"And they came through."

She smiled. "It was between them and the affiliate in Bangor, Maine."

"Also far," I said. "Also cold."

213

"I know." She stopped smiling. "And . . . we'd just met and I thought we had a really good thing going."

"We still do," I said.

"And here I go and get another job." She smiled by pressing her lips together. "I didn't want you to think it had anything to do with you."

"I don't."

"They have any comedy clubs in Anchorage? I looked for one when I was up there, but . . ."

"I think there's a one-nighter."

"You ever played it?"

"Not yet," I said. "I'll see if I can get booked. Tack a few days on to the front and back."

"Okay."

I pushed my plate away. I wasn't hungry anymore. Neither was she.

"I'm sorry," she said. "I didn't know how to tell you. I guess this was a bad time."

"I was kind of preoccupied," I said.

"I figured."

"When do you start?"

"A week from Monday," she said. "What's today?"

"Thursday."

"Oh. Wow. It's Thursday? My parents are coming in tomorrow. They're going to help me pack and rent a U-Haul and drive me up there."

"So this would be our last day together anyway."

"Yes."

"Hey." I turned to her and forced a smile, taking both of her hands in mine. "This is great news. What are we acting all sad for?"

"Because it is great news," she said, "but this is the sad part."

I took each of her hands in mine and kissed them. "You're doing the right thing," I said.

"I know." A tear slid down one cheek behind her librarian glasses. "It's just some times the right thing to do is the hardest, you know?"

"Your parents are coming in tomorrow?"

She nodded.

"What do you need to do today?"

"I have to go into work and wrap up some paperwork," she said. "Hand over everything to my associate producer. She's the one that's going to be doing the postproduction and delivering the final script and segment to Kyle. Then I start packing."

My turn to nod. "So I guess this is it."

"I didn't plan it this way, Biff, I swear."

I took her shoulders in my hands. "I know."

"If there was another way . . ."

"There isn't."

The waiter came and cleared our plates. I laid a twenty down before the check even appeared. Ten minutes ago I was having breakfast with my new girlfriend and now she was walking out of my life forever.

We stood in the center of Farmer's Market, between a store that sold nothing but coffee cups and another one that sold only incense and candles.

Bells rang in the clock tower. Ten o' clock. "I'm supposed to meet my editor," she said.

"Don't be late."

"I already am."

"Then kiss me good-bye," I said.

She closed her eyes and pressed her lips to mine and I kissed her once and just as the first one ended we started another. The third was the last one. Then she held me tight, hugging me close.

"I hate this," she said. "I've never gotten good at it."

"Just walk away," I said over her shoulder and into her ear. "Don't turn around. Don't look back. Just walk away."

I didn't say my next sentence. She sobbed once and kissed me again on the cheek and I watched her leave me. Her head was down and she had a hard time putting her sunglasses on and she almost ran into an old woman with a cart full of groceries and she slowed and excused herself but she didn't stop. She rounded a corner to the parking lot and I stood there waiting for her to turn around and come back and say she wouldn't take the job in Alaska, I was more important to her than she thought, but she didn't.

I stood there between the coffee cup store and the candle shop until I realized I was once again alone. Then it was my turn to walk away and not look back.

THIRTY

I got in my car and drove. I didn't know where I was going and I didn't care. The first turn I hit coming out of Farmer's Market was south on Fairfax and I took it. I drove past Tom Bergin's and wondered if it was open and if I could start drinking at this hour without ending up in a worse state of mind than when I started. Maybe that wouldn't have been a good thing. Never stopped me before.

Fairfax went under the 10 Freeway and then fed into La Cienega and before I knew it I was on the 405 South, edging past the airport. I thought about pulling in and getting on a plane and showing up at any of the comedy clubs on the road where I had an open invitation. There were a couple of dozen cities where I could arrive unannounced and—if not find a paying gig—at least get some stage time. Tampa. Austin. Chicago. Vegas. Nashville. Seattle. Kansas City. Frisco.

Go. Just go somewhere and shake off this feeling that L.A. was poisoning me. Hit the road for a week, a month, a year, just like the old days, no home but the stage, a new pretty face every night, free drinks at the bar and a roomful of strangers to listen to all my troubles as long as there was a punch line at the end.

I stayed on the 405 going south. It didn't matter. There were other airports between there and San Diego. Was I going to San

Diego? There were a few clubs down there. I could drop in at the La Jolla Comedy Store, get a guest set, crash at the club's condo and wake up looking at the ocean. I could drive into Mexico. I could turn left and start heading through Arizona, New Mexico, Texas. I could do anything I wanted or needed to. I had nothing holding me back.

I thought about places near and far, friends living and dead, the past and the present, letting my mind wander over the course of my experience and just as I was about to wonder where to go to next I saw the exit for the Long Beach Freeway.

This time I put on my blinker and eased over into the other lane. There was someone I could see in Long Beach. Rather than wallow in my own misery, I should concentrate on helping someone else with their loss. Maybe that would do me some good, to say nothing of what it might do for him.

Belmont Shores Dog and Cat Grooming was on Second Street, the main thoroughfare of Belmont Shores. Traffic on a Thursday morning was thickening up and I held Max Colton's business card in one hand while I drove with the other, looking for the address he'd written on the back. I found it on a street corner underneath a sign that had the business name painted in crooked letters over a trail of paw prints. I parked a few metered spaces away.

The sea air smelled good as I walked the two blocks back. I looked in the window before going through the front door. I saw Max Colton inside, blow-drying an English sheep dog.

He looked up when I walked in, giving just a glance without recognizing me and then he looked up a second time and held my gaze longer. I nodded at him and he nodded at me without smiling back. I approached him cautiously. "Am I bothering you?" I asked over the high-pitched whine of the hair dryer.

The sheep dog barked in response. His hair hung in his face so far it touched his muzzle.

"I don't think Caesar likes that you're interrupting his bath."

"Sorry, Caesar."

Caesar barked again. I couldn't see his eyes but his face was pointed right at me.

"If you can wait a few minutes—" Max said.

"Sure."

Caesar barked. Then growled. He didn't like me.

"Outside?" Max asked.

"What Caesar wants," I said, "Caesar gets."

Barking followed me out the door. I stood outside and watched the pretty girls cross the street. There was never a lull in the quality or quantity by the beach. I might have to move down here.

After a few minutes, Max Colton stepped outside, shaking a cigarette out of a wrinkled pack. He offered me one and I shook my head. "I'm an ex," I said.

"But you don't mind if I . . . ?"

"We're outside," I said. "The world is your ashtray."

He lit up, inhaled and blew out gray smoke. He was wearing white coveralls flecked with water spots and dog hair. "You just in the neighborhood?"

"Not exactly."

"You got something to tell me." It wasn't a question.

"Yeah," I said. "Then I got something to ask you."

"Tell me first."

I told him about what had happened to me last night.

"So both these guys are dead?"

"No," I said. "Just one. Whiteside. Agar's in custody."

"So you think these guys killed my father?"

"They say they didn't."

"But do you think they did?"

"I don't know."

He finished his cigarette. His second. Getting my life threatened by two escaped convicts is a two-cigarette story. "So what did you come down here to ask me?"

"Your father ever mention anyone by the name of Gary Ross?"

Max shook his head. "Who is he?"

"A manager."

"Of what?"

"Comedians."

"Never heard of him."

"Didn't mention him in passing?" I asked. "Ever mention a manager he was doing business with?"

"No."

"He was also an executive producer of a TV show."

"Doesn't ring a bell," he said. "What show?"

"*Class Dismissed.*"

"Don't get a chance to watch much TV," he said, "when you're living out of a van."

"It hasn't aired yet," I said. "He ever mention a comedian named Peter Marling?"

"Who is he?" Max asked. The tone in his voice shifted upward. "Is he the star of this *Class* show?"

I nodded.

"Peter Marling . . ."

"You heard of him?"

"Maybe. When is this show going to air?"

"It's a mid-season replacement," I said. "The first thirteen episodes are being shot now."

"Maybe I read an article in a magazine or newspaper, but the name sounds familiar . . ."

"Your father ever mention him?"

"He mentioned somebody . . ."

"Tall guy," I said. "Plays a schoolteacher. Used to be a prop comic. Actually met your father through your—through Ellen Alexander."

"Really?"

"She was showing him a condo he was going to buy in the Peninsula."

"No, I know who he is. I'm just trying to remember how Bernie mentioned him to me." He chewed on his lower lip. "Maybe in the letter."

"Letter?" I asked. "What letter?"

"Remember how I told you my father asked me for money?"

"Yes."

"He asked me in a letter," Max said. "And I think he mentioned Peter Marling in that letter. Saying he had something going on with him, some deal in the works and that was how he was going to pay me back." He took another cigarette out of the pack, and then crumpled up the empty pack and threw it into a sidewalk trash can. "He signed it 'Dad.' Most of his letters he signed 'Bernie.' "

"Can I see it?"

"Sure." He pocketed the cigarette. "Step into my office."

I thought we were going to go back inside but instead Max headed around the corner and we walked another block to where his van was parked at the first metered space on a side street, facing Second Street. "Home sweet home," he said. I made no comment. He brought out his keys and unlocked the passenger side, holding the door open for me. I got in and then he came around the driver's side and let himself in.

"Now let's see . . ." He rummaged through the glove compartment which was stuffed with bills, notices, envelopes and papers. The van smelled of shampoo and animal hair. I looked over my shoulder. There was a clean canvas mat laid out on the floor of the van. Harnesses dangled from the sides, bolted in place to immobilize someone of Caesar's strength and stature. Organized into small plastic boxes were clippers, scissors and shears, soaps and shampoos, snack foods for his four-legged clientele, leashes and ribbons. There was a plastic filing box with the lid open, folders with numbers and letters denoting different matters of business. Pasted to the top of the box was a license of some kind.

"Nice," I said.

"Try sleeping in it," he said. "Is this it?" He pulled a letter out of the glove compartment, folded inside a Flugelhorn's stationery envelope. He opened up the letter and scanned it. "No . . . this isn't what I was talking about, but this was when he . . . here. Take a look. I'll go check in the back."

He left me alone in the passenger seat. The letter was dated a year ago, and started with the salutation *Dear Max.*

Since I haven't heard from you for a while I wanted to let you know that I have decided to sell the club unless I can get some financial assistance. The bank, your mother, all my relatives and even the comedians I helped have turned me down. I'm only asking a loan, to keep open the club that made them a star. How quickly people forget when—

Suddenly a ribbed hose from a hair dryer whipped around my neck, tightening like a rubber snake. I dropped the letter and put both hands to my neck, but Max's strength was too great. I could feel his foot against the back of my seat as he strained to cut off the air and blood to my brain. He had the element of surprise on his side. My neck was still sore from the rope Whiteside had looped around it, and my left arm was still hurting from the knife wound.

I went up and out of my seat to relieve the pressure, unable to speak, already feeling my face redden and swell. Max jerked me back between the seats, to the floor of the van. I went kicking for the horn to make some noise, my ankle catching on the gearshift mounted on the steering wheel. I shoved the transmission into neutral with my foot. My hand found the emergency brake between the seats and let it go.

The van started moving.

I went over the back of the passenger seat and sprawled onto the canvas mat on my hands and knees, the ribbed hose still around my neck. Max cracked a hair dryer onto my head twice, connecting with the stitches still in my head. He seemed to know exactly where they were. I fell onto my chest, stunned. He dropped the hair dryer and put a loose restraint around my left hand. I started to resist and realized that it was meant for an animal, so each movement caused the loop to tighten. The circulation was being cut off at the wrist. Max scrambled around to the rear and grabbed my ankle. I turned my head and kicked him in the chin. It had little effect. I lashed out again and this time my heel landed on his nose and I felt something crunch and give. He gave a snort and fell against the back of the passenger seat.

The van was gaining momentum.

I looked up. The back doors were loose and swinging. If I could free my hand I could make a run for it. My wrist was bound to a leash that was attached to a snap bolted into the side of the van. I reached to unhook it but saw Max dip his hand into one of the little plastic buckets and bring out something sharp and pointed, which he proceeded to try to stab me in the leg with.

I gave up on undoing the leash and rolled over on my back, kicking back at Max. His nose was broken and bleeding, but the once-pathetic shlub had turned into a fierce opponent. The tool in his hand was some kind of sharp thin spike, used to clean under doggies' dirty toenails. He had broken the skin on my leg once in a scratch, and was going for a deeper wound.

I kicked at his face again. He grabbed my pant leg by the

cuff and before I could pull free he planted the toenail spike into my calf. I yelled and reached out to pull it free, but that was exactly what he wanted me to do. He picked up one of the little buckets—this one was made of metal—and swung it at my face, smashing its hardest edge into my jawbone. My head snapped back and in the few seconds I was dazed he looped a larger harness that hung from an overhead pulley around my legs and hung on it with all his weight.

The lower half of my body lifted up off the floor. Now all I had free was my one good arm. I flailed around, trying to keep my shoulders and head from falling back on the floor.

"Now, Mister Comedy," Max said, "since no one's figured out who killed Bernie, let's see if anyone's going to be able to figure out what happened to you."

I stopped trying to escape long enough to look him in the face. "You?" I said. "You killed him?"

"Didn't figure that one out, did you?" His eyes were red and burning, his nose turning purple, swelling with blood. "Nobody did."

"Why'd you do it?" I gasped. At that moment I cared more about my own life, but if it kept him talking . . .

He fumbled in a small box for a bottle and a cloth. "The money," Max said. "He said he had the ten grand for me and when I showed up, he shorted me. Paid me less than half."

"He did that to everybody."

He dipped the bottle into the cloth and moistened it. "What are you talking about? You're just a comedian. What'd he short you? A hundred bucks? I was supposed to be his son!" The van lurched as it scraped against another car. I heard tires squeal, horns honk. "Now I have to park on the street in front of where I used to live!" We were heading out into traffic, into Second Street. We slowed, then kept rolling. People were yelling at us: stop, stop, stop.

Max got up on his knees, the cloth in hand. I could smell it from where I was lying. Ether.

"I'm talking thousands! We were family! He was supposed to love me!"

The van lurched again. "Got to hurry," he said. He threw his upper body on top of mine, pinning my shoulders with his weight and he clamped the cloth over my mouth. I held my breath. "Nighty night," he hissed. "We're going to Mexico. I'm going to bury you in the sand dunes."

I had maybe thirty seconds to a minute before I ran out of air. With my right hand, I made a fist and started punching him in the face, aiming for his broken nose. He tightened his grip on me like a python and turned his hand, the blows landing on his ear and skull.

I heard rubber screech just outside the van walls and then came a bone-jarring collision as a car struck us from the side. Max was thrown off of me. I sat up, finding where I'd dropped the toenail cleaner. One edge was sharpened and serrated. As Max struggled to his knees I grabbed the leash around my legs and sliced through it with one stroke. I slashed my left hand free and turned around, ready to face Max, but he had jumped free of the van, the back doors banging open, running out into the street.

The van had stopped moving, but I still heard honking and braking sounds. I jumped out of the back doors and into the street. Max was running in and out of traffic, waving his arms, beating on windshields, trying to flag down a car.

"Max!" I yelled.

He turned and saw me. I started running toward him, my speed hobbled by the fresh wound in my leg. Two Long Beach police officers on bicycles saw the lone madman darting through traffic and dismounted, drawing guns and shouting commands for him to stop running.

Max saw the police on one side and me on the other. He didn't have much of a chance of escape. A siren began to wail in the distance. He looked up in the sky. No helicopters yet.

Traffic was still moving in the opposite lane. A semi was cruising along, headed toward the 710 Freeway, oblivious to all the excitement. Max watched it come, hanging back, ready to make his move. Just as the truck was about to pass him, Max looked at me one last time, smiled sadly and said something I couldn't hear. I only saw his lips move. Then he stepped in front of the semi before the driver had a chance to even blast the horn.

The truck blocked my view of what happened next to Max. I didn't see the impact. The truck braked and honked, the driver leaping out of the cab before his rig had even stopped moving. I ran into the street toward the accident and saw that Max had been struck down by the force of the truck, but mercifully spared the crushing force of the wheels. One side of his chest was dented in, as though it had collapsed on itself. He was breathing blood out of his nose and mouth, closer to death than life.

I was the first to reach him. "Max," I said as I knelt by his side. "Lie still."

His eyes fluttered in his head. He tried to focus on my face. "Remember . . ." he whispered in a wheezing groan. "He was . . . never . . . my real . . . father."

The driver of the truck was the second one there. "He jumped out in front of me," he said. "I swear I tried to stop but I couldn't."

I looked up at the driver and nodded once and then I looked back down at Max. He was dead.

"Did you see it?" the driver asked. He looked around for other witnesses but couldn't find them so he kept talking to me. "He stepped right in front of my grille. It was like he wanted me to hit him."

"I believe you," I said.

THIRTY-ONE

It was visitor's day at the Los Angeles County Jail. I wasn't on the inside; I was there to see someone. Despite all the mayhem I'd found myself in, I had yet to be locked up or face any charges. I think Detective Gilmore was getting a little tired of hearing my name and seeing my face, but tough; someone had to get their head beat in for no good reason. I offered a convenient target, and apparently on a regular basis.

Max Colton was dead. The murder of Bernie Coleman was solved.

That left one dead body unaccounted for, and that was why I was there to see someone in jail on visitor's day.

I sat on one side of the scarred Plexiglas barrier and waited. To my right and left, lovers were reuniting, families were meeting and tears were shed. I was asked by a guard if I was here to see family or friends and I said neither. When he asked my relationship to the inmate I replied, "Assailant."

The door to the holding facility opened and Sam Agar came out, dressed in an orange prison jumpsuit. His hair had begun to stubble in patches on his scalp, his thick features holding no curiosity or remorse. His face looked like it had been molded out of flesh-colored putty and needed someone else to form an expression on it.

He sat down and looked at me like a television set that wasn't working right.

"Sam, do you recognize me? I'm Biff Kincaid."

He nodded.

"Are they treating you all right in there?"

Sam shrugged. Jail was jail.

"I wanted to let you know I found out who killed Bernie Coleman."

Sam cocked his head. That interested him.

"It was his adopted son, Max. Max Colton. He confessed to me before he committed suicide."

Sam nodded slowly. Ahhh. That made sense.

"So I know who killed Bernie Coleman," I said, "but I don't know who killed Rick Parker."

Sam blinked.

"Was it you?"

Sam shook his head, no.

"Did you know Rick?"

Nodding. Yes.

"Was he a friend?"

Shrug.

"Was it Johnny?"

Sam hung his head.

"I'm sorry about Johnny. I know you miss him."

Sam's eyes remained downcast. A single tear tracked down one side of his face. He sniffled.

"But you're telling me Johnny didn't kill Rick Parker?"

Eyes still down, he shook his head, then he pointed at himself.

"You killed Rick . . . ?"

Again he shook his head, and pointed at himself.

"Oh, I get it," I said. "Johnny would have had you kill Rick."

Vigorous nod. Sam looked up on that one.

"Johnny would not have killed him alone."

Much nodding.

"Did you ever hear anyone talk to Johnny about Rick Parker?"

Sam's face and head remained very still. He looked at me cautiously, then sneaked a glance over his shoulder to make sure the guard wasn't watching.

Then he nodded. Once only.

"Who was that?"

Sam looked around for something to write with. From another inmate he got a crayon and a piece of paper and scrawled a message. He held it up to the glass for me to read.

PETR.

The "R" was backwards.

"Peter," I said. "Peter Marling?"

Sam nodded.

"What did he say, Sam? Did he tell Johnny to . . . no, wait. If he told Johnny to kill Rick, Johnny would have had you do it."

Sam nodded.

"So . . . what did Peter tell Johnny?"

Sam wrote another note.

RIK KNOS.

"Rick knew what?"

A BOT GUS.

"Rick knew about the Gus Fletcher murder?"

Sam nodded.

"Who was this Gus Fletcher?"

Sam shrugged.

"You don't know?"

Sam shook his head.

"Was this before you met Johnny?"

Sam nodded.

"So you never met Gus?"

Nod.

"Did you tell the police any of this?"

Sam shook his head.

"Why me, then? Why are you telling me?"

A final note:

U NICE 2 JONY.

I guess he meant when I talked to Whiteside about comedy. Wish I could say the same for him, I thought. "Thank you, Sam. How long they have you in here for?"

Sam shrugged, then put the fingertips of both hands together and pulled them apart. A long time.

"Back to Ojai?"

He shrugged. He didn't know.

"Okay." I rose. "Look, I know it's none of my business, but are you mute, can you not—?"

Sam opened his mouth and I saw inside that all there was was red tissue. He had no teeth or tongue.

"Oh . . ." I sat back down. "I'm sorry. How did that happen?"

One final crayon-scribbled note for me to read:

JONY WANTED ME 2 SHUT UP.

"Okay," I said. I stood up again. I had to get out of there. "Take care, Sam."

He made a hooting sound, like a chimpanzee. I turned around. He had his lips formed in a long "O," like an ape. He kept looking at me as I walked out the door, and it was only when I was out of his sight I realized what he was doing.

He was laughing.

THIRTY-TWO

The offices of Ross Entertainment were at Sunset and Doheny, across the street from Sylvia Henn's at the Marsh Agency. I parked farther east on Sunset, at a meter, and walked back. I didn't have an appointment with Gary Ross. It wasn't for lack of trying. I had called his offices for the last three days, getting only voice mail. I had spent my weekend staking out Peter Marling's condo in Palos Verdes, my nights hanging out at the clubs, looking for him. I had missed him so far. I would be hanging out at the Comedy Store when he was at the Improv, or he would have dropped in at the Laugh Factory just after I'd left.

I walked into the office building, smaller than the one where Henn's agency was. Up the street was a shipping store. I'd stopped in and bought a cardboard box and written Gary Ross's name on top, and used an overnight form as an invoice. Instead of my beret, I wore a baseball cap with the logo from a messenger service on it. It was left over from a corporate gig. Biff Kincaid, master of disguise.

I walked past the security guard in the lobby. He was watching a Dodgers game. I leaned over as I signed in a fake name and looked at the screen, wincing at a foul ball. Shaking my head, I walked away backwards and got on the elevator.

Gary Ross's office was on the fifth floor. I stepped off into the hallway and walked past a travel agency and a dentist's office until I found Ross Entertainment. I knocked on the door. No answer. I looked through the mail slot. The lights were on. Past the reception area were large cardboard cartons, open and ready. Someone was moving.

I held my breath as I heard a door open down the hall, letting out the sound of water flushing. The men's room. I held my ground and as Gary Ross rounded the corner—in a T-shirt and jeans far removed from his Hollywood power suits—he saw me and slowed.

He stopped ten feet away from his own door, keys in hand.

"Who are you?" he said.

"A messenger." I took off my baseball cap and chucked the fake delivery props onto the carpeted hallway floor.

"I'm not expecting any deliv—" He cut himself off in mid-sentence and peered closer at my face. Without the baseball cap on he recognized me. "I know you."

"Biff Kincaid," I said. "We've spoken before."

"You're that comedian who asks too many questions."

"That would be me."

"What are you doing here?" He took a step backwards. His eyes went to the cardboard box. "What's in there?"

"Oh, this?" I stepped on the box to show him it was empty. "Darn. When I'd left home this morning I'd filled it full of hissing rattlesnakes."

"Don't joke around," Ross said. He was shorter than I was and he was trim from workouts, but he didn't have the look or the stance of an experienced brawler. His weapon of choice was the cell phone. "I have a gun," he said.

I made a show of looking him up and down and from side to side. "Where?" I pointed at his office door. "In there?"

He didn't say anything.

"You want me to wait out here while you go get it and point it at me?" I asked. "Or can we go inside and talk?"

He jostled the keys in his hand.

"Asking too many questions gets you some answers," I said. "If we pick each other's brains, we might find out something."

"About what?"

"About who killed Rick Parker," I said. "About why two murderers were freed from jail. About why your client makes voodoo dolls out of people who then turn up dead. You want to talk about this in the hallway where the dentist and travel agent and whoever needs to go to the bathroom can hear me, that's fine."

He stepped forward with his keys, hesitant at first. I gave him room and he unlocked the door and let us both inside.

The reception area had been stripped, the contents sparingly packed away into boxes with bubble wrap. Lots of paper had gone into a large metal bin marked *"Basura."* Trash.

We walked past the bin and into Ross's office. It still had the view that had been described in *Show Business Weekly*. There were still a few pictures on the walls, a couple of mementos on empty bookshelves. Some framed nomination certificates for Emmys and Golden Globes. A People's Choice Award.

He sat on the edge of his desk. There weren't any chairs.

"Going somewhere?" I asked.

"I'm relocating my offices to New York."

"How's Peter Marling feel about that?"

"I'm no longer in business with Peter Marling," he said. "I'm not his manager and he's not my client."

"Is Sylvia Henn still his agent?"

He laughed in a hitching tenor. "You run into her, too?"

I nodded.

"Sure," he said. "I guess. This week."

"She going to be his manager?"

"She sure as hell thinks she's going to be," Ross said. "But that depends."

"On what?"

"On what happens with *Class Dismissed*. The pilot tested well with audiences. Focus groups love it. Advertisers think it's going to be the big breakout hit of the spring. The network has doubled its promo budget."

"So why walk away now?"

"Because there are too many questions I can't get answers to."

"Such as?"

Ross folded his hands and looked out the window at his view. "You ever been in a pilot that's gotten picked up by a broadcast network?"

"No."

"Know anyone who has?"

"Sure."

"Then you know that what the network has seen so far is the pilot, the test scores, the advertiser's reports . . . and if those are good, they don't need to see much else. Everyone smells gold. A hundred episodes! Syndication! We'll all be rich! So the machinery kicks in: promos, marketing, publicity. Peter Marling seems a dream. He has an act that's killed on the road for the last five years, or so he says. He gets standing ovations at colleges and clubs all across the country. The other night when you dragged me out of the Main Room at the Comedy Store I was showcasing him for a dozen studio executives. They loved him. I got calls the next day. Let's make a deal. The network heard about it and they think they have a gold mine on their hands. They can't wait to make Peter Marling a star. There's only one problem."

"What's that?"

He folded his hands and tucked his head into his chest. "I don't know who he is."

"Pardon me?"

"I met Peter Marling six months ago, and signed him as a client. Business has been great. But in all that time I've yet to learn anything about him. Who is he? Where did he come from?" Ross spread his hands. "He doesn't seem to have any family, any friends, any past. He won't name a hometown, he won't say where his parents are and I just found out Peter Marling is not his real name. This wouldn't be a problem except he has just informed the television network and the production company that's producing his sitcom that he will not do any interviews. He doesn't want to talk to any reporters, and he doesn't want any profiles done on him. His solution is that they interview him in character as the teacher he plays on the show—as long as they submit questions in advance."

"Have you told the network?"

"Yes. And they need him to change his mind. This isn't a road gig where you can blow off the *Lubbock Avalanche-Journal* or the *Tuscaloosa Tribune*. We're talking *Time, Newsweek, People,* and *In Style,* not to mention *Entertainment Tonight, Access Hollywood,* the Fame Channel, CNN and E! Haven't you seen the magazines and television features done these days on celebrities? They want to know the name of your fifth-grade teacher, show a picture of your report card and then go and talk to your classmates. You have to give away pieces of yourself to promote a product. It's the way it's done. That's part of being famous. It turns out his bio and résumé are false—the same bio and résumé I've been using for six months as a press packet—and the articles in it which contain supposed interviews with him were faked. He wrote them himself and dummied them up at a Kinko's. It was a marketing researcher who found all this out."

"What's his real name?"

"I don't know!" Ross shook his hands in front of him in frustration. "The social security number he gave me was a fake. The IRS bounced it back to my accountant. All moneys had been going through my office, and I'd been writing checks to him. I can't clear my books without a taxpayer ID number. I asked him for another social security number and that turned out to be a fake, too! Jesus Christ, who was I in business with? SAG and AFTRA called, wondering what was up with him, and told me he's in danger of being bounced out of his unions! I sat down with him and said, 'Peter, we've got some serious problems. I know you've lied to me in the past, but from this point forward you've got to play it straight with me and we can both be millionaires.'"

"What was his response?"

"He fired me." Ross slapped his hands on his knees. "He gave me my walking papers. We're done. He's probably going to sign with Sylvia Henn now. Well, good luck, sister. When this whole thing crashes like the *Hindenberg*, I'm going to be in New York, three thousand miles away. It'll make headlines in the trades, and hopefully my name will be real small, toward the end."

He got up and stood in front of the window, looking out at the horizon of the Hollywood Hills, his hands clasped behind his back, his face calm, his voice soft. "I came out here ten years ago thinking I was going to be the next Bernie Brillstein. Comedy was getting people rich. I thought it was going to be easy, like finding oil. Dig until you hit a gusher." He looked back at me.

"I did okay. I'm not hurting. I made some money and I saved it." He turned his gaze back out to the Hills. "It's not the money that's driving me out; it's the people. They lie. They cheat. They steal. And they kill."

Silence for thirty seconds.

"You think Peter Marling's done something bad?" he asked.

"Yes."

"Well, so do I. I don't know what. But I want to get out of here before he makes me into one of those voodoo dolls of his."

I let another thirty seconds go by.

"I'd like to see the materials he gave you," I said. "The ones you said were faked."

Ross turned away from the window and looked at me. "All right."

He opened and closed a few cardboard boxes until he found what he was looking for. He handed me a pocketed folder. Taped to the front was one of Peter Marling's headshots, his expression a kind of shrugging helplessness, as if to suggest that life was too much for him. It was a cute cuddly pose, completely non-threatening to the camera. He looked a lot different with a gun in his hand.

I opened it up and fingered through the press clippings and other headshots to find Marling's résumé. I pulled it out and scanned the list of comedy clubs he had listed as where he had headlined.

"Hm," I said.

"What is it?" Ross asked.

"All these clubs have one thing in common," I said. I turned the résumé over and looked at the back. The list was continued.

"What?"

"They're all closed. Even . . . well, I'll be damned."

"What? What?"

"Flugelhorn's is here," I said. "He lists Flugelhorn's as a club he played. But I heard he didn't know of the place, that he had never met Bernie before . . ."

"So what are you saying?"

I put my hand out. "Thank you," I said. "You've given me something to go on."

"What?" Ross followed me to the door. "What have I given you?"

I held up the press packet. "A voodoo doll of my own," I said. "And this one's going to work."

THIRTY-THREE

I called Peninsula Properties and asked for Ellen Alexander. I got an assistant who said she was out showing a house. I claimed to be an interested buyer, got the address in Rolling Hills and drove out there, taking the Harbor Freeway as quickly as traffic would allow.

My destination was a Victorian perched on a bluff at the top of Crest Drive. The city was splayed out before me on one side of the street, the vast expanse of the Pacific Ocean on the other. There were parts of the house yet to be finished. It was still under construction. A FOR SALE sign was out front, with Ellen's name on it. A cold front was moving in, and the sign was being blown back and forth.

I parked my car and waited for Ellen to appear. Her clients left first, a couple near retirement age. They drove a Cadillac.

I was up and out of my car as soon as Ellen shut the front door of the house behind her.

She saw me first. "What do you want?"

"Why didn't you tell me Peter Marling had played Flugel-horn's before?"

"What?"

"It's on his résumé. Why didn't you tell me?"

She looked at her car. She thought about getting in her car

239

and driving away. I don't know why she didn't. I wouldn't have stopped her.

"I didn't know."

"When we talked?"

"No. At first." She looked at the horizon. "It's windy. Can we go inside?"

"Sure."

She unlocked the front door and I walked into a house that was bigger than some apartment buildings I've lived in. "There's chairs in the kitchen," she said, and led the way to a breakfast nook that had two benches facing each other but no table in between yet. We had to angle our knees so they didn't touch. To my right was a pane of glass that looked out on the seashore below. The wind howled by like a dog that wanted to be let in out of the cold.

"I didn't know at first," she said. "I wasn't an expert on the history of Flugelhorn's. Bernie was. When Marling said he was interested in playing a local club, I put him in touch with Bernie. When I asked Bernie how it had gone, Bernie said Marling had a little history with the club. I asked if he had played there before and Bernie said something that just went right past me at the time—I didn't even mention it to the police—but now that you're asking . . ."

"What did Bernie say?"

"He said in a previous life he had."

"A previous life?"

"His words."

"So he must have had something, some kind of records that he checked that Marling wouldn't have known about."

Ellen looked at the space between us where the table should have been with her arms folded. "There were the records from before he took over the club, when Mel Sikorsky owned it."

"What records."

"Old headshots, pay stubs . . . Mel was a real pack rat."

"Where are those kept?"

"In the basement."

"I didn't even know Flugelhorn's had a basement until you told me that's where Mike Gallahan slept."

"It's beneath the kitchen."

"Is it locked?"

"Usually."

"Do you still have keys to the basement?"

"I might."

"And to the club?"

"At home. What are you thinking of doing?"

"Bernie knew something, something Marling didn't want anyone else to know, something Bernie knew just by virtue of being in the comedy club business for twenty years."

"And what would that be?"

"I don't know. Marling's ex-manager tells me that his client is being very evasive about his past. He won't do interviews to promote his new show. He won't give biographical details to reporters. He's refusing to reveal himself to the press."

"So what does that mean?"

"It might mean that Bernie was blackmailing him."

"What?"

"Here's the chain of events: Peter Marling needed a club to work out at. He mentioned this to you. You put him in touch with Bernie. Bernie has some kind of dirt on Marling—maybe something Bernie doesn't know is that valuable—so Marling concocts a scheme to get rid of Bernie. But he doesn't want to do it himself. He goes to Agar and Whiteside and contracts them to kill Bernie. Their price? Freedom. In advance.

"So Marling stages a prison comedy show where two convicts escape. These are the baddest hombres Marling knows, and they can do the job. But Bernie tapes the show and sells it to *Eyewitness Crime*. That makes Marling more nervous. He needs Bernie out of the way more than ever. He tells Whiteside and Agar to get the tape.

"But fate intervenes. Bernie is killed. Whiteside and Agar go after Rick Parker, thinking he has the tape. Rick comes to warn me, but it's too late for him. Marling kills Parker, thinking no one will find him in the storage space for some time.

"But whatever Bernie originally had on Marling as blackmail still exists. And it's either in Marling's hands or inside Flugelhorn's."

"Aren't the police handling this?" Ellen asked.

I nodded. "The cop working on this is good—very good. But he might not know what he's looking for."

"What do you think you are looking for?"

"Something that shows Peter Marling—or whoever he is—is not who he says he is. Whiteside and Agar said he had them kill someone before. They gave me a name. Gus Fletcher. If I can prove that, I can put him away. Will you help me?"

"What I don't understand is why you are so hot on this guy's trail. He didn't kill Bernie, like you said. Parker was an ex-con. Who's going to miss him? The police are working on it. Marling's about to have a hit sitcom. So what do you care?"

"Because people like him shouldn't be in comedy," I said. "You ask any comedian anywhere; L.A.'s the end of the yellow brick road. Some comics turn around and go back, some comics hit it big, and some just stick it out. It's tough, it's harsh and it's brutal. A comedian can spend a lifetime just knocking at Hollywood's door and never get in. Some buy their way with a famous name and family money. Some hype themselves to success with the right agents and managers and publicists. I've had guys who didn't have five minutes of material pass me like I was standing still. That's part of the game. But I sure as hell am not going to sit back and watch another comedian come off the road and think he can murder his way to the top. Not on my turf. Not in my town."

Ellen Alexander reached for her purse and stood up. "The keys are at my house in Huntington Beach," she said. "We need to get going if we're going to beat traffic."

THIRTY-FOUR

I waited until ten that night.

I drove over to the west side of Los Angeles where Flugel-horn's was and parked my car. I skulked around the parking lot for a bit, then walked up to the back door—still sealed with crime scene tape—and used the keys Ellen Alexander had given me to open it.

I walked in and shut the door behind me.

The club was completely dark. I'd brought a flashlight and two chemical flares with me, and I turned the flashlight on to see. The interior was untouched since I'd last seen it, the flashlight casting long eerie shadows. I looked down the hallway toward Bernie's office. I wondered if he haunted it now.

The kitchen was in the opposite direction, past the bar. I walked slowly. I heard glass crunch under my feet. The broken bottles had yet to be cleaned up. I passed the spot where I'd fallen, unconscious.

The kitchen had two swinging doors. I eased one open with my elbow and shone the light inside at the cool burners and empty pots. There was a faint smell of garbage left out.

I looked again to my right, by the freezer, where Ellen said the basement door was, behind a blue curtain. I'd never noticed the curtain before. I hadn't been in the kitchen much. When I'm in a comedy club, I usually don't go looking for hidden passageways. I spend more time checking out the waitresses.

I found the blue curtain and pushed it aside. Behind it was a wooden door with the paint just beginning to peel off of it. Another lock. Another key. I wondered if Gilmore had been there before me.

I opened the basement door. Cool air wafted up from below, smelling of earth and concrete. If I thought Flugelhorn's empty at night was creepy before, now it seemed positively warm and inviting compared to going underground. What was I going to find down there? Another dead body? Great.

The stairs were wooden, and I kept a hand on the railing as I toed my way down, one step at a time. I stopped and used the flashlight to scan around, to make sure there weren't any corpses hanging from the ceiling or other surprises.

It turned out the basement was rather small, with about half a dozen metal file cabinets set against the wall. In one corner was the furnace. A fire ax was hung from a hook on the wall. A dusty cot was folded up and set against the wall. There should have been a sign: Mike Gallahan slept here.

I reached the floor, a dusty slab of concrete with whorls and ridges still set in it from the pouring twenty years ago, now lined with dirt. I made my way over to the battered file cabinets, turned on the lone overhead bulb and started looking.

The history of Flugelhorn's was kept in those file drawers, from pre–computer age ledgers all the way up to laser-printed forms. There were bar receipts, invoices, processed paychecks (some with some very famous signatures), old flyers, contracts, menus . . . nothing that gave me what I was looking for. I spent about a half hour on each cabinet and in the third I found where the old headshots were kept.

Before Bernie Coleman got the club, Mel Sikorsky owned and ran Flugelhorn's—if not with an iron hand, certainly with a precise one. He kept a meticulous file of comedians' headshot submissions, along with a detailed form outlining an analysis of their tape or showcase performance. Mel's handwriting was neat, curved and precise; Bernie's was jagged and he scribbled in the margins.

I went right for the "M" file.

The file tabs were yellow and the pictures packed in so tight I had to lift them out in bunches and sort through them by hand. At one time they must have been in perfect alphabetical order, but the comedy explosion of the eighties had impacted the organizational process. Over the years some of the Ns and Ls got mixed in with the occasional Q, or M filed on a first-name basis. A lot of comedians had sent in more than one headshot.

A half hour later I found a picture of Peter Marling.

Only it wasn't Peter Marling. At least, it wasn't the face of the man I knew as Peter Marling. This man was shorter, stockier and had more hair. His face was rounder, his eyes brighter. He looked to be in his mid-twenties. The shot was taken outdoors, the focus not at professional level. A first headshot, done by a friend or a neighbor.

My pulse began to beat in my ears. I'd found what I was looking for, but I wasn't sure what it meant yet.

I looked at the résumé stapled to the back. It listed an area code and address in Lubbock, Texas. He'd put down that he was a graduate of Texas Tech University and had gotten a master's in the theater department. His credits were scant—local clubs, TV stations and conventions mostly—and the evaluation form Mel had attached indicated he'd sent in a tape as a submission for playing the club. The comments were that his comedy was prop-oriented but too regional. Jokes about Tech's football team, the Red Raiders and so forth. Lacked polish. Seemed as if he was just starting out. Cover letter mentioned he'd heard of Flugelhorn's through a cable television special taped there.

I set that headshot aside as carefully as if it was made of nitroglycerine, and then I went to another file drawer, this time looking for the one marked "F."

It took me almost another hour, but I found the headshot for Gus Fletcher. It wasn't even an eight-by-ten; he'd had someone take a Polaroid and blown it up. A one-of-a-kind item. No name on the front of the photo, just a handwritten résumé on the back, which was more of a letter of introduction. He, too, had seen the club on television. He had just started out. He was certain he was going to be a star. Just give him a chance.

In the picture, looking back at me, was the man I now knew as Peter Marling. In his face there was none of the goofy schlemiel that was now starring in his own sitcom. His eyes were level and cool, his mouth set. His hair was shaved close to his head, as if it had been done in an institution. He looked hard, mean and tough. It was the face of the man who had held a gun on me.

We helped Peter take care of old Gus, Whiteside had said. *This was about ten years ago, before anyone had ever heard of Peter Marling. Peter owes it all to Gus. Got him started in his comedy career, you might say.*

Something bad had happened, ten years ago, in the dim and dusty past, and the only proof of it was in my hands.

Then a light went on upstairs, and I knew I was no longer alone.

THIRTY-FIVE

A sliver of light was visible under the door that led from the kitchen to the basement. I could hear footsteps overhead. I decided now would be a good time to act invisible. I scooped up the headshots, tucked the flashlight into my pants after I turned it off, quietly closed the file cabinet drawer I had been looking in, and, just before I slipped into the shadows of the far corner of the basement behind the stairs, I took the fire ax off the wall. It was the only weapon I had. I wish I had brought my gun.

The basement door had been left unlocked. I heard footsteps overhead walk toward it, slowly and deliberately, and then stop. I heard a fumbling with the lock, and then the knob turned and the door swung open, letting in a shaft of light from the yellowed bulbs in the kitchen.

"Kincaid?"

I didn't answer. From where I was hiding, I couldn't see who was standing there, and I didn't recognize the voice. Not right away.

I heard a metallic click, and then a gunshot rang out, echoing off the concrete walls of the basement so loudly my ears rang. I smelled gunpowder and heard glass tinkle.

He had shot out the light.

"Kincaid, I know you're in there. Ellen Alexander told me you'd be here—just before she died."

I set the headshots down on the floor and gripped the fire ax with both hands, the cool rough wall of the basement at my back.

"It's me. Marling." He chuckled. "Of course, by now you know that's just a stage name."

I looked around. There was no other way out. I was trapped in the basement of a comedy club with a murderer at the top of the stairs, and I hadn't told Gilmore what I was doing. Stupid, stupid, stupid.

"I know you're down there," he said. "I saw you come in. I knew it was you who would lead me back here."

His voice was calm, reasonable. Unafraid.

"I've had you in my power since we first met," he said. "I knew you wouldn't be able to do me any real harm, and would, in fact only end up destroying yourself. I wanted to make sure you took certain secrets with you."

He picked up something that sloshed inside itself. A container of liquid.

I heard him unscrew a metal cap. "I willed you here, Kincaid. I commanded you to help me. You haven't been free for some time now. Bernie Coleman, Rick Parker, Johnny Whiteside . . . they all served my purpose to the end. And so will you."

He kicked a red metal can down the stairs. It tumbled, spilling fluid along the way as it fell, end over end, to stop within a foot of the staircase, where its contents spread along the concrete floor, soaking into the ridges and curves, lapping at the base of the file cabinets.

I smelled it. Gasoline.

Marling picked up another can and began to unscrew that. "Right now you're wondering—is there any way out of this? There isn't. There's only one door to the basement. Parker told me, before I killed him. There will be pain for you, Biff, but pain is like fire. It cleanses. It purifies. I tried to teach Whiteside that, when we first met, in prison, ten years ago. Pain is a tool, nothing more. I don't think he ever got it, but I tried."

He pitched the second can harder. It bounced against one of the file cabinets with a metallic bang and began to drool along the floor.

I wasn't just going to stand there in a corner in the dark and die a horrible death. I silently edged toward the staircase, staying in shadows, the ax in my hands. I was behind where Marling was standing. If I could get a clear shot at him with the ax . . .

I ran my thumb over the edge. Sharp enough.

"But Whiteside was like you, Biff. He was a simple, foolish man. He thought the world operated on a balance system: good on one side, bad on the other. It doesn't work that way. There's only power and pity. I found power, and I pity those who haven't learned how to use it."

I stepped under the staircase as he tossed a third open can of gas into the basement. He was standing on the entrance from the kitchen, his feet out of sight. There were spaces between the steps, big enough for the ax head to slide through. If I could just get him to step forward, I would have a shot.

"I'll do you one last favor, Biff. If you'll step out now, I'll shoot you dead where you stand. Otherwise, you're going to burn alive and that's going to be slow and painful. All you have to do is renounce your pride and ask for something it is still in my power to give."

I had the flashlight stuffed into my pants pocket. I switched the ax to one hand while I slowly pried the flashlight out. I had to set the ax aside as I turned the flashlight on, keeping the beam covered with one hand.

"Mercy. That's all you have to say. Just like in the old days, when my kind was burned at the stake as witches. Ask for mercy, and it will be granted."

I chucked the flashlight so it hit one of the file cabinets with a bang. He fired his gun instinctively, taking one step down to aim.

I picked up the ax and swung.

The blade sank into the soft arch of his left foot, cutting through the shoe and flesh with equal ease.

He screamed and dropped his gun. It bounced off the wooden steps and fell to the concrete floor. I let go of the ax and reached up to grab his foot, gushing blood, and pulled. The ax fell out of his foot and stuck between the steps.

Marling lost his balance and fell forward, tumbling down the steps to land with a grunt next to one of the gasoline cans, rolling in the pool of gas, soaking his clothes in it. He started to get up, but I wrenched the ax free and ran around and knocked him back down with the blunt end.

Marling went down and stayed down. I felt through his pockets for other weapons but all I found was a cellular phone. I took it. I picked up the gun and the flashlight, pointing both upstairs to make sure there was no one else. Marling had come alone.

I walked backwards up the steps, dragging the ax beside me, not taking my eyes off Marling as he slowly blinked his eyes open and sat up. There was a circle of blood around his foot the size of a coffee table. He tried to put his hands on the wound but he couldn't reach it.

He looked up at me. "I'm bleeding."

"I can see that."

"You don't have anything for it, do you?"

I took off my beret and threw it at him. "Use that."

He let the hat hit him in the chest and fall into his lap. "You're not just going to sit there and watch a man bleed to death, are you?"

"I've done it before," I said.

"When I looked into your soul, I saw death in your past."

"Actually, that was from a show on Long Island I did two years ago. I never got that crowd." I took out his phone. "I call 911 when you tell me what I want to know. You might die, but I'll know the truth."

Marling worked off his shirt and tied it around his ankle in a tourniquet. "I'll talk," he said.

"Where's the real Peter Marling?" I asked. "What'd you do with him?"

"He's dead."

"You kill him?"

He nodded. "Me and Whiteside."

"Why?"

"Whiteside and I met in prison in Texas. Both of us got out the same day. Both in for armed robbery. Both on probation. Couldn't leave the state. So I needed a new name. More than that, I needed a new life. Someone who traveled. Someone who wouldn't be missed. Someone who could be taken into my power."

"So you chose a comedian."

He nodded. "He was doing a week in Amarillo. I sat and watched his act every night for a week. Started buying him drinks. He was going on his first big road tour. Going to be gone for three months, all over the country. Just a kid, twenty-two years old. No family. Some props. Some magic. I tape-recorded his act and memorized it. Then the last night of his show, Whiteside and I took him down. Beat him to death with a baseball bat. Switched driver's licenses. Destroyed his fingerprints with a blowtorch. Weighted him down and dumped him in a lake."

"You make a little doll of him?"

Marling smiled, but in his pain it looked more like a rictus. "That was the first thing I did."

"So Gus Fletcher died, and Peter Marling lived on."

He nodded. "That's right."

"And Whiteside?"

"Whiteside followed me across the state line into New Mexico, then California. He got busted six months later for assault and sent back to Texas. Texas prisons got too crowded and he got transferred out to Ojai."

"So then what? You do Marling's gigs?"

"First as a cover. I just wanted to be out of state. Start over. Clean slate. But . . . it turned into something more."

"You liked it."

He nodded. "That feeling onstage . . . when you could get the audience to do what you wanted. . . . that was real power. You can feel like you're Hitler or Kennedy."

"I'd rather be Kennedy," I said. "He did better with the ladies after the show and I always thought Adolf's material was weak."

"You mock the power I worship," he said, "but it still rules your fate. The lines of force may be invisible to you, but they are there all the same."

"If I wasn't the one with the gun and the good foot, I'd really think you knew what you were talking about," I said. "So you kept doing comedy. You became Peter Marling."

"But not the Peter Marling that was," he said. "The Peter Marling I was meant to be. He was booked as an opener. I went on to headline."

"You did better at it than you thought you would."

"I did better at it than most comedians," he said. "I got clubs, cruises, colleges. I made money. I had women. I got laughs. And then I got a show. A TV show. All my own. I was going to be a star."

"You just forgot one thing," I said. "Your past."

"It was Whiteside who found me first. He said he was prepared to spill the beans unless I did something for him. He saw how well I'd done. He wanted to be a star, too."

"I saw his act," I said. "Don't think that was going to happen."

"I devised a plan to get Whiteside and his new friend Agar out. I recruited Bernie Coleman to help me, and the next thing I knew he was telling me he'd heard of another Peter Marling. Nothing specific. Just vague enough to let me know what he wanted." Marling looked around him. His face was pale. Beads of sweat were on his brow. "I didn't know if he had talked to Agar, if some tabloid reporter had found something, if there was a lawman back in Texas still working the case. All of that would have happened if he had released that old headshot."

"Double blackmailers," I said.

"Bernie didn't know what he had on me," Marling said. "But Whiteside kept his end of the bargain."

"Not quite," I said. "He told me, but that's because he thought I was a dead man walking."

"So how much do you want?"

"For what?"

"Silence. About this. I need to find a doctor. One who'll keep his mouth shut. I can get you ten thousand tonight and tomorrow—"

"No, tonight the police come," I said. I pulled out the phone. "You go back to jail for the murder of Rick Parker."

With a grunting effort, Marling got up on one knee. He had lost a lot of blood. He was getting his strength from sheer will. "I . . . kind of figured . . . you'd say something . . . like that."

I stood and took another step backwards. "Stay where you are," I said. "I'll call for help."

"No need," he said. He reached into his pocket and pulled out something too soft and small for me to find when I searched him.

A book of matches.

I went up the steps behind me so fast I almost stumbled. "Marling, don't." I felt fear clutch in my chest.

"Purify and cleanse," Marling said as he worked a match loose and closed the book. "Purify and cleanse."

I dropped the phone and leveled the gun at his chest. "Marling!"

"Mercy?" Marling asked. He kept the match just inches from the striking surface. "Is that what you're offering me? See, Kincaid, I won't really die. I made a doll of myself. It's in a safe place. My spirit resides there, awaiting my return. But first, I have to discard this"—He looked down at his wounded body, his legs and arms soaked with gasoline—"host."

"Wait," I said. "If the police—"

He struck the match.

I fired.

THIRTY-SIX

Marling staggered back as he dropped the match. The floor burst into flames, orange fire racing up his legs and back. My shot had been to warn or wound, and I had done neither. If I'd hit him, I couldn't tell. It didn't matter. He rolled his eyes downward and his mouth went oval as he realized he was burning alive.

The gasoline ignited with a *whoosh*, the heat from it hitting me so hard and close I felt hair singe. I turned around and ran up the stairs as the flames found the spilled fuel on the staircase. I stopped at the top to turn around and look for Marling.

The basement was ablaze from floor to ceiling. The staircase itself was burning like kindling, the steps themselves dancing with flame. I saw movement in the inferno, but couldn't tell if it was from a human or from the heat. Suddenly, a column of fire broke away and fell on the steps, hissing and smoking.

It was Marling. His face was red and swollen with blisters, the hair was burned off of his head down to the scalp, his tongue red and swollen, his eyes the only feature left unscorched. His clothes were charred into his blackened skin. I could smell his flesh crisping. He lifted one seared hand as he clutched a step with the other, choking and gasping, and uttered a final word:

"Mercy . . ."

I lifted the gun and aimed, standing on the top steps of the staircase. He lowered his head, ready to receive the bullet. My finger tightened on the trigger.

Suddenly the staircase gave way and collapsed to the floor of the basement. Marling went with it, lifting his head in surprise, his eyes wide with horror as he realized he would not be spared his final agonies. I fired, but my shot went wide of the mark as the steps gave out underneath my feet, too.

I dropped the gun, twisted around in midair and heaved myself into the kitchen, catching my hands around the doorframe. My legs dangled into the basement and I could feel my shoes warming, the rubber on the soles melting as I pulled myself up and through the doorway. I beat at the sparks that had landed in my jeans and, on my hands and knees, turned and took one last look into the conflagration.

I saw only red heat, burning and eating everything below. It was like looking into Hell's waiting room.

And then I heard Marling scream, a howl of pain and penitence I didn't know a man could make. It lasted for one breath, and then was gone.

I closed the door.

I ran to Bernie's office. I called 911 from there. Then I called Gilmore. When I left the office I saw the club was beginning to fill with smoke. I ducked my head and looked in the kitchen. The basement door had caught fire. Flames licked around its edges. I turned to the back door and let myself out. I could see orange light glowing in the windows of the club as the fire spread from the basement to the kitchen. I stood in the parking lot and watched Flugelhorn's burn.

The fire trucks came and they did what they could. By the time the fire was under control it had spread to the showroom. The club was gutted. Parts of the roof had burned through.

By that time Gilmore had shown up. I told him what had happened. He found Marling's car parked less than a block away from the club and had his men search it.

"We found this," he said, handing me a small wooden black oblong box, bound by a length of twine. He opened it up and showed me what was inside.

It was a doll. Pinned to the head was my face, cut out of one of my headshots. The strands of hair Marling had taken from my beret were glued to the top.

"You know what this is?" Gilmore asked.

"It's a voodoo doll," I said. "He made it so he could have power over me." I looked at the detective. "You didn't find one of him, did you?"

"No," Gilmore said. "Why would someone make a voodoo doll of themselves?"

"So they'd be protected from earthly harm."

"Marling believed in black magic?"

"Not anymore," I said.

It was long after midnight when I left Flugelhorn's. Gilmore and the fire investigators were still working the fire scene, looking for Marling's body. I'd seen enough. I didn't need to see that.

I got in my car and headed home, taking surface streets back to Beachwood Canyon. I was driving down Olympic when on impulse I turned left on Beverly Glen and took it up to Sunset. When I got to Sunset I turned right.

I pulled into the parking lot of the Comedy Store at a quarter to two. No one was even watching the lot at that time of night. A light was still on in the Original Room, and I glimpsed someone onstage, in front of a mike. The show was still going on.

I parked and got out, heading in the back. I looked at the stage again and saw the emcee I'd seen through the window, Kevin Soames, bringing up another comic, Tom Platt. Platt I didn't know that well. Soames I did. He was tall and preppy-looking, younger than me.

I checked the list hanging by the back staircase. Platt was second to last. Last was Jennie Rush. I looked around. I didn't see her. Maybe she had canceled. That would mean there was an opening in the schedule. A fallout. I hadn't been onstage in a week.

I caught Kevin Soames as he headed for the bathroom.

"Soames."

He turned and saw me. "Kincaid, hi—" He stopped. "What happened to you?"

I looked down at my clothes. They were streaked with soot. My beret was gone. My stitches were showing.

"I had a little excitement earlier this evening," I said. "I'm all right, though."

"You look like hell."

"I know," I said. "Jennie here?"

"No."

"She call in?"

"No, she just didn't show up."

"Can I go on if she's a fallout?"

"There's only two tables left," Soames said. "Five people total. One guy's fallen asleep."

"I don't care."

"I've got to shut it down at two in the morning," Soames said. "Platt just went on so . . . I can only give you ten minutes."

"That's fine."

"All right." Soames sighed. "And I thought I was going home early."

"Sorry."

"What do you want me to say about you?"

"Regular at the Store, clubs and colleges all across the country."

Soames chuckled. "The usual bullshit, huh?"

"Please. With a side order of fries."

"Okay." Soames looked at the stage and checked his watch. "I'll give Tom the light in five minutes."

I nodded and walked up the back stairs into the Original Room. Soames was right. It was just about empty. Platt was trying new material, then old stuff, then just talking to whoever he could find, trying to get a response, anything, from what was left of tonight's crowd. It wasn't working.

I heard snoring. I turned and looked. Soames wasn't kidding. One guy was asleep, and his date was nodding off beside him.

Platt got the light, and when he left the stage the one remaining table of conscious patrons did, too. That left the sleeping guy and his date. Fine. I'd wake them up. Platt walked by me, shaking his head. "You're not going on, are you?" he whispered.

I nodded.

He clapped me on the back. "Good luck."

Soames wasted no time on my intro, saying it like one long run-on sentence. He was tired and bored and wanted to go home.

I could have turned and walked away, but I didn't. There wasn't anything for me there, but I was going to hunt for it anyway. I wanted to feel the mike in my hand, the lights in my eyes and the stage under my feet. If I could get a laugh out of the one table left, if I could make a waitress shake her head and smile as she cleared the glasses off the table, if I could get Soames or the guy working the ticket booth to chuckle as they waited for me to close down the show . . .

I heard the emcee say my name and headed for the stage.

DAN BARTON is a professional stand-up comedian. He began his comedy career at the Comix Annex in Houston, along with Bill Hicks and Sam Kinison. He currently lives in Los Angeles where he is the supervising producer for *Wild On* at E! Entertainment Television. He is the author of several other novels, including the Biff Kincaid mysteries *Killer Material* and *Heckler*. He can be reached at dan@killermaterial.com.